NOW I KNOW

RED FOX DEFiniTiOnS

PREVIEWS

Stars spinning
he points the compass.
His hands bear the universe.

A man jogs round the curve of earth,
white shorts and sweating white sweater.
He breathes cloud embryos into the dawn,
seeing only the narrow path.

Again Nik sees her
striding behind her antinuke banner,
grinning, drenched.
(But not marching, not her, ever.
Process, yes; belong, protest, yes.
But never march against marching.)
No matter all those other hundreds
Loved on sight
Of all her.

The explosion lifts him up
hurls him down
a crotch-hold and body-slam.
Out.
Conditioning him for death.

Tom said to the duty officer, 'I'm on the crucifiction, sarge.'

'Super's off his head,' the sergeant said. 'Set a kid to catch a kid.'

'That your guess?'

'Kids anyway. Take more than one to do a thing like that.'

'What about the one they strung up?'

The sergeant consulted a report. 'According to the only witness, he's about seventeen.'

'Where's he now?'

'Gone.'

'Gone!'

'Vamoosed.'

'How come?'

'You're the one playing detective.'

STOCKSHOT: *The best in this kind are but shadows; and the worst are no worse, if imagination amend them.*

NIK'S NOTEBOOK: This by Simone Weil:
Hitler could die and return to life again fifty times, but I should still not look upon him as the Son of God.

Good, that. Ms Weil quite someone. Also says we must get rid of our superstition about clock time if we are to find eternity. What does she mean? ETERNITY? Time no more?

Things happen one after the other, yes? Or do they? But that's not how we remember them, is it? I don't. I asked Julie. She doesn't either. Who does? Life only makes sense when it's out of order. Ha!

Also: Things happen simultaneously. Julie says everything is now. Making the connections is what matters.

Selah.

By the same author

BREAKTIME

DANCE ON MY GRAVE

THE TOLL BRIDGE

POSTCARDS FROM NO MAN'S LAND

Aidan Chambers lives in Gloucestershire with his American
wife, Nancy, who is the editor of *Signal* magazine. He divides
his time between his own writing and lecturing which he does
extensively in Australia, the USA and Europe. His provocative
and challenging novels for teenagers and young adults
have won him international acclaim.

Postcards from No Man's Land is the fifth novel in what he
perceives as a sequence; this starts with *Breaktime*, continues
with *Dance on my Grave*, and carries on through *Now I Know*
to *The Toll Bridge*.

A sixth book is planned. Each novel stands on its own exploring
a different aspect of contemporary adolescence.

aidan
chambers

NOW I KNOW

RED FOX Definitions

To Margaret Clark

A Red Fox Book

Published by Random House Children's Books
20 Vauxhall Bridge Road, London SW1V 2SA

A division of The Random House Group Ltd
London Melbourne Sydney Auckland
Johannesburg and agencies throughout the world

Copyright © Aidan Chambers 1987

1 3 5 7 9 10 8 6 4 2

First published in Great Britain by
The Bodley Head Children's Books 1987

Red Fox edition 1995

This Red Fox edition 2000

Printed and bound in Great Britain by
Cox & Wyman, Reading, Berkshire

Papers used by The Random House Group Ltd are natural, recyclable products made from
wood grown in sustainable forests. The manufacturing processes conform to the environmental
regulations of the country of origin.

THE RANDOM HOUSE GROUP Limited Reg. No. 954009

ISBN 0 09 950301 8

ALL WRITING IS DRAWING

IN THE BEGINNING
THERE WAS A YOUTH GROUP
who decided to make a film about
GOD
AFTERWORDS
no one could remember
how they came to make such a decision.
None of them could remember being concerned about
God at the time.
But for one of them
what happened is here
NOW

BEGINNINGS

There were three beginnings.
From the beginning, you see,
we are to be given our words' worth.

The beginning of the beginning

One evening, Nicholas Christopher Frome was lying idly in his
bath when the thought struck him that eventually he would die.

He had of course thought this before. He is no fool.

But that evening it penetrated his consciousness with a
terrible clarity. A clarity so pure, so undeniable that, despite the
pleasant heat of the water, he turned cold inside.

What made the thought so terrible was not the knowledge of
his eventual death, but the realization of the separateness of his
being.

He was not, he understood completely for the first time,
merely his parents' son, nor just any seventeen-and-one-month
year old youth, nor simply another member of the multi-
tudinous human race.

He was *him self*. A separate, individual, unique and self-
knowing person who would one day snuff it.

I am not, he thought, anyone else. Only me.

The cold inside froze his body. He stared, amazed, at the
bathroom's perspiring ceiling.

I am me, he thought, and one day this Me will come to an
end. I shall not be.

His stomach curdled.

He sat up and spewed into his bathwater.

There is never one particular moment, one small event,
whether in life or in a novel, that is the only beginning. There
are always as many beginnings as anyone cares to look for. Or

9

none at all of course. But when Nik was thinking afterwards about what happened, he decided that the moment when he sat up in his bath and spewed his guts out came as near to being the beginning of his story as any.

The beginning of the end

Thomas Thrupp. Keen, ambitious, a would-be chief constable and yet only nineteen. Naturally suspicious, he trusts nobody, not even his granny, possesses a certain dangerous charm, and is said to be at his best in tight corners. Tom would never throw up at the thought of his own death.

One morning Tom was summoned to his superintendent's office. Earlier that day a young man had been found crucified on a rusty metal cross. The cross was not stuck in the ground, after the manner of ancient custom, but was dangling from a crane in a scrap yard across the railway tracks from the centre of town.

The super believed a gang of yobs had perpetrated the crime and that a young copper might sus them out more quickly than an older man. So despite Tom's lack of qualifications he ordered him to investigate. Besides, the super reckoned him a likely lad, attractively hungry for success. What Tom lacked in experience he'd make up for in ruthlessness. The super admired ruthlessness as much as he admired desk-top efficiency. (There were no papers cluttering his desk, just a closed file, a calendar and a photo of his wife.) He had Tom marked out as good at both. Tom also reminded him of himself when he was a young plod. (The super could be very sentimental on occasion. Sentimentality is, of course, the flip side of ruthlessness.)

Afterwards, in the briefing room, Tom said to the duty officer, a man of years, 'I'm on the crucifiction, sarge.'

'Super's off his head,' the sergeant said, entering up the duty book.

'Thanks for the vote of confidence.'

'Got all the confidence you need.' The sergeant sniffed. 'Set a kid to catch a kid.'

'That your guess?'

'Kids anyway. Take more than one, a thing like that.'

'What about the one they strung up?'

The sergeant consulted a report. 'According to the only witness, he's about seventeen. Five-eightish. Short brown hair. Thin face. Pale, but who wouldn't be under the circs. Slim build. Bony. Attired only in his underpants. Dark blue y-fronts with white edging. Very natty.'

'Marks and Sparks,' Tom said, scrupulously jotting the details into his notebook. 'Could be anybody.'

'Not quite,' the sergeant said.

'Where's he now?'

'There you have me.'

'Sorry?'

'Gone.'

'Gone!'

'Vamoosed.'

'How come?'

'You're the one playing detective.'

'This kid was hanging there and we lost him?'

'Quick on the uptake, I'll grant you that.'

'Jeez!'

'Could be him you're after.'

'Very funny, sarge. What else is news?'

'Wouldn't hang about if I was you.'

'Another good one. On form today.'

'Crack this, could make a name for yourself.'

'That's what the super said.'

The sergeant grinned. 'No slouch, our super. You fail though, and it'll be all your fault. Know that, don't you? Incompetent trainee officer ballses up, etcetera. You win, and the super takes the prize for daring use of bright young man. 'Course, he'll let you bask in the reflected. Get your pic in the *Police Gazette*.'

'You're a real encouragement, sarge.'

'As I say, I don't think you need any. So long, lad. Givem hell.'

The end of the beginning

JULIE: Hello . . . hello? . . . one two three . . . Is it working?
[*Pause.*]

Dear Nik, this is a Julie tape-letter. It's all Nurse Simpson's idea. Blame her. She's hung a microphone from my bedhead. She says all I have to do is talk quietly and the microphone will hear me. Which is just as well because I can't do much else but talk quietly.

So now, though I can't write to you, Nik, I can talk to you. And if you want to reply in the same way, Simmo says she'll put headphones on me so that only I can hear what you say. But it'll be a slow-motion conversation because of the post. And you won't be able to interrupt and answer back.

[*Pause. Tape surf.*]

I still can't see. My eyes are still bandaged. Most of me is still bandaged. I feel like a shrink-wrapped jelly-baby. The consultant says I'll be like this for a few days yet. In doctor's language I think 'a few days yet' means 'for a long time yet'. But she sounds nice. She has a gentle middle-aged voice and is sometimes with a squad of young students who go very quiet when they reach me. Simmo says that's because I'm such a knockout, but I know the sort of knockout I must be, and so must you.

Which reminds me: thanks for coming to see me. All that way! Why couldn't it have happened nearer home? There can't be much to see of me either, wrapped up the way I am. And wires and tubes and gear hanging off me as if I were one of Frankenstein's monsters in the making.

In fact, I don't feel I have a body any more. I feel more like a mind inside a carcass. Just now, all I am is a mouth saying words because I've just guzzled the dope they give me to kill the pain and keep me docile. I can't even feel my body. It might as well not exist. So I'm having an identity crisis. How do you know who you are if you've no body to speak of? I'm working on the answer. I'm nothing but words in my head all day. And dreams all night. Sometimes harsh words and usually horrible dreams. They say the dreams will go away, but what about the words?

[*Long pause.*]

Other people are only voices too of course. You can tell a lot from people's voices when that's all you've got to go on. Their voices give them away and they don't know it. You can hear when they're being genuine and when they aren't, and whether they're naturally kind or cruel, or thoughtless or strong or weak, and if they're being brave. And if they're hiding something. If you listen very carefully, you can hear the lies hiding behind the words.

That's how I know I'm not the knockout that Simmo pretends. And that the consultant doesn't mean a few days when she says about the bandages coming off my eyes. I can hear the lie in their voices.

I don't ask whether I'll be able to see again when the bandages do come off. I couldn't bear it if they lied about that. And they would lie, wouldn't they, if the answer was no?

[*Long pause. Sound of deep breaths being taken in and slowly exhaled.*]

Sorry. Didn't mean to say any of that. Promised myself I wouldn't. Doesn't mean anything. Just came tumbling out. Haven't talked to you for so long. Seems years. Lost track of time and days. Seems like I've been here for ever and won't ever leave.

So nice to talk to you . . . Nice . . . Silly word. I mean . . . such a relief . . . to be able to talk to you and say some of the things churning in my head, even if they have to be recorded and take two days to reach you, knowing the post, even if sent first class, and that'll cost the earth.

Sorry . . . there I go again . . . I've tried talking this letter twice today already but made Simmo wipe the tape. Neither time was right, because I went off all over the place, saying things I didn't mean . . . The drugs, I expect . . . And not actually having you here . . . Seems ridiculous, talking blind into thin air. Well, this time I'm making myself see your face, as though you really were here, and not letting myself think of anything but your face and what I want to say. But even so I . . .

[*Pause.*]

Where was I? . . . Oh, yes—your visit. I knew you were here. I felt the touch of your hand. But I couldn't say anything. I tried very hard but nothing happened. Like one of those dreams when you strain to move but your body won't budge.

Well, what I want to tell you is this. Your touch, the touch of your hand, made me believe I could live again. Till then I hadn't believed and was praying for the end to come quickly. But your touch, and knowing it was you, made me believe I could make it. And made me want to. Thank you for that gift, dear Nik.

[*Pause.*]

Being ill, I mean being very ill, makes you feel useless. Makes you feel you're a burden to everyone. You feel all of life is passing you by. Your own life becomes meaningless. There's no sense in it any more.

[*Pause.*]

What you believe matters. I'm learning that the hard way. I believe everybody matters. Being ill or being well shouldn't have anything to do with it. Everybody has a part to play in building the world God has given us. I'm a Christian because I believe that, and I believe it because I'm a Christian. But how do you play your part when you're trapped by illness?

If you were here, Nik, you'd be interrupting like mad by now!

What I'm trying to say is that I've decided that perhaps it's my job while I'm like this to work out what illness . . . means. And why not? There's nothing else I can do.

[*Pause.*]

I can't talk for long at a time because even talking tires me. I must stop soon. But I wanted to ask if you'd do something for me. Simmo has brought me some Talking Book tapes of the Bible. She says there are other books—novels and poetry—she can get for me but she doesn't know what I'd like. If she sends you the list, would you choose something? I'd like you to because then it will be like you giving me a book you want me to read, the way you've done before, and I can imagine you're listening with me. Then we can talk about it in our tape-letters. If you'd like to, I mean. Only if you'd like to.

[*Pause. Deep breaths, in and out.*]

I know that must sound pretty silly. Such a little thing. But you've no idea how such pitiful little things mean most when you're in my predicament.

Something else, while I'm on silly things. I quite often burst into tears. Into sobs, I mean, because my eyes can't cry. Reaction, I suppose. 'Just your nerves, love,' Mum says. She says it so dolefully that I can't help laughing. Between crying and laughing for no reason, I'm sure Mum thinks I've gone off my head.

Anyway, I'm making such a big production out of it because if I start howling when I'm recording you'll hear. And it'll sound ghastly. I hate the idea of you hearing it. I don't mean to cry. I'm not looking for sympathy. There's just nothing I can do about it. Simmo says, 'Forget it, he'll understand.' And I know you will. But I wanted you to be prepared. I can't edit out or press the pause button or anything like that. A case of 'look, no hands'. It's just that suddenly everything comes over me in a great overwhelming wave . . . and the wave breaks . . . and . . . *nurse! . . . quick! . . .*

†

The day after Nik threw up into his bath he was asked by his history teacher, Leonard Stanley, if he would like to help a youth group who were making a film. The group needed a researcher.

They were making a film about what would happen if Jesus Christ returned today. They weren't a church group—far from it. But one evening they had had a long discussion about the politics of the Middle East and the arguments for and against the state of Israel, and they had arrived at the conclusion that the world was no better now than it was at the time of Christ's first visitation in Palestine two thousand years ago. They had agreed that if Christ returned today, and lived in their own West of England town, never mind in Palestine, he would be treated no better, and possibly even worse, than he was treated then.

The group's idea was to use their film of Christ's second coming to make strong criticisms of life today. They supposed that staid old fogies could hardly get upset if Christ was the person who showed up the bad things that go on and the old fogies responsible for them. (They considered anyone over the age of thirty to be an old fogey. One of them wore a sweatshirt that said so.)

Truth to tell, though, only a small minority of the group were in the slightest interested either in the life of Christ (now or two thousand years ago) or in politics. They would have been hard put to say which they found more boring. What interested the majority was being together and having some fun. Within the group there was another minority who were not interested in politics but were interested in film-making, and wanted to use cameras and sound equipment and create spectacular special effects, and generally wanted to carry on as if they were big names in Hollywood. So as usual in human affairs, as well as in youth groups, the decisions were thrashed out between the few vocal members of each minority while the rest waited with as much patience and as little attention as necessary till the most determined ones got their way.

In all this the group was led and encouraged by their organizer, a man of twenty-seven called Frank Randwick, a motor-mechanic by trade and a youth leader by desire. He it was who first suggested the idea of making the film, and he immediately appointed himself its Director.

Of course the political hotshots gave themselves the job of writing the script. And early in the discussions they realized that none of them knew very much about the life of Christ or about Palestine in his day. The script-writers did not want to be bothered about such insignificant details. But they found themselves opposed by three of the so-far silent girls.

As it happened (and rather appropriately, you might think) the girls were cast to play the three Marys: Mary the mother of Christ; Mary Magdalene, who legend has it was a converted prostitute; and Mary of Bethany, the sister of Martha and of raised-from-the-dead Lazarus, who is celebrated in the Bible for anointing Christ's feet with balmy oil and afterwards wiping them clean with her presumably long and luxuriant hair.

These three suddenly vocal girls declared that if the group was going to film Christ's story they should at least get the facts right. The script-writers said to hell with facts, what mattered was the message. It wasn't the facts of Christ's life that interested them, they said, but telling people about life now.

The girls were determined, however. Check the facts or they wouldn't take part. And as it seemed a very neat way of getting their own back at the script-writers for being so boring about politics, a number of the rest of the group supported the girls.

In the face of this opposition and with the astuteness of born politicians, the script-writers said okay, the facts would be verified. But later, in secret, they agreed with each other that they'd do what they liked anyway, whatever the facts were, just as soon as shooting started and everyone's attention was occupied by the excitements of filming.

They demanded, however, that a researcher be appointed to help them. As no one in the group wanted such a thankless and unglamorous job, the Director approached the Head of Nik's school, who passed the buck to the head of the history department, Leonard Stanley, who nobbled Nik, because Nik was one of his better history students.

But Nik was not keen.

He said, 'I'm not bothered about religion and I don't believe in God.'

Leonard Stanley said, 'But think what a marvellous project it will make. History in action. You can submit your notes and an essay about the whole experience as part of your exam assessment work. No one else is doing anything like it.'

Nik said, 'I'd prefer black holes. I'm interested in black holes. They're more important than God nowadays.'

'Black holes,' Leonard Stanley said, 'don't have a history.'

'Everything has a history,' Nik said. 'At least, that's what you tell us.'

The teacher shrugged. 'Nobody knows much about black holes yet. That's what I mean.'

What he really meant was that he didn't know much about black holes himself and didn't want the bother of finding out in order to grade Nik's work.

'Now God,' he went on quickly, 'God has been around a long time. We know quite a bit about him. About religion, anyway.'

Nik smirked. 'God has never been around at all. He's an

invention. God's a fiction, sir. Just a story. In the past people needed some all-powerful being to explain things they couldn't understand, and to calm their fears. Or to blame for the awful things that happened to them, like illnesses and earthquakes. And sometimes they used God to scare other people they didn't like. But it's no good any more. It doesn't work. We know better now. God is dead. If he was ever alive, that is. That's what I think, anyway.'

Leonard Stanley snatched a winning point, poking a finger at Nik's chest. 'In that case,' he laughed, 'God's all history. Isn't that right?'

Nik couldn't help nodding an unwilling agreement.

Leonard seized his advantage. 'And you can't have a better subject for a history project than a subject that is nothing but history, can you?'

Nik said, 'I still prefer the history of living things, if you don't mind, sir.'

'Look,' the teacher said, turning on his serious manner. 'People are living. People have histories. People have a long history of believing in God. A history that goes back to the beginning of people. And a lot of people, probably the majority of people in the world, still do believe in a God of some kind.'

'And look where they've got us,' Nik said. 'They fall for this God stuff and before you know it they're fighting each other about whose God is the real one. Then they start torturing their enemies to try and convert them. And they end up fighting holy wars and killing each other, and anyone else who doesn't agree with them. All in the name of this God they think they own and who gives them the right to murder in his name. It's not on, sir. I don't want anything to do with it.'

Leonard Stanley liked nothing better than this kind of heated argument from his students. He believed it helped them discover how exciting history is. Not that he expected anyone actually to do anything as a result of the arguments. Talk was one thing, action another. But this time he had quite mistaken the character of the student he was arguing with.

Leonard rubbed his hands and said, 'Listen, Nik. People do all those things for other reasons as well as religion. For politics, for example, and family feuds, for money, or food, or to gain territory, or because of jealousy, or even for love. All you're saying is that religion includes the whole of the human race, the good and the bad. Which makes it a perfect subject for a historian to study.'

'But,' Nik said, 'the Christians say God made people in his own image, don't they? So if there's a God, and if he made people in his own image, and they go round murdering each other and doing horrible things, then it's all God's fault that the human race is like it is, and the sooner we ditch him the better. But if there isn't a God, then there's no point in doing history about him because it's a waste of time.'

Leonard said, 'I'm not saying whether there's a God or not. Historians don't answer questions like that. What they do is tell the story of people and how they got to be the way they are. It's people who interest historians. All I'm saying is that religion is one of the most powerful forces—maybe *the* most powerful—in the history of people everywhere. So we should study it.'

Now it was Nik's turn to shrug. 'Maybe.'

The teacher took a step closer, a sign the argument was over. 'Don't give me any maybes, Nik. You know I'm right. This project is a perfect opportunity to investigate first hand one of the most potent forces in human life. And you can do it by researching its effects on real, ordinary people of your own age. Anyway, it'll be fun. And it'll get you in amongst others. You spend too much time on your own.'

'I'll think about it,' Nik said, not happy at the turn the conversation had taken.

'Don't think about it. Do it. Okay?'

Nik knew he'd be badgered till he agreed. 'I'll give it a go, sir. But under protest.'

'Protests I can live with,' Leonard said, and stalked off, thinking force of argument had won the day.

He was wrong. Nik knew, without admitting it to himself just then, that throwing up in his bath at the knowledge of his own separateness had much more to do with it than argument.

EYE DEES

Nik's first few meetings with the group were interesting enough. The historical information they needed was easy to find; and he mildly enjoyed the joshing and jokes which seemed to be what most of the group came for.

He quickly fell into the habit of arriving just in time for the film-making part of the proceedings, and of avoiding the whoopee afterwards by saying he had school work to do and dodging away. A few people teased him for this, hinting at darker, sensational reasons for his leaving. 'We've heard that before,' they'd say with winks and nudges and obscene fists. 'Who is it? Come on, tell us.'

Some, he knew, thought he didn't hang around like the rest because he was snobby and standoffish. But Nik was used to this. From infancy he had never felt comfortable with large groups, worst of all when everyone was his own age. One of his earliest memories was of standing in the middle of a swarm of babies at nursery school and screaming till his mother took him away. Later he always kept clear of gangs and parties. And these days he felt particularly suspicious of what he called 'teenage playgroups', unable to imagine why anyone needed them or why any sane adult wanted to run them.

A teacher once accused him of being 'chronically unclub-bable', as if this were a dire ailment. Others often called him a loner, their tone of voice leaving no doubt that loners were never approved of. He both resented this and was proud of it.

In self-protection, and out of cussed principle, he had encouraged this view of himself as an oddity, making an aggressive virtue of being an outsider. He even acquired a kind of following of boys, and of girls too, who admired his remoteness and tried to imitate his slightly aloof manner, his wary look through his glasses, the bite in his talk, and his disdain for any physical activity.

Recently, this body of admirers had become vocal. Someone

had given them what was intended to be a scornful name, the Nikelodeons. Others, both for and against, took it up and with startling speed Nik found himself the unwilling focus of a fashion which people took sides about. Even second- and third-years were soon calling themselves Nikies. They could hardly be called a club as the whole point of Nikishness was to be unclubbable and fiercely individual. But they took to standing about together and off-handedly acknowledging each other when they crossed paths in corridors.

Then one day NIKS SCORE ALONE was found scrawled across the team lists on the soccer notice-board. And the next day N = 1 was sprayed on the maths room wall. After that Nik-graffiti appeared everywhere. The best of it was collected and printed in the school newspaper.

THE NIKELODEONS OF LIFE PLAY THEIR OWN TUNES

BETTER A NIKEL THAN A KNUCKLE

NOW I KNOW I WON

Secretly, of course, Nik enjoyed his temporary notoriety. Everybody likes to be noticed. But he never openly confessed it, nor that being a loner had one enormous disadvantage. It literally meant that he was frequently alone, when the truth was he would have liked companionship now and then.

This partly explains why he stayed with the film group. His project gave him an excuse for being there without his having to acknowledge any other reason. He thought of himself as an outsider, an observer, one of the group without belonging to it. So he didn't feel he was giving in to any of those human weaknesses he scorned.

In his role as observer, and on Leonard Stanley's instructions, he kept a notebook in which he recorded the events of each session, wrote up the information needed for the film and for his essay on religion. But very soon he began to use it as a kind of journal of his secret thoughts and comments on what happened to himself. (Though it must also be admitted that his notes became as long as they did because he had just been given a word processor and using it was a novelty.)

But there was another reason why Nik stayed with the group. This is how it came about.

At Nik's sixth meeting the Director settled the casting of the film. There was plenty of crude joking, about, for example, the appropriateness of the boy who was Judas, and whether the girl who was Mary Magdalene was experienced at certain aspects of life that would fit her for the part of a reformed prostitute.

Towards the end of the evening the Director said, 'Agreed, then. That's the cast.'

Mary Magdalene said, 'Except for Jesus.'

'Yeah, what about him?' Saint Peter said. 'We can't make a film about Jesus turning up again if we haven't got anybody to act him.'

The Director said, 'Why not? He could always be just out of shot. Or the camera could be him. Everything seen from his point of view. I've considered it.'

General uproar.

'Arty-farty,' John the Beloved shouted.

'Gimmicky,' Doubting Thomas yelled.

'You have to see him,' John the Beloved went on. 'I can't eat the last supper with a camera for Christ.'

'All you ever think about is your stomach,' Mary of Bethany said.

'That's all you know!' Jason the clapperboy said with a mock simper.

'Trouble is,' the Director said, 'we don't know what he looked like.'

'Handsome,' Mary the Mother said. 'He'd have to be, wouldn't he? He'd not be ugly, not the son of God.'

'Why not?' Lazarus said.

'Like you!' Doubting Thomas mocked. 'Type cast, you are. Won't need no make-up. Like death warmed up without any.'

'You leave my brother alone,' Mary of Bethany said.

'What I mean,' Lazarus said, ever undaunted, 'is that God might of let Jesus be ugly to show that ugly people matter as much as handsome people.'

Groans.

'Depends what you're after,' Brian the camera boy said.

'We all know what you're after,' Sally the continuity girl said, grinning, and not at all resisting the yoke of Brian's arm.

The Director said, 'What's ugly and what's handsome anyway?'

Doubting Thomas said, 'Can't say I have much trouble deciding,' and looked lasciviously at Mary of Bethany, whose luxuriant black hair had landed her the part and Thomas's obvious admiration.

'All I'm pointing out,' the Director said, 'is that everybody has their own idea. And then there's fashion. Ideas about what's ugly and what's beautiful change from time to time.'

'Yeah,' Rachel the sound recordist said. 'In the eighteenth century they liked fat women and men dressed in long curly wigs and lacy clothes.'

'Dishy,' Jason the clapperboy said, only, as usual, to be ignored.

'We ought to have some idea of what Christ looked like though, oughtn't we?' Judas said. 'We've got to cast somebody.'

'I think he'd have nice eyes,' the Magdalene said.

King Herod yawned, never one for discussion, and said, hoping to put an end to this one, 'Nik ought to know. He's the researcher.'

Nik said, 'That's the trouble. We don't know much about him at all.'

'Tell us anyway,' the Director ordered.

Nik flipped pages in his file. 'It'll be easiest if I read you a summary.'

Mary Magdalene said, 'Not long, is it? Want to be home early tonight to wash my hair.'

This was taken as an incredibly funny joke. The Magdalene frequently had this effect, though she never quite understood why. (The Director had cast her as the Magdalene expecting she'd have this effect on audiences too, for his secret intention was to direct the film as a send-up of religion, he being a rabid atheist himself.)

When everyone had quietened, Nik said, 'Only a page. You can survive that.'

'If it isn't boring,' Doubting Thomas said.

'Can you tell the difference?' Nik said, and went on, 'Extract from—'

'Never mind the frills,' script-writer Tony muttered.

Mary the Mother said, 'He's only trying to be accurate.'

Nik read.

STOCKSHOT: *Jesus of Nazareth has been the central figure of the most widespread religion of the past two thousand years, yet almost nothing is known of his earthly life. We can confidently state that he lived in Palestine in the time of Herod Antipas, tetrarch of Galilee, and that he was crucified under Pontius Pilate. Beyond that, we have only the devout literature of his disciples and followers, and we see and hear Jesus only through their record. Our lack of historical information is due in part to the fact that to his disciples Jesus was not a memory but a living Lord, and when they came to set down his story they presented him not as the Jesus of past history but as the Christ of their living faith.*

'That'll do,' Thomas said.

Nik said, 'There's more.'

'Not about how he looked?' the Magdalene asked.

'No.'

'Then we might as well make him look any way we want. And I don't care, as long as he isn't one of them wallies they put in pictures in churches.'

'How would you know?' script-writer Harriet said. 'You never go into a church.'

'I do! I was in one when our Jim got married four years ago.'

Laughter.

Mary of Bethany said, 'I don't want no creeping Jesus neither. I'm not wiping his feet with my hair if he's one of them. I'd get the giggles anyway. If I'm going to act the part I have to believe in the characters. I couldn't believe in no weeping-willy.'

'No weeping-willies,' the Director said. 'Promise.'

Nathaniel, quiet as ever, said, 'Ought to look ordinary. He must have looked like the people where he was born, mustn't he? So he should look like the people round here if he's born here. He'd look like everybody else till God called him, then he'd look special.'

Brian, sneering, said, 'You make him sound like a religious Clark Kent.'

'Who's Clark Kent?' Nathaniel asked, and was bewildered by the cries of mockery.

'You laugh,' the Director said, 'but there's a lot in what he says. In any case, I think I know who I'd like to play the part.'

†

NIK'S NOTEBOOK: ME play JESUS. Five thousand exclamation marks.

He said he didn't want anybody to play the part who also wants to be an actor. He wants a non-actor. Someone, he said, who can just BE. Someone who can just be an idiot, Judas said, as he would, he having wished to play Jesus himself.

Our Beloved Director is out of his leptonic mind.

Selah, as they say in the Godbook.

All this Bible-reading research is going to my head. I just looked up *selah* in the dictionary. A Hebrew word of unknown meaning, it says, which is a lot of help. Except I do like words of unknown meaning, because then they can mean anything you want them to mean. The dic. does say, though, that *selah* probably had something to do with an instruction in music. Like saying: Pause here. Which makes it very suitable for this songandance.

Also: Suppose Our Beloved Director has more than a lepton for a mind after all. Suppose the only leptonic thing about him is his leptosomatic body. He is all of 1.46 m. in his legwarmers, and is about as thick as a leptocephalus when last seen in a suitable state to be measured for swimming trunks—a service I observed the costume person of female gender performing for him last week behind the counter in the nosh bar when OBD thought we were all doing relaxation exercises in the drama hall. No wonder they call him Randy Franky, as he is so frankly randy. (I was hunting for a packet of Smarties at the time, finding the consumption of Smarties more relaxing than re-laxation exercises with a bunch of sweating would-be superstars. Also: what the ding do women see in him, when there's not much to see of him at all? I still have not understood about sexual attraction and must make a special study of it soon.)

OBD is leptocephalic in other ways as well: like slippery and wriggly. He also looks slimy to the touch. I have no intention of finding out if he really is. But withal he is fascinating in a primitive kind of way. The gang say he is okay when you're in the bad and that persons of youthful age who find themselves in trouble flock to him for advice and assistance. Being sheep, they would. All I can say is I hope I'm never in trouble with no one else to bleat to.

Selah.

I am without any doubt whatever a NON-actor. For a start, the gushing pretension of would-be actors puts me off. Ergo ego. I watch them preening in front of the rehearsal mirrors in the drama hall. Just waiting for applause. All they want is to be liked. Plus admired, adored, idolized, flattered, etc. And they're more groupy than glue. If they're on their own for more than five minutes they get withdrawal symptoms and go walkabout, looking for kindred lost souls to coagulate with.

Why me? I asked OBD.

His reply: Many are called but you is chosen.

Very convulsing. I told him he himself should play a small but perfectly formed Almighty, as he already seemed to ALMOST know the lines.

Reply: All right, you big Dick—I mean, Nik!—get on with it because you're cast.

Much laughter from the groupies.

Me: I have been told my natural curiosity is one day likely to land me in hot water. Despite this warning, I joined your crazy filmthing because you wanted a researcher to save you the trouble of doing the work yourself. This I don't mind. I enjoy researching, and God turns out to be quite interesting in an uninteresting sort of way. But me play Jesus! Pick on someone your own size!

OBD, riled by this second reference to his diminutive stature: Look, Lord Bighead, you joined this project because your history teacher told you your work on the film could be submitted for exam assessment, and you thought what a nice

26

easy option it would be. So just do your researching and quietly think of playing Jesus Christ, okay? There's weeks yet before shooting starts so you'll have plenty of time to turn us down if you don't want to do it. In which case, your researching will be finished and you can seek pastures new among people of a better class who are more worthy of your superior talents than this our humble company.

Etc. yammer yammer yak yak. Quite took off with the putdowns.

I said I'd think about it, just to shut him up.

Well, he does kind of breathe at you. He wriggles close and exhales up at you from beneath your nostrils, he being minuter than everyone else in the movie except that pricky clapperboy. And his breath stinks of mints. He chainsucks those nasty little mints with the hole in the middle. This habit he makes even more attractive by spearing the mint through its hole with the sharp point of his pink little lizard-like tongue and then sticking his tongueyed mint out at you while he listens to what you're saying. Distracting. He was doing it during our heated exchange, which is why I couldn't think of any speedo-witty retorts to his insults.

The rest of Our Gang enjoyed this no end, naturally, and orchestrated it with much hooted laughter in the manner of a Greek chorus gone off their heads. Especially when OBD said that I was exactly his idea of the sort of anybody person who can't act and wouldn't be noticed in a crowd even if everybody else left.

A sort of renta-nobody, John the Baptist quipped.

Mintbreath breathed: A nobody would suit my idea of Jesus Christ exactly. And you, he said to me, will make a very successful nobody.

Selah.

If he was trying to rile me in revenge for being turdy with him, he succeeded. But:

I AM NO NOBODY

And I have a passport to prove it. Required last year when Grandad took me to northern Sweden to meet some old buddies from his days at sea.

There is a terrible picture of me staring at the Qwik Foto camera on Paddington station. Even my own mother wouldn't recognize me. And my passport says in official government printing that I am Nicholas Christopher FROME, British Citizen and Student, 1.75 m. taille, with no distinguishing marks.

When I come to think about it, this just shows how useless a passport is at telling who you are. For example: 'No distinguishing marks'. Ridiculous. I'm covered in distinguishing marks! Not that I'd want other people to know about most of them.

Like the brown mole, 1 cm. diameter, just below the hip bone on my right thigh. And the scar, 3.4 cm. long on my left kneecap, where I fell on a jagged stone at age nine yrs four mths while being chased by cruds in the playground at school, their intention being to tie my arms and legs into reef knots, they being good little boy scouts busy learning their tenderfoot and desirous of practising brotherly love and scouts' law on me. This experience has left me with serious reservations about boy scouts and brotherly love. As churches of all kinds often run scout troops and talk a lot about brotherly love, this also makes me suspicious of churches, apart from my difficulties with God.

Circumcised. 9.6 cm. limp, a slim 13.3 cm. when roused. (Last checked two nights ago, when I was disappointed to find no further development since the previous measurement a month ago. There's more hair though—and about time.) My mother was fanatical about cleanliness and thought my father a dirty old man, even at thirty, which is old, I know, but not old enough, surely, to class him as a DOM. Anyhow, my fifth member was given the chop shortly after my second birthday (or so I've been told; I've no memory of this presumably painful occasion) to make sure I could be kept germ free and could be thoroughly inspected for any signs of DOMishness by Mummy in the bath at night, which she insisted on right up to the time when she . . .

I prefer not to remember that distinguishing mark. Forget it.

Why am I spewing all this out here? It has nothing to do with God and Our Gang. Must be this word processor. You just keep writing like you were talking to someone, when really it's

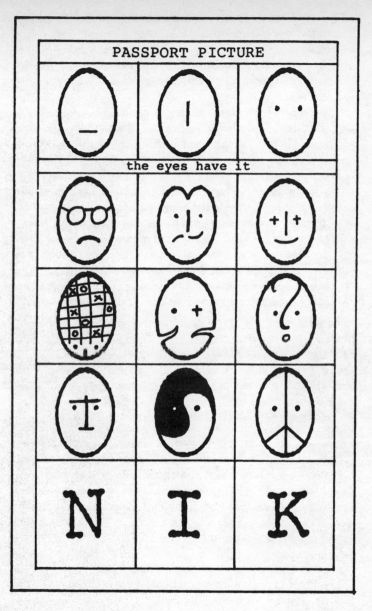

only a dumb machine. It's the gazing face of the VDU that does it, and the green fingertip moving across, writing words. And having writ moves on. You just can't stop.

STOP damn it. Where was I? Oh yes: Distinguishing marks. Also: light brown hair, grey eyes, glasses (not all the time), etc., all 'visible'.

The point I'm making is that there can be nobody else anywhere in the whole spacedout world who has *exactly* the same combination of physical attributes, thus proving how unique a somebody I am.

Which is a nice thought till you remember that everybody else is just as unique a somebody. Which also means, therefore, that being unique is the most commonplace thing you can be. Which seems a contradiction in terms. But never mind.

What's more I haven't even started to list the things *inside* me that are never ever visible, even to myself, and which nobody knows about except me, and which are more me than any of the visible bits. None of these ever gets on a passport, or any kind of form, so how does anyone ever know about anyone else?

STOCKSHOT: *And as the mole on my [right thigh] is where it was when I was born, though all my body has been woven of new stuff time after time, so through the ghost of the unquiet father the image of the living son looks forth . . . That which I was is that which I am and that which in possibility I may come to be. So in the future, the sister of the past, I may see myself as I sit here now but by reflection from that which then shall be.*

The idea of me playing Jesus is also ridiculous because I do not believe in God. OBD said this didn't matter.

He said: You don't have to believe in God, ducky. All you have to do is behave like you're the son of God. And judging by your normal behaviour you shouldn't have any difficulty doing that.

Har har har and good-night.

The evening so happily concluded, Mintbreath sent us all home to work out who or what our Bible characters would be if they returned today. Caiaphas equals the Archbishop of Canterbury, Judas equals the Chancellor of the Exchequer: that kind of thing.

Not me. He wants a nobody for Jesus, he can have a nobody. A nobody who refuses to be anybody who is not the somebody he already is. If I'm going to play Jesus (which I'm not) then Jesus Christ is going to be me.

Selah.

Who cares anyway? As far as I can tell from my researches, the only thing you can say about Christ is that he never turns out to fit anybody's idea of how he ought to be. Everybody tries to make him into what they want him to be. In my opinion, nobody wants to know what he was REALLY like, because they all know instinctively that they wouldn't like what they found if they did.

I'd cop out of this movie right now, but I keep wondering WHY. Why do people believe all this guff about God? And what does it feel like to believe it? What does it DO to you? I mean, even *intelligent* people fall for it! It must DO something. Mustn't it?

That's the trouble with being too curious. Once you're hooked you can't give up. I keep churning it over in my mind and I know I might as well get it out of my system right now. I mean, it would be such an indignity to get old, like in your twenties, and still be interested in God. You'd never live it down. It's so juvenile. So I'll tackle God and Jesus Christ now and then get on with black holes, which is at least something worth looking forward to. (Question: Is God the Father a black hole? Is God the Son a white hole? Is God the Holy Ghost a quasar? Explore and discuss.)

Selah.

Anyway, I told Mintbreath I'll play Jesus if I can convince myself Jesus is important enough to bother about, but that I'd only be doing it under protest.

To which OBD replied: You think Christ was willing? So who wants to be crucified?

Har har har and a second good-night.

ACTION: Fixed interview with Revd Philip Ruscombe BA, Vicar of St James, tomorrow, 7 p.m., at the vicarage, to ask Important Questions About God.

Start with the priests. If they don't know about God, who does? How does anybody know?

Not that Christ had much luck with the priests, come to think of it. They were the ones who wanted him dead.

†

Only one witness, an insurance agent, Brian Standish, reported finding a young man hanging from a cross. Later that same morning Tom sought him out in his office.

'Don't look much like a policeman,' the insurance agent said. 'And I went through all I know half a dozen times at the station.'

'Helps to hear it first hand, sir.'

'Have to make it quick. Up to the eyeballs. Coffee?'

'No, sir, thanks.'

'Well, let's see. As I told the sergeant, I was jogging. Morning stagger, do it every day. Same route: along London Road, left past the council depot, under the railway viaduct to the canal, along the towpath, up into Cheapside, along Rowcroft, up into town and back home along London Road. Some days do it twice, if I'm feeling strong, which isn't often. Today I did it twice, though I'm beginning to regret it. Didn't see him first time so don't know whether he was there or not. I'm not one for the scenic beauties. Anyway, it was a bit foggy this morning and parky. But the second time round, the fog had cleared and the sun was bright. That's why I spotted him. The sun caught him. He was swinging, you see, turning slowly like a life-size crucifix on the end of a wire. The sun flashed on his face, I think. At any rate, it was his face I saw first, hanging up there, right above me, over the hedge along the towpath. Stopped me dead in my tracks. But I mean dead. Took my breath away for a second. The look on his face. The pain. But smiling. Grinning more like. Mad almost. Weird anyway. I thought he was a gonner. But then I heard him say something. Saliva slavering from his mouth. His body was shining with sweat, ribs sticking out, belly sucked in. Like a chicken carcass hanging in a butcher's shop. And his legs! Bent, very awkward. And those underpants! Not a pretty sight!'

'Blue with white trimmings?'

'Shouldn't laugh, but the underpants were comic somehow. Not that I laughed then. Too stunned.'

'And he said something?'

'Blabbering. Couldn't make head or tail.'

'Important, sir.'

'Sorry, not a word. Delirious, I suppose. Not that I stood there listening. As soon as I realized what I was looking at, I scrambled up the bank, pushed through the hedge into that dump—which, by the by, it's time the council made them clear, junked cars piled all over the place, rusty scrap everywhere, a bloody eyesore, a blot on the town, the sooner the bypass goes through the better ... Where was I?'

'Pushing through the hedge, sir.'

'Right. Wasn't till I was in the dump I realized he was dangling from a crane. Couldn't believe it! Fifteen feet off the ground on a cross made of rusty metal hooked onto the end of a crane! He was strapped on with strips of polythene round his arms and legs. Looked at first like there was nothing holding him at all. It was only then I realized I'd expected nails and blood streaming out. When I saw there wasn't, it was almost as big a shock as seeing him first. And I panicked a bit, I suppose. Funny thing, you expect the worst and when you don't find it, you go to pieces. Usually a calm person myself. Have to be in my line of business. But you don't find people on crosses every day, even in insurance. And we don't do a policy covering crucifiction.'

'So you did what, sir?'

'Ran about like a spooked rabbit. I was going to try and get him down. But then I thought, what happens if I push the wrong levers and he goes twanging up into the pulley or crashing to the ground? Pole-axed or pile-driven, that's what. Either way, a big claim against yours truly. So I started thinking whether to fetch the fire brigade, the ambulance, or the police. Or all three. But I couldn't believe what I was seeing, and I thought, if I don't believe it myself, who's going to believe it when I tell them over the phone? So there I was dodging about and getting nowhere while the kid was babbling on like he was in Parliament, spouting a lot of hot air that didn't make any sense.'

'But you finally went for the police.'

'Daft, I know, running all that way. Could have dialled the three nines. But somehow I just had to *see* somebody to tell.'

'You arrived at the station at six thirty-three, according to the report sheet. Told the duty officer what you'd found. He sent you in a car with two officers back to the scene.'

'And he'd gone.'

'But the officers believed your story?'

'The driver knew me. Stan Fields. Belong to the same bowling club. He could tell I wasn't joking. And of course there were the footprints. The cross was lying on the ground directly under the crane and strips of polythene were scattered all round. They'd been cut. But that wouldn't have made a case, would it? The footprints did though. Very fresh, and all round the cross. I knew mine because of the pattern of the soles. I was wearing new running shoes, expensive, with an unusual pattern on the instep. We could see the print of them all right. But the other prints crisscrossed over mine, so they must have been made after I'd been there.'

'You were at the station by six thirty-three. How long to run there from the scene?'

'Oh, eight minutes. Ten at most.'

'You were back at the scene by six fifty according to PC Fields' report. So there was a maximum twenty-seven minutes for whoever it was to get the boy down and away. And you didn't see anybody anywhere near the scene all the time you were there?'

'Nobody.'

'And you can't identify the boy?'

'Sorry. Never seen him before, as far as I know. Not that I go round looking at kids his age. See enough of my own two, thanks.'

'They about his age?'

'Fifteen and sixteen. He might have been seventeen. Hard to tell under the circs. Certainly not younger than sixteen, I'd guess. Too well hung—if you'll pardon the pun.'

'I've the other details you gave the sergeant, sir. But perhaps you've thought of something else since then?'

'Sorry. Would help if I could.'

'Then I'll not hold you up any longer, sir. Thanks for your time.'

'Best of luck. Hope you catch them. Need to crack down on this sort of thing. Too much violence everywhere these days.'

†

JULIE: Dear Nik. Can't start without saying a name, as if I'm talking to thin air and not to another person. When I pray I start Dear God. Same thing. Somebody . . . *other* . . . has to be there. So: Dear Nik.

[*Pause.*]

Funny about names. At the beginning, when I thought I was dying, names suddenly seemed very important. I used to say my own over and over to myself. Julie . . . Julie . . . Julie. JulieJulie-Julie. And Sarah . . . Sarah, because that was the name my father called me when I was little. I was christened Sarah Julia, did I ever tell you? But when I was twelve I took against Sarah because I read in the Bible about Sarah being childless till she was very old. I thought, I want children when I'm young, so I won't let anyone call me by a name that might put a hex on me. As if names could work bad magic. I told everybody they had to call me Julie, and everyone did, except my father, who said I'd always be Sarah to him. Sarah my solace, he'd say.

When I thought I was dying I thought: There you are, you're going to die without any children after all. Dad was right to call you Sarah. SarahSarahSarah, I said. And saying it over and over made me feel like I used to feel when I was little, as if all my childhood was inside that name, and saying it made me into a child again.

[*Chuckles.*]

SarahSarahSarah I said in my head until it stopped making any sense at all but was just a sound that didn't mean anything. As if I'd worn it out. And then my childhood faded away too

35

and I was in hospital again, thinking I was dying and feeling the pain.

I thought I was only saying those names in my head but Simmo told me I was saying them out loud some of the time. She told me this last week when we were talking about you. She said yours was one of the names I kept repeating. Nik . . . Nik . . . Nik. I shouted it sometimes, as if I was calling to you. That's why they sent for you to come quickly. But most of the time, Simmo says, I just said Nik . . . Nik. Quietly, like it was a magic spell that would make something good happen.

And names do, don't they? Even babies know that. They soon learn if they say Mummy they get fed or hugged or looked at. If you speak a person's name they come to you or look at you. And when someone else speaks your name you feel pleased. You feel wanted. You feel *there*. Alive. Even if they're saying your name with dislike, at least you know you're you, that you exist.

Once, when I was little, about eight, I asked my dad, 'Is there a God, Daddy?' Dad said, 'I'm not sure. I think so.' And I said, 'But there must be, mustn't there, because he has a name.'

Anyway, that's why I kept saying your name and my own name when I thought I was done for.

Does this mean anything? Am I just rambling? The drugs make me ramble sometimes.

[*Pause.*]

I'm only trying to explain that names make sense of the nothing you feel you're going into when you think you're dying. At least they did for me. Thinking you're going to die is like setting out on a long journey that frightens you to a place you know nothing about. And saying the names of the people you love seems to bring them to you, to be with you. And your own name is like a space suit you live inside. While you've got it on you're all right. You live inside it. Without it you'd melt into the nothingness and be nothing yourself and never reach your unknown destination.

[*Sounds of Julie drawing in and exhaling deep breaths.*]

Sorry! Simmo says if I breathe in deeply when the pain comes and let it out slowly I'll feel better. As if the big breath comes inside, wraps up all the pain and fear and sadness like broken glass in cotton wool, and carries it away when you breathe out. Sometimes it works. This time it left some glass behind.

[*Breathing in. Breathing out.*]

I never knew pain is so . . . consuming. I mean *real* pain, not just hurt. Real pain sort of eats you. Gnaws you all over like a thousand rats chewing at your bones. And it burns you with sharp flames.

Now I know why people in the old days talked about hell being a place of fire and torture. Real pain is a kind of hell.

I've been trying to think about what pain *means*. Why do we have to have it? Why do people suffer?

I haven't got far yet. Except to hate it with a deep deep loathing. I've never felt such hate for anything before. Perhaps I have to get rid of the hate before I'll be able to think about what pain means? Just as I had to stop thinking I was dying before I could begin to get better. I managed to take that step thanks to you, Nik. Perhaps I have to do this thing about pain on my own? Perhaps that's what it means – what it's for. For learning to be on your own. Do you think it could be?

Doesn't sound right somehow. If only you were here we could talk about it, like we talked from the first time we met I remember our first time together, every moment. Frame by frame, you might say—or your leptonic Director might!

[*Quiet chuckles.*]

That's another thing I'm discovering about illness. And about not being able to see anything, or move, or do anything at all. You remember a lot. Memories come flooding back—like remembering myself so vividly as a child when I say Sarah-Sarah. In the last few days I've remembered things I haven't thought of since they happened years ago.

Which reminds me of that poem . . . how does it go? . . . I expect you think it's trite . . . but, there, you see, I've suddenly remembered it when I haven't thought of it for ages . . . I've got it:

> I remember, I remember,
> The house where I was born,
> The little window where the sun
> Came peeping in at morn;

He never came a wink too soon,
Nor brought too long a day,
But now, I often wish the night
Had borne my breath away!

[*Pause.*]

Heavens, it's much gloomier than I thought! How funny! I only remembered the sun peeping in at dawn. That's why I liked it. I learned it when I was . . . what? . . . nine, I suppose. I found it in a book, and thought it was specially for me because the sun came peeping into my room at dawn too.

But I didn't remember the night bearing my breath away. Just shows what you don't notice when you don't need to! There've been plenty of times since what Simmo calls my little mishap that I've remembered the house where I was born and wished the night would bear my breath away so there would be an end to the pain.

I don't remember the rest of the poem, and now I'd rather like to know how it goes on. Could you find it for me?

I wonder if the poet lived in her memories as much as I'm living in mine? I'm beginning to think we only know who we are, only know ourselves, through our memories. I mean, think what it would be like if we couldn't remember anything. We wouldn't be able to do most of the things we like doing, never mind the things we don't like doing. We wouldn't be able to learn anything. We wouldn't even be able to learn from the mistakes we make all the time, because we wouldn't be able to remember our mistakes no matter how painful they were.

Grief! We wouldn't know the people we loved, either! We wouldn't have any memory of them so we wouldn't be able to think about them, or what it was like to be with them. We couldn't love them because we wouldn't be able to remember what we liked about them so much.

And how could we trust anyone? We'd have nothing to go on, no past experience to tell us this person is honest and this other one tells lies. If we could remember nothing of our past could we be anything now? Except confused, I suppose. And frightened, because we wouldn't know what was safe and what was dangerous. We couldn't believe anything because we wouldn't remember anything to believe in. Not that we'd know what belief meant anyway. We wouldn't know what anything meant.

I've never thought memory was quite as important as that! But I suppose it is.

[*Deep breathing.*]

I'm tired out. Time for another drug-scoffing session. I eat more drugs than I eat meals. Till the knockout pills arrive I'll think of you, Nik, and the memory will keep the pain away. You, the first time we met. All that rain! You, the first time I took you to church. Disgracing yourself! You the night before . . .

[*Snatched-at breaths.*]

Sorry, have to stop . . . *Nurse!* . . .

[*Cries of pain. End of tape.*]

MEETINGS

NIK'S NOTEBOOK: The vicar of St James is pathetic. St James was the son of Zebedee, brother of John the Beloved, called Boanerges. Boanerges means 'son of thunder'. St James's vicar is no son of thunder. Son of silence more like.

Except when speaking of golf (said: goff). Waxes chatty then. Goff clubs are the first thing you meet inside his front door. Along with pong of mouldy wellies and decomposing dog. Dog a podgy black labrador with watery eyes, slavery mouth, and a limp in the left foreleg. Turns you off animal rights. Vic calls him Bugsy when not calling him Old Chum.

Vic is a bachelor. Tall, balding, pink-faced, smelling vaguely of Old Spice and musty incense. Also large-bellied. Rumour says he's oathed to celibacy. But what woman would have him? He came along the path from church in flapping black cassock, like a converted Dracula, Old Chum hobbling along behind.

The vicarage is occupied by neglect. Cold even with sun shining in. Took me into what he called his study, a sort of religious knocking shop. Large gooky pic of Virgin Mary in fetchingly soulful pose staring from one wall. A fairly explicit full frontal crucifix made of carved wood hanging over the fireplace. A jumble of bookshelves crammed with heavy dull tomes, mostly holy manuals, tombs for dead words, covering most of the walls. A bulky desk big as a snooker table piled with controlled disaster of paper. (He should persuade the parish to stump up for a word processor, he'd save himself a lot of garbage, but maybe God wouldn't approve? Is there a God in the machine? If there is in mine he-she-it only says what I tell him-her-it to say. That's the sort of God I like.)

He waved me into one of two exhausted armchairs beside the empty fireplace. The fplc mouth blocked by an old head-stone, from the churchyard I guess, its inscription worn unreadable by weather. Made the room seem ominous. The room a tomb. Sitting with a memorial to your own death in the great reaper's waiting room.

Selah.

Vic says, suspicious: Wanted to ask about God, did you say?

Me, nervous: Wondered if you could explain belief.

Vic's left eyelid twitches: Belief! Tricky subject. What was it you wanted to know exactly?

Old Chum collapses between us like a whale expiring on the beach. The way he lies, the headstone becomes his. Maybe it is, because I'm not sure he's alive even when he's limping about.

Me: Not sure, *exactly*. What belief means, I suppose.

Vic smiles. Ah! he says with relief.

He picks up a large dog-eared vol. from a stool beside his chair. (Underneath the dog-eared vol. lies *The Times* folded at the crossword puzzle, mostly finished.)

He flips dog-eared pages and says: The dictionary tells us, let's see: *Belief. Noun. One: a principle, idea, et cetera, accepted as true or real, especially without positive proof. Two: opinion, conviction. Three: religious faith. Four: trust or confidence, as in a person or person's abilities, et cetera.* There you are.

Thumps book shut, replaces on top of *The Times*.

Silence except for heavy breathing from Old Chum. Vic bends forward and pats him. Decomposing doggy pong rises like a gag.

I gag. Cough. Try not to breathe. Fail. Say: Might need a bit more, if you wouldn't mind. I mean, how does belief feel?

Vic, looking startled, sits back in chair and says: Feel! Good lord! Can't say one honestly *feels* anything. Rather . . . that is . . . one does not *feel* belief . . . one . . . *accepts* it.

I stare at him. He toys with a pen lying on the stool at his side and stares at Old Chum. Old Chum pluffles in sleep.

Selah.

Vic is not a man in a hurry. Eventually looks up, smiles, says: Warned you it was a tricky subject. I don't mean one doesn't feel anything about one's beliefs, only that one doesn't feel belief.

Silence. Stares at pen as he toys with it.

Then goes on: One decides that God is, by and large, bad

days taken with good, more likely *to be* than not. This . . . one believes.

Pause.

STOCKSHOT: *Canst thou* [Vic says] *by searching find out God? Canst thou find out the Almighty unto perfection? It is as high as heaven; what canst thou do? deeper than hell; what canst thou know?*

He looks up at me. Says: If you understand me.

Pause. I stare at him.

Not quite, I say.

Vic says: No, thought you mightn't. He sighs (sounding so like Old Chum I wonder if Vic ventriloquizes the dog, or maybe even vice versa. Then also realize they look pretty much alike as well, except Vic doesn't have the watery eyes yet). He slumps further into his puffy chair and his own bulgy waist.

Silence again. Vic stares between his hillocky knees at Old Chum's hillocky body for so long I think he's forgotten me or eternity has begun without me noticing.

But then he stirs himself, glances up, says: Look, er . . . Nik? What's all this about? Thinking of asking for confirmation?

I explain. He laughs. Quite revived, he seems for a minute. (Old Chum lifts his head at the sound of Vic's laughter, takes a bleary glim, and flops, comatose again. The millennium is not yet.)

Vic: How splendid! A reluctant Jesus in search of belief in himself! That does appeal, I must say!

I'm laughing too, because it is pretty funny.

Don't be upset, says he, I'm not laughing at you, dear boy.

(I love the dear boy bit.)

I say: It's okay. I think it's a pretty stupid idea myself.

Not at all, no no, says he. Then, perking up even more: You don't happen to play goff, do you?

Sorry? say I.

Pity, says he. You know . . . Nik? . . . what I'd do if Our Lord walked through that door this minute? After the required pleasantries, of course.

I shake my head.

42

Vic says: I'd say, My Lord, will you honour me with a round? And, you know, Nik, it has always seemed to me that He would reply, My dear vicar, I'd be delighted. Or words to that effect.

I say: Maybe we can make that a scene in our film. (I'm only half joking, I realize as I say it.)

You could, Vic says in all seriousness, do worse. Better than pretending to perform miracles. More likely. More real. More to do with belief, in fact.

But, I say, how would you know he was Christ?

Ah! says he, now there you have it, you see. That's what belief *is*. I'd know because of believing. It doesn't feel like anything. It's just *there*, a fact of one's life.

Now it's my turn to stare at Old Chum while trying to sort out this nugget. Then: Sorry, vicar, but I don't find that very clear.

Vic slumps even further into his own and his chair's upholstery and looks deeply disappointed.

He says: Convincing is what you mean.

I do? say I.

He nods, sighs: I'm not very good at this, I'm afraid . . .

I didn't mean . . . , I say, feeling embarrassed.

Vic, flapping a hand: I know, I know. But I'm not. One must have the courage to acknowledge one's limitations. And I have to admit that I'm not too good at talking about God. Never really have been. Every week I hold confirmation classes. Mostly young people of thirteen or fourteen, and mostly attending because their parents want them to. Rather like baptism, you know. Parents want their children done just to make sure. Hedging their bets. If God exists, having it done might get him on your side. If he doesn't, who cares?

He chuckles. Chummy fluffles and slobbers.

Well, Vic says, I talk to them. Tell them as best I can about church and prayer, and about God. They listen – rather dutifully, I have to admit, and politely. Too politely, I sometimes think. Might be better all round if they argued. They do ask the odd question now and then, but just to show willing and to be kind, I'm sure.

He smiles, but sadly, and goes on:

Some drop out. But mostly they stay the course and go before the bishop in their best new clothes for the laying on of hands. All very pretty and pious and their mums and dads looking proud. But as I stand at the bishop's side and witness the performance of this holy rite I know that six months later they'll mostly have given up any pretence of being in the slightest interested in God or church or anything religious. And I wonder how much their falling off is a failure of mine.

He pushes himself up in his chair, not looking at me. I sit stone still. I'm not sure he's talking to me now. He might not even remember I'm in the room. Is he just talking aloud to himself? I feel a bit guilty, like I'm eavesdropping on a private confession.

He speaks so quietly I strain to hear: Of course, if you suggest to them that they aren't Christian any more, they're most indignant, quite insulted in fact, and tell one sharply, and not so politely any more, how Christianity isn't the same as being a church-goer, and how, if it comes to that, the church has betrayed Christ because it's more interested in old buildings and out-of-date customs than in people and their needs, and how the church supports evil rulers and amasses wealth while people die in oppression and hunger and terrible poverty. And frankly, Nik . . .

He does remember I'm here after all!

. . . I have no answer to such accusations. I'm quite inadequate to the task of explaining that what we're really talking about is the Being who, by definition, is so all-containing of ourselves and the world and the entire universe, as well as whatever unimaginable wonders lie beyond, that it is impossible to say anything meaningful at all. God is a being who is beyond being. How can one speak of such a . . .

He raises his hands, shakes his head, shrugs.

I nod, meaning: I understand the difficulty.

He sighs again. Says: And now you come, asking me to tell you what belief is. What am I to say?

Now I have to shrug.

And it's his turn to nod and smile sympathetically: You're quite right to ask, I don't mean you aren't, dear boy. But I find myself in a quandary. I'm like a man who's found a sack of gold but can't tell anyone where he found it because, if he ever knew,

44

he's forgotten now. And whenever he tries to share his gold with others, it turns to sand even as he pours it into their hands. You can imagine how embarrassing that is! For a vicar especially.

He laughs, but for some reason I can't join in.

One even gets to the point, he says, of hiding the fact that one possesses gold oneself so as to avoid the embarrassment of people asking for some. One even sometimes tries to pretend that not having is the same as having. That the gold is an illusion. Which is a painful kind of betrayal. Of those people, like you, who ask, and of one's faith. Worst of all, it is a betrayal of God.

He mutters the last sentence so quietly, so shamefaced, that, though I sit forward to hear, I look away from him at once.

Silence. Long, long silence.

Broken at last by Old Chum. He wakes like a canine Lazarus, staggers to his doddering paws, shakes decomposition into the airless air, and hobbles to the door.

Vic comes to and says with bluster: Sorry, dear boy, not much help to you, I'm afraid.

It's okay, I say. And it's time I went. Things at home . . .

Of course, yes, Vic says. I'll see you out.

At the door he slips a goff club from its bag and putts a pebble from the step. Old Chum lumbers after it like a geriatric caddy and disappears among the overgrown garden bushes.

Pity you don't play, Vic says. Easier to talk on the fairway. Fresh air. Exercise. Should try it. Strongly recommended. Give you a lesson, if you like.

He is a different man from the one I've just been talking to. More lively but less likeable. The real Vic is hiding behind a shield of hearty gamesmanship.

Thanks. Sometime, I say, and retreat towards the gate.

You've only to ask, he calls, waving his club in farewell.

I wave a non-committal hand and escape through the gate, thankful that a high wall makes it unnecessary for me to look back.

†

Nik—Sorry to have been so little use last evening. After you left, a thought occurred that might be helpful. I suggest you see some friends of mine. They are a kind of monk. Don't let this put you off. They're quite sane. They're called The Community of the Holy Innocents. C H I for short. (We do have monks and nuns in the Church of England, though most people don't seem to know!) I think they might be able to answer some of your questions better than I.

If you can stay a day or two you might even discover some of the answers for yourself. Seek and ye shall find, as the saying is.

Whether you do or not, I think you'd have an interesting time. The brothers will put you up free of charge. (Though you may be expected to help with a few small chores.) And without any religious obligation of course. I mean you don't have to promise to let them convert you in order to qualify for free bed and board!

Do try. You won't regret it. I spend a spell there every year and always return refreshed. Write to Brother Kit C H I, at the address overleaf. Say I suggested the idea.

God bless.

Philip Ruscombe

✝

Lacking clues, Tom visited the scene-of-crime.

No one was there when he arrived. The cross lay in between a battered mobile crane and a pyramid of old tyres. He poked about, finding nothing except a confusion of footprints drying in the mud. Whatever else there might have been would, he supposed, have been carted off for lab treatment.

An old man, hands in pockets, came wandering up.

'After something?' he said, unwelcoming.

Tom flipped his identity wallet.

The old man was small and stocky with high, hunched shoulders. He wore a grubby cap and a torn old pullover that might once have been green and was covered with flecks of wood shavings and a powdering of sawdust. His trousers were baggy, tired grey, probably part of an old suit. His face was clean shaven, though spiky bristles grew in the creases of rugged lines. A prominent nose—almost a beak, Tom thought—and pale sharp eyes. He looked about sixty but could have been older. A hawk-like man.

'Thought your lot had finished here,' the old man said.

'You know what all this is about then?' Tom said.

'Roughly.'

'Work here?'

'Now and then.'

'Meaning?'

'Now and then. Supposed to be retired. Bloody fool idea. Retirement is for the dead. I keep a workshop. Do a few odd jobs. Nothing regular.'

'Here early this morning?'

'How early?'

'Six o'clock?'

'Too early for me, that is. These days any road. One benefit of being retired, you see. Can please yourself.' The old man laughed.

'But you know what happened?'

'There's plenty of gossip.'

'And what does the gossip say?'

'That some kid was strung up on a cross during the night but disappeared after he was found this morning. Something like that.'

'Does the gossip say who did it?'

'Hooligans, likely.'

'And who the kid was?'

'No. Nothing about him.'

Tom nodded. He felt he was being stonewalled.

'And what do you think, sir?' he said with too careful politeness.

The old man sniffed and grinned. 'Nothing much.'

'You don't seem very bothered.'

'Why should I be bothered?' the old man said, looking away. 'Anything can happen these days, and mostly does, if you wait long enough.'

'Could I have your name, sir?' Tom said, taking out his notebook.

'Is it that bad!' The old man chuckled.

'Might need to talk to you again, that's all.'

The old man, shrugging, said, 'Arthur Green.'

Tom said, 'You don't own this dump?'

'No!'

'Who does?'

'Wouldn't know. Fred Callowell runs it.'

'Is he around?'

The old man nodded towards a hut where the access road ended. 'That's his office. But he's often out, buying and selling.'

'Was he here earlier, would you know?'

'Better ask him.'

Tom looked round at the wilderness of scrap metal and pyramids of corpsed motor cars.

'You'll be here all day?'

'Can't think there's anything more I can tell you.'

'All the same, you never know.'

Tom walked away, past the closed hut, along the access road to his unmarked car parked out of sight by the railway bridge.

Arthur Green watched him go, then hurried to his workshop, two buildings along from Fred Callowell's hut.

†

The day after Nik visited the vicar of St James's, he read a notice in the local rag, headlined:

CHRISTIAN CND
PEACE RALLY

Demonstrators were invited to form up in Field Road, near the maternity hospital (how the new mums would love that), at three o'clock on Saturday afternoon, before marching through town (how the shopkeepers would love that) to Stratford Park (how the bowls players would love that) for the inevitable speeches from local and (minor) national notables.

A good chance for Christian-watching. Besides, he approved of the cause if not the method. Crowds and slogans never succeeded in convincing him of anything except that they were likely to be wrong.

Nik stationed himself in the park well before time on high ground in front of a large lean-comfortable tree, from where he would have a good view of the proceedings. When he arrived few other people were there. Six or seven young men and women wearing armbands printed with M (for Marshal) were busy being important around a scaffold platform draped with Christian and CND posters. An older man in a baggy suit was giving them orders from the platform, calling everyone 'Brother' or 'Sister' in a way that, Nik thought, gave Christianity a bad name and mixed it up with loony trade unionists. A knot of policemen and one policewoman stood to one side, trying to look dispassionate, and muttering jokes to each other, which, from their side-glances, Nik could tell were about Baggy-suit.

Five minutes before the demonstration arrived, a blaring out-of-tune brass band heralding its coming, the already grey and overcast sky started pouring rain as if to douse a fire. This settled, after its first enthusiasm, into a steady, drizzling fret. Under his tree, and dressed in his usual, though dishevelled, ex-army combat jacket, Nik was bearably protected. The police, ever prepared for the worst, donned waterproofs snatched from their van. The marshals, exercising Christian fortitude, made no concessions but laughed a lot and moved about even more busily.

Baggy-suit tested the microphone, tapping and blowing on it, saying, 'One, two, three . . .' and then intoning, 'He maketh his sun to rise on the evil and on the good, and sendeth rain on the just and on the unjust.'

'Matthew five, forty-five,' shouted one of the marshals from the ground and the others cheered.

He at the microphone said, 'Hallelujah, brother. The Lord reigneth; let the people tremble.'

His acolytes groaned, mocking his pun.

'Psalm ninety-nine,' yelled back he of the memory.

'Brother,' Baggy-suit called, waving at Nik, 'can you hear me up there?'

Cupping his hands to his mouth, Nik shouted, 'Mark four,

nine,' this happening to be one of the few quotations that had stuck in his memory from all his recent reading.

'What did he say?' he at the microphone asked aside of a marshal.

Marshal of the memory shouted, 'He that hath ears to hear, let him hear.'

Baggy-suit coughed. 'Thank you, brother,' he said and climbed down.

JULIE: All that rain! And me holding up that silly poster someone had pushed into my hands while we were forming up. Rain was running off the handle straight down my arm. My hair was soaked and streaked in rat tails all over my face so that I could hardly see, and water was streaming down my neck. I remember you telling me afterwards that I was beaming great smiles and you thought I must be alight with the vision of God or something. But really it was only the rain trickling between my boobs and making me nearly giggle. Nothing holy.

NIK'S NOTEBOOK: Carrying a poster

Made me laugh. Saw her straight off, even before she was near enough to see her face or even tell that she was a girl. A kind of energy or something. Don't know. Also, most of the others were playing at being demonstrators, looking around with a kind of pretend humility, but at the same time saying: Look at me, I'm protesting. As if protesting made them better than the people who weren't.

Note for history essay: If you're protesting something – a belief or an opinion or an injustice, or anything – does your protest only 'work' if there are a lot of other non-protesting people to see you? Suppose it depends a bit on this, or who's to know? But it oughtn't to. And if protesting only depends on the publicity value, and isn't worth anything *in itself*, is it worth anything at all?

But this girl wasn't being anything but herself. You could tell she *meant* it. Felt it. Her thoughts were her own. I mean were part of her.

Seems to me most people don't/can't think. They only think other people's thoughts. People who enjoy being in crowds are mostly like that. They like speeches and demos because they are told what to think. And because they are with a lot of other people the same as themselves, which makes them think they're thinking for themselves and doing something about what they think. But they aren't. It's all a trick, a con. What they're really doing is giving themselves up to somebody else who is just using them.

Selah.

This girl. Couldn't take my eyes off her. She was so *her*. But she was taking part in this demo. How could she? She wasn't just a goggle to look at. There was more to her than that. Why was she there at all?

She was dressed in a floppy blue sweater that was too big and jeans you could see, even from the odd glimpse of them I got, had been worn by a male (or else she was hermaphrodite). As the sweater got wetter and wetter it hung heavier and heavier on her, and clung to her, showing her top half was indisputably female. She kept brushing the hair out of her face, and looking round with this slightly silly grin, as if she was observing what was happening as much as she was taking part. And what she saw was amusing her.

Even before the trouble started I was thinking maybe I'd try and talk to her afterwards.

STOCKSHOT: *Who is there?*
I.
Who is I?
Thou.
And that is the awakening—
the Thou and the I.

The trouble Nik mentions started five minutes into the first speech. A couple of hundred demonstrators were crammed together in front of the platform. On the platform nine or ten people were trying to look godly and peaceful. Two press photographers were darting about like sheepdogs herding a flock. The police, about twenty by now, were scattered around the edge of the crowd like blue fence posts, listening and watching with professional poker faces. Nik, under his tree uphill from them all, had a view of the whole scene and, by panning right, of the road from the park entrance.

He was paying little heed to the speech, being too busy watching the girl. She stood in the middle of the crowd, her back to him. But even this hedged back view fascinated him. He willed her to move just for the pleasure of seeing it. Most of all, he willed her to turn and see him, and be as eager for him as he was for her. He wondered about tracking through the crush till, standing beside her, he could see her close up and be ready to speak.

And would have done had he not been distracted by the sudden appearance along the road from the entrance of an open truck driving fast and festooned with Union flags and flapping posters bearing such messages as:

NF
KEEP BRITAIN SAFE
BRITAIN FOR THE BRITISH

and biggest of all:

NF v COMMIE NUKE DEMOS

Paraded on the back was a rampant squad of jeering, stamping men, late teens and early twenties, geared in bovver boots and black leathers, bullet heads shaven close, fist-pumping arms tattooed and harnessed in studded bands. The rain gave them an armoured glaze and spumed in their wake.

What happened next happened very fast, of course, and took everyone by surprise, as it was meant to, which also added to the confusion, causing people to behave irrationally, against their convictions and even against their natures.

Some of the nearest police and demonstrators, hearing the

truck's approach, turned to look. One policeman walked towards it, his arms spread wide, flagging it down. The truck skidded to a halt in front of him at the edge of the crowd. As it stopped five or six of its squad jumped down from the side nearest the crowd and advanced, jeering, towards the approaching policeman.

This, however, was a blind. From his vantage, Nik observed six or seven more squaddies jump down from the other side, split into two groups, and sprint round the crowd, one group heading one way and one the other.

Before anybody had quite grasped what was going on, the leading squaddy had reached the platform, leapt onto it, snatched the microphone from the speaker, and was shouting into it himself:

'This demonstration is another communist-inspired attempt to undermine the will of the British people to protect itself against foreign aggressors and against those who have no right to live here . . .' Et cetera, ad lib.

Julie at first thought this was part of the demo, some kind of stunt arranged by the organizers to help liven up the meeting and make their point in a dramatically ironic way. So she laughed and booed and mocked, thinking she was joining in the fun. Others around her must have thought so too because they reacted with similar amusement. But very soon, several events happening at the same time forced everyone to realize this was no stunt but was brutally real.

Before the invader had said much more than is quoted above some of the platform party surrounded him, shouting objections, and trying to wrest the microphone from his grasp. This brought two more squaddies leaping up in support of their man. Their intervention turned the disagreement into a scuffle and finally into a brawl with fists as well as words being thrown. (Thus in minutes providing a graphic demo of how wars begin: provocation; angry objection; resort to physical violence; and so to battle.)

Just as soon as his leader was interfered with, a squaddy stationed at the side of the platform for this very purpose grabbed the wires trailing from the mike and cut them with clippers.

Meantime (mean time indeed) the gang of squaddies who had jumped down on the side of the truck facing the crowd were approached by three or four of the nearest police, coming to the aid of their mate who had flagged the truck down. The squaddies let the police reach them then dodged away in all directions, bulldozing through the crowd and snatching at banners, which they flailed above their heads, thus turning posters for peace into weapons of war (and demonstrating the neutrality of matter). As they bludgeoned swathes through the protesters, people scattered, shouting, stumbling, falling, ducking away, the squaddies yelling and whooping, and raising Cain by way of yet another demonstration that all men are not brothers.

During this riving diversion the oldest (he was forty if he was a day), biggest, most fiercely and expensively leathered squaddy of all, who had so far sat watching from the truck's cab, climbed onto the back, and from there, using a bull-horn, continued the speech begun by his platform henchman.

A couple of police, hearing this, detached themselves from the keystone kops pursuit now in progress against the crowd busters, and turned their attention instead to the silencing of the truculent orator. Only to find, as they ran towards it, that the truck moved off just fast enough to prevent them reaching it, circling skilfully, zigging, zagging, curling along the edge of the disintegrating crowd, thereby leaving the bill behind, sloshing about in the mud churned up by its wheels, and causing further mayhem among the protesters now fleeing outwards from the mêlée.

NIK'S NOTEBOOK: Planned. All of it worked out beforehand and executed like a military op.

She was trapped. And stood her ground, still holding up that gormless banner. Others near her scattered. But not her.

One of the black leather boys came right at her, shoulder charging. She went flying, arms spread-eagled, legs kicking. Her banner rocketed out of her hands. He caught it in mid air, swung it, and batted her across the buttocks like she was a shuttlecock, sending her pancaking flat-faced into the mud.

That did it. Observer turned activist. Pacifist turned belligerent.

I've never felt anything like it. Me, I'm a watcher, not a doer. The world is splitting at the seams with doers. People who think they know best, who want to be in charge, want to be the ones who make the running for the rest of us. Mighty Mice dressed up as Supermen.

One of the reasons I like history is that it tells about the doers. And it seems to me the bigger the doer becomes the more he/she turns into a murderous, power-hungry, hypocritical, self-righteous, arrogant prig. While ordinary non-big-doers like me and Grandad and all the tellywatchers of the world, who want only to live our lives unmolested, are supposed to be thankful, and admire these Big-Doer creeps, who always pretend they're doing what they're doing for the sake of the rest of us, when they're really only doing it for themselves. And they pay ad-people (who are no better) to make ads and T V programmes presenting them as heroes.

I HATE HEROES.

Selah.

But when I saw her splattered into the mud by a turd in black leather, something happened I'd never felt before. A Doer made me so angry I did something about it. Without thinking. That split-second. Even as his body hit hers. It was a violation against me as much as against her. Just because there was something ... I don't know ... different ... intense ... separate about her. Something I wanted. Wanted to ... *know* I suppose is the word.

Right now, just an hour after leaving her, I don't understand.

But anyway, I piled in.

Geronimo!

JULIE [*Singing*]:   Mud, mud, glorious mud,
There's nothing quite like it
for cooling the blood.

[*She laughs.*]

Mum has an old record of that. I think it's called 'The Hippopotamus Song'. When I was little I used to play it over and over and end up hysterical.

When I hit the mud and felt the mess on my face and hands and the stickiness squeezing through my clothes that song flashed into my head. They'd frightened me when they started running through us, yelling and thrashing about. But the mud and the hippo song cooled my blood and I thought, 'Let them come after me again and it'll be the hippo song for them this time.'

Well, you know what happened then! [*Laughs.*] If my face hadn't been covered in mud so that I couldn't see, I would have known at once whose side you were on, because they were all in leathers and you were in your usual sloppy outfit. But I couldn't see and you were yelling, 'Get up! Come on, get up!' One thing I can't stand is people yelling at me. It infuriates me. I was trying to get up anyway. But you grabbed my arms and pulled at me, and that angered me even more because I don't like people grabbing me either, so I struggled. And what with you pulling and me tugging to get loose we both went off balance and then I slipped in the mud and we both went flopping down, me onto my face again and you onto your bum.

[*She laughs so much she starts coughing, and breathing heavily, and has to pause to recover.*]

'Excrement!' you said, using the crude word.

'Don't you swear at me, you barbarian!' I said, or spluttered rather, because I got a mouth full of mud, and that made me furious with myself as well as with you, which, of course, only made things worse.

And I know what you're thinking right this minute, Nicholas Frome, as you listen. You're thinking how prudish I still am about ruderies, despite all your efforts to corrupt me. But I don't care. I don't like them, and that's that. I don't see any need for them. In fact, I think they're a kind of violence. You say rude words are just explosions that relieve tension. Well, I've some experience with explosions remember. And I don't think any kind of explosion is meaningless, or is just a relief of tension, not even if they are only explosions of words.

Words can't ever be just explosions anyway. They're always words. They all mean something. They all affect people somehow. The people who use them and the people who hear them. And I don't just mean their dictionary meanings.

Saying that makes me think words are like people. They have bodies. You can see them, and you can like the look of them or not, just as I like the look of Nik. It's as interesting back to front as it is front to back. Kin as well as Nik. And the two tall letters protect the little eye. Like a spine. You. Always there. The core. The DNA of Nik. And you, the eye, the ee-why-ee. Watching. A lovely, neat, playful word. And just like you!

And words have intellects as well as bodies. Their dictionary meanings, and their meanings when they're put into sentences. Like these sentences I'm saying to you now. They make some sort of sense, I hope!

And words have emotions just like people do. The things they make you feel when you hear them or read them. Like the words in the sentence 'I love you' which you have to admit no one can ever quite explain just from dictionary meanings, but which get you pretty stirred up if they're said to you.

And sometimes their emotional meanings don't have much to do with their dictionary meanings. Just as sometimes what people think about something is quite different to what they feel about it. They aren't thinking words, they're feeling words. Isn't that right?

So I don't know how you can say that any word can ever be just an explosion that relieves tension. Though I expect, as usual, you'll find some argument to use, because you just love arguing for arguing's sake. But really, in your heart you know I'm right. The truth is you like using ruderies for their shock effect.

Hey, I'm starting to argue with you again! That's a good sign, isn't it? I must be getting better!

[*Pause.*]

Now I've forgotten what I was talking about before I started rambling on about words! None of which I'd thought before now, by the way. So that's one good thing about being ill—it gives you time to think.

INTERCUT: *Crowd scattering in every direction. Police chasing squaddies. Platform party in disarray, scuffling among themselves while squaddies vandalize the scaffolding under their feet. Vocal truck continues its erratic course, ranting still.*

Arrests being made of belligerent members of both parties, who are frogmarched to a police van and bundled inside.

JULIE: Oh yes! Us in the mud.

'I've had enough of this stupid game,' I thought, and my anger turned red. I've a dreadful temper, if I give in to it, as you've good reason to know.

Then you started pulling at my arms and yelling at me again, and I thought, 'This barbarian won't give up!' So I grabbed a nice pat of mud in each hand and plopped them in the general direction of your face. You let out a terrible squawk so I knew I'd hit the spot. [*Laughs.*] I ought to feel sorry for doing such a thing. After all, I might have blinded you—she says with feeling! But I don't so I'll have to work at it. Please God, I'll be sorry, honest—but not yet, because it's still funny to remember, and I need all the laughs I can get.

Whoops! Gloom and doom showing again.

[*Deep breaths.*]

'Hell!' Nik said, letting Julie go, he recoiling bottom down as before, and she, released, slithering onto her front again.

'I'm trying to help you, goddammit!' he cried, wiping gritty mud from his face so he could see again.

'Don't you swear by God to me, you pagan!' Julie spluttered, biting on mud and wiping her eyes.

Nik spat. 'I'm only trying to get you away from this.'

'I can look after myself, thank you!'

She could see him now and sat back on her haunches. 'I thought you were one of those barbarians,' she said, grudgingly.

Nik, outraged, said, 'One of that mob!'

'Well, I couldn't see!'

'Excuses, excuses!'

The rain began falling in torrents again.

'Go and boil your head,' Julie said, slithering to her feet.

'A good Christian thought,' Nik said, pushing himself up too.

'I don't feel very Christian,' Julie said. 'Not after being attacked by people like that and being soaked in mud and being pulled about by—' She slipped again, and sat with a bump on her behind. 'Dear God, give me strength!' she shouted in anger, striking the ground with her hands.

Nik broke up.

'Thank *you*!' Julie said, glaring at him, but then could not help herself smiling.

'Here,' Nik said, 'give us a hand.'

She did, pretending reluctance. He helped her, slitherily, to her feet. But at once she took her hand back; and without difficulty, for the mud greased their palms.

Nik regretted this loss.

'Come on,' he said. 'Let's go.'

'Go!' Julie said, a fierceness returning. 'Go! You mean run away from . . . [*nearly speechless*] . . . *them!*' She looked Nik accusingly in the eyes. 'Run away yourself. I won't.'

Nik stared back. Then held out his lonely hands, cruciform, and asked, smiling, 'Run from what?'

By now they were an island in a lake of mud. What action there was scuttled about on the shore. No one marauded near them. The platform was a shambles of collapsed metal and torn posters, the party gone. The demo demolished, ended.

Nik could watch Julie close up at last. She was smaller than he, and smaller than he expected. Slight even. Her clothes clung, soaked, to her frame, modelling her small breasts, and bulgy, too thick buttocks, and fleshy thighs. Her triangular face, and cap of bobbed black hair, close-gripping from wetness, set off her round strong skull, which shone, for him, as if in a halo, out of which her blue-grey eyes stared fiercely at him.

She was to Nik, quite simply, beautiful. A being he wanted to take hold of and fit to him.

His limbs began to tremble. He hoped that if she noticed she would only think he was cold from the wet.

'We might as well,' he said. 'Go, I mean.'

Julie did not move, except to turn her head and look disgustedly at the scene around them, her dripping hands held comically out from her sides, as a penguin holds its flippers.

'There's nothing to stay for,' Nik said, unable to think of anything brighter. His intelligence wasn't working, or rather had slipped from his mind to his body. All he could think of was wanting to touch her. She had pale skin, almost bleached in this rain-cloud light. His eyes fixed on a small round scar indented into her left cheek near the corner of her mouth. Shaped like an O, it made him think that the blunt end of a pencil had been jabbed there. But the blemish only made her more attractive. He wanted to finger the mark and ask how she got it.

As he drank her in she blinked and sniffed and sucked at her lips. She might almost have been cosseting tears, but he knew she was only placating the rain coursing her eyes.

He was so engrossed he did not notice a young policeman running towards them.

(Tom coming between them.)

'Are you okay, miss?' he asked, but he was sussing Nik.

'We're all right. I was knocked down. He came to help.' Julie smiled, showing her teeth. One of the two front ones was chipped to a guillotine angle. She tongued it as she smiled, a habit of hers, Nik soon learned. He longed to kiss her mouth, tongue and all.

The policeman waited a moment, summing them up before saying, 'If you're sure you're okay?' He turned to run back to the van waiting for him. 'You'd best be getting home,' he said, and trotted off.

Nik resented him. Not so much for giving orders as for his intrusion.

Tom gone, Nik and Julie, statuesque in the rain, looked at one another, aware now of how wet and cold they felt, how clarted in mud. But neither moved.

Julie ended their silence. 'He's right. I ought to go home.'

'I'll take you,' Nik said. 'If you like.'

'Don't put yourself out. Only if you're going my way.'

'I'm going your way.'

'But you don't know which way is mine.'

'Yes I do. Whichever way you go is your way. And I'll be with you, so I'm going your way.'

Julie laughed at last, indulging him.

NIK'S NOTEBOOK: I mean—it's grotesque. All that puppy-dog stuff. Can't believe I behaved like that. As if I'd lost control of my mind, as well as of my body. All a-tremble and saying

60

pukey things. She must have thought I was some kind of schoolboy idiot, drooling over her like that. Not drooling exactly. Blethering.

I daren't think about the things I said on the way to her place. And I'm certainly not tapping them into this wp. The VDU would turn red from embarrassment (instead of staying green from envy of my brilliant mind, fantastic good looks, etc.).

Naturally, I just *had* to tell her about this batty film, didn't I! And she laughed, as any intelligent person would because it is unquestionably one big joke. So I came on all ho-ho-ho and smart-assed about it, which can't have been any more winning. I can't stand supercilious creeps, even when I myself am the supercilious creep I can't stand. She must have noticed. But she took it well.

I hope.

Selah.

I parted with the immortal words: Can I see you again sometime?

Gawd!

Yes, she said, and I nearly piddled myself. (Nearly relieved myself from relief!) Sunday morning, she said.

I knew from the way she said it what the catch was.

So long as I go to church with you?

Why not? she said. It'll be good for your research if not for your soul.

At least I didn't tell her, thank heaven, that I couldn't care less if it wasn't good for anything because I'd do anything for her right now.

But why would I?

It's not that she makes me randy. She does make me randy, no question. But her body wouldn't make me randy on its own. She isn't like the girl playing the Magdalene. Her body does the trick all on its own. What does it with Julie is something . . . *inside* . . . her body. Something I want to reach in and take hold of. The sex would be a way in. A pleasant way in, sure. But it wouldn't be for itself, like it would be with Mary M. Not just for the sensation, I mean.

I think I mean.

But what's the 'something' inside her that I want to get hold of? And how do I know it's there if I don't know what it is?

Come to think of it, it's like a black hole in space. We know it's there but we don't know what it is, and we don't really know yet what happens if you go into it. Maybe if you go into that dark magnetic space you suffer a total change. Become the opposite from everything you are now. Male to female. Weak to strong. White to black. Human to—what? Inhuman? Superhuman? Maybe you pop out through the binary white hole into a whole new universe? A bit risky. Or, of course, none of those things might happen. You might just vamoose. But fantastic. Worth the risk.

†

JULIE: I lie here now remembering that day. After you'd gone, looking so pleased with yourself, I got straight into a hot bath and soaked away the mud and soothed my bruises and thought, 'Oh dear, what now! Have I done the right thing?'

You see, even after just that first sopping hour together I knew you'd get serious about me, and that I'd have a job keeping myself from getting serious about you. And the trouble was—the trouble is—I hadn't planned on boyfriends. Not serious ones, anyway.

You weren't part of my scheme of things, dear Nik. Not at all.

INTERCUT: *Julie's room. An upstairs bedroom in a small terraced house. The walls are painted brilliant white, and are bare of all decoration except for a slender cross made from two pieces of sea-scoured driftwood which hangs in the middle of one wall. Beneath the cross stands a prayer desk of plain oak on which lies a Bible and a loose-leaf file containing passages from books, poems, and other writing Julie has copied out for use during meditation.*

Against the opposite wall is a single bed with a white-painted tubular frame. The bed is covered with a light blue counterpane that matches the curtains hanging at the only window. In the corner between the window and the prayer desk is a small armchair. Against the fourth wall, by the door, is a light wood bookcase full of mostly paperbacks. One shelf contains religious books; the other three hold novels, poetry, some biography. After that is a door to a wall cupboard where Julie keeps her clothes.

The bare deal floorboards are stained a shining dark oak colour. A strip of cheap, dark blue carpet lies by the side of the bed. The window looks out onto a small back garden—a garden shed, square of lawn, carefully tended vegetable patch chock-a-block with plants—and beyond, over the roofs of terrace houses stepping downwards, to the other side of the valley where some fields, then streets of houses, rise up to the skyline.

The window is open and sun is streaming in, but the curtains are not blowing in a breeze, summertime sounds cannot be heard. Only now do we realize that we are looking at stills. But the noise of a football match being shown on television seeps into the room from next door.

JULIE: I haven't told you this before. Didn't want to. Couldn't bring myself to, if I'm honest. But now I have to tell you, I think. It's time. Because whatever happens when they take off the bandages—whether I can see again or not— nothing will be the same as before, will it? Can't be.

[*Deep breaths in and out.*]

I think about it a lot. About when the bandages come off. And about the future after that. When we know for sure what's left of me. [*Chuckles.*] Not that I'm any the wiser for thinking about it so much. More confused, if anything. Except, I know some things that weren't decided before will be then. What you are to me, and what I am to you. That'll be the important thing the great unwrapping will make me—us—sure about.

You see, dear Nik, what I haven't told you is that for years I've thought that I want my life to be all for God.

[*Laughs.*]

I know, I know! But don't give yourself a hernia from hilarity. Lots of girls go through a nunnery phase just the same as they go through having crushes on hockey sticks and horses and pop stars and even on yummy teachers. I know that. But I got over those things before I was fourteen. This is different. The same way it's different when people decide they'd like to become doctors or computer programmers or scientists. I want to be a God something. I don't know exactly what kind of something, but something for God.

I was trying to work out what that something would be when you came along. I was looking for the best way. A way that would be right for now, for today, and not a way that used to be right years ago but isn't any longer.

Not that I've said anything about it to anyone else. Mum knows, of course, and Dad, and my brother. Oh yes, and Philip Ruscombe. But no one else. I like to be sure of myself before I say anything to other people. And being a God-something isn't the sort of subject people talk about very easily without . . . well, without laughing, I suppose. They find it hard to believe you mean what you say, or that anyone could seriously want to do anything like that these days. So I was quietly sorting it out for myself. Till you came along.

Suddenly there you were, and I couldn't think why I cared. Not at the time. I remember lying in my bath that Saturday afternoon, half of me still smouldering with anger at the pagans, and the other half wondering what on earth it was about you that disturbed me so much. I mean, you aren't especially good looking. Sorry about that! You're fairly clever, I suppose, but you aren't a genius. And you're younger than I am. I don't mean only in years, but in yourself. You're still a schoolboy.

So I'm no fashion plate, and I'm not even as clever as you, but I do have a job, however lowly, and have had for two years. I feel like a grown-up woman, not a schoolgirl any more. [*Laughs.*] Yes, I know. But everyone can be wrong!

Apart from those things, you were big-headed. All the way home you made fun of everybody else. The leptonic OBD, the kids in the film group, Leonard Stanley, the CND organizers, the NF mob, the police. You were quite funny, I admit, but you were unkind too. So when you asked if you could see me again I only said yes because I thought you'd give up when you knew going to church was part of the bargain.

It wasn't until I was in the bath that I realized I wanted to see you again, and wanted to see you in more than an ordinary way. I worried about that for a while, feeling as if I were betraying God or myself in some way. But then I thought, 'That's ridiculous. God will just have to take her chance.' And so will I. Because if I can't survive a crush on a bigheaded schoolboy, then I'm not likely to survive all the difficulties that'll be thrown at me if I work for God. So, I thought, 'Perhaps this quirky schoolboy is a sort of test, perhaps he's a temptation I can use to find out how determined I am. In which case, I might just as well relax about him and get on and see what happens.'

If I'm honest, though, I have to admit I didn't think you were much of a challenge. Didn't think you'd last long after church, even if you actually turned up. But here I am weeks later, still battling! And I've enjoyed every minute. Truly.

[*Pause.*]

What I'm trying to tell you is that I've got the same sort of feeling now that I had about you in my bath. And just like then, I don't know why. But this time the feeling says the test is near its crisis. That there'll be an end . . . No, that's wrong. Not an end but another beginning . . . Very soon. Which is why I want you to know, before it happens, the way things are. So that whatever happens there's no deception, and no pretence. Only honesty and truth. Or the truth as near as I can get to it.

Does this make sense? Do you understand?

I'll worry till I know.

REVELATIONS

That first Sunday morning, when Nik met Julie at her front door, she said, 'I don't mean to be rude, but would you mind if we didn't talk at all till after church? I'll explain later.'

'If that's what you want,' Nik said.

So they walked side by side, unspeaking, along empty streets, up through town to St James's, set on a hill above the hospital and below the cemetery.

Nik smiled to himself as they approached, thinking, 'On the trip from sickness to death stands the church of God, and it's uphill all the way.'

Julie plodded along with such abstracted concentration that she might have been by herself. Her gait was urgently mechanical, her eyes fixed on the ground ahead, unseeing.

What was going on? Nik wondered. What was she thinking about? Was she worried? Or feeling ill and forcing herself to church? Or fed up? She certainly didn't look pleased or happy.

No, she looked more like someone utterly absorbed in a book. Consumed. That was the word.

Julie yomping to church puzzled him. Which made him all the more curious.

NIK'S NOTEBOOK: Must the insides of churches be like deep-freeze warehouses? St James's is a late-Victorian stone pile with walls painted white to try and brighten the place up. But all this does is make it look cold as well as feel cold. Is this what Jesus Christ intended for his fans?

'Thou shalt build in my name large, cold mausoleums that shalt cost thee a bomb to keep up. These thou shalt perfume with the odour of damp dust, dirty underwear and dry rot. There shalt thou gather with glum faces, sit near the back, utter long prayers in mournful voices, sing tedious songs out of tune and very slowly, and generally give thyselves a thoroughly bad time.'

Not that I've been in many churches. None at all for ages, in fact. Maybe they've changed. Maybe they're terrific fun places now. But not St James's, that's for sure. I think the people who go there must be masochists. Or else they all have terrible guilt complexes and think going to church is a penance that they suffer for their sins in order to keep in with God.

One of the troubles I have with Christianity is that I don't feel guilty about anything. Maybe I'm a religious defective?

Selah.

There were sixteen people. I counted while Julie was kneeling down, doing her kick-start prayers after we got settled in a pew near the back. She wanted to take me nearer the front but I wouldn't let her. Who might be there and see me? I'd never live it down.

Early morning communion. You'd never get me up before ten on a Sunday morning for anything normally, and sitting there with the shivers waiting for the performance to start while Julie did her hands-together act beside me, I began to wonder why ever I'd got up so early this morning. Is Julie worth such sacrifice?

Mostly the sixteen were old women on their own. One young couple carrying a nearly new baby. Nobody paid any attention to anybody else. I thought Christianity was supposed to be about brotherly and sisterly love and doing unto others etc. Going by this morning's evidence, what Christians want others to do to them is pretend they aren't there. Not that I was there long enough to find out if things warmed up because I disgraced myself soon after the service started.

The trouble was caused by an old nun kneeling in the pew in front of me. Julie said afterwards that she was on holiday from her convent. I knew she was a nun because she was dressed in a dowdy grey frock and thick wool stockings and black clod-hopper shoes. Her head was covered in a blue scarf-thing with a white face band. Nothing like the old-fashioned nuns in books, who always look weirdly fetching to me. I mean the ones in flowing robes tied with rope and with crucifixes and beads and holy baubles dangling all over them. And their faces peeking out from their fly-away wimples. The climb-every-mountain sort of nuns.

Well this modern C. of E. nun wasn't anything like that. She wasn't just dull, she was actively unattractive. I expect they think they should look as unfetching as possible so as to avoid dreadful temptations of the FLESH. The sins of the flesh always sound so cannibalistic. Not that you'd want a nibble at this old dame or make a pass at her of any kind unless you were ninety and feeling pretty desperate.

I wouldn't have paid her much attention except she was right in front of me and her insides kept gurgling like a water system with dicky plumbing. After a while, the eruptions went into another phase. She'd rumble, then there'd be a short pause. Then she'd let off a string of three or four very lady-like little farts. Nothing gross. And very quietly. So quiet in fact that I don't think she could hear them herself. But I could, being in direct line of fire. Maybe she was gunning for the heathen spy behind her.

At first I just smiled. Things got started. Old Vic came in dressed in a white nightgown with a piece of green curtain like a poncho over his shoulders and pottered about at the altar. He looked a lot better doing that than he looked when I talked to him. More at home, really. I could see he believed it all, just the same way you can tell when a good actor likes his part and is really into it. Completely absorbed. So I was getting interested in what was happening, and forgetting about the cold and how early it was. Meanwhile, old rumble-tum was bubbling and popping off in front of me.

But then the prayers started. I managed the Lord's Prayer all right. It's a great piece of writing when you come to think of it because it's so easy to remember and always seems okay to say even when you're not in the mood and don't actually believe all the other religious stuff. Like a great poem, I suppose.

At any rate, we got through ₁ ₁t without any trouble. But then Old Vic launched into: 'Al₁ ₁ghty God, unto whom all hearts be open [*rumble, gurgle*], a₁ desires known [*glug*] and from whom no secrets are hid [*pause*]: Cleanse the thoughts of our hearts . . .'

And she pooped.

That did it. I started to get the giggles. Julie gave me the kind of sideways glare your mum does when you're little and being naughty, which didn't help. So I buried my face in my hands like a humble sinner having the thoughts of his heart cleansed, and hoped the noise of my half-stifled guffaws would be taken for the sound of a holy purgative at work.

Which I'm sure would have done the trick. Unfortunately, just as I was composing myself again, there came an ominously prolonged growl from the old girl's innards, followed by a cliff-hanger of a pause. Then she let loose a very unlady-like raspberry.

This Julie also heard. She gave the old girl a startled look, then glanced at me, who was watching events through my fingers. We eyed each other for a second. And then she broke up. She stuffed the knuckle of her thumb in her mouth and hung on to the prayer position, eyes front.

This sight did nothing for my equilibrium. Which was not at all helped, either, by my memory recalling at this inopportune moment that hymn they make you sing at infant school: 'God be in my head, / and in my understanding; / God be in my eyes, / and in my looking; / God be in my mouth, / and in my speaking; / God be in my heart and . . .' *Poop-poop.*

At which I really collapsed. I flung myself down behind the pew and rammed as much of my sweater into my mouth as it could take without suffocating myself. Here I slunk while the bout of laughter wracked my tortured frame.

O God, I thought, don't let me . . . don't let me . . .

(I've just realized this was the first time I've prayed since I was ten and asked for Mum back. When she didn't come, I decided God wasn't there after all or he'd have done something about it. As if God was nothing more than a megastar Santa Claus.)

So there I am, doubled up in this prayer box with a mouth full of sodden sweater, shaking with frustrated giggles, while Julie kneels beside me as rigid as a memorial, and the old nun goes on happily rumbling and pooping, and at the altar Old Vic tells the lord we're humbly sorry for all our sins, when this wizzened old guy appears in the aisle bending towards me with a worried look on his face and a glass of water in his hand and hissing: All right? . . . Like a drink?

Had to leave, nothing else for it. I'd have died if I hadn't or had hysterics. Death or cachinnation. Neither quite the thing in church. Not that church anyway. And I didn't want to make life worse for Julie, did I. A knave in the nave.

'I'm not sure you're fit to be let out in public,' Julie said afterwards.

'Why?' Nik said. 'Doesn't God have a sense of humour?'

'As she made you, I suppose she must have.'

'She?'

'Why not? If God is everything, that must mean God is a she as well as a he, mustn't it? So if you call God he, I don't see why I shouldn't call her she.'

'Or it, as he/she is everything and must therefore be stones and stars as well as male and female?'

'Why not?'

Nik shrugged. 'It's your God. But I didn't know you lot went in for such explosive worship.'

'She's a very old nun and a bit deaf.'

'And full of the power of the lord.'

'See what you're like at her age. If you live that long.'

'The trouble was, I thought maybe you'd want us all to join in with a rousing chorus of—'

'You're not going to turn crude, are you?'

'Is it a sin on Sundays?'

'No. Just tedious.'

'You weren't exactly the soul of solemnity yourself.'

'D'you always talk like that or only on your off days?'

'Depends on the company I keep. But it was funny, though. Admit it.'

'It was funny. But she's a dear old woman, and a friend of mine, and very devout. She'd be horrified if she knew.'

'Won't say a word, honest.'

They were walking back to Julie's house.

'Tell you what,' Nik said. 'You've taken me to your church. Now I'll take you to mine.'

'Surprise, surprise! Where?'

'Selsley Common.'

Julie laughed. 'With the kite flyers and the babies being aired and the dogs out for walkies.'

'And the cows. Don't forget the cows. Free range cows as

70

well. None of your battery farm religion up there. Not like your place, with everybody stuck in a pew being fattened up for heaven.'

'So you're a closet pantheist really. That explains your mucky mind.'

'No, no. You've got me all wrong. I'm not a pantheist. I'm a *pen*theist.'

'Oh dear!'

'Well, actually, if you must know, I just like a good view. Besides, when we get back to your place you might not invite me in, whereas, if we go up on the common—'

'It'll take the rest of this morning and half this afternoon, and I've promised to help with the cooking. So we'll go in my car, if you don't mind, and be back by eleven. Will that do?'

'You've got a car?'

'Don't get excited, it's not a Porsche.'

'I don't care if it's a motorized orange box, it's better than my leg-powered bike.'

'Never mind. When you're grown up you can put an engine in your pram and be just like all the other big boys.'

'Wow, thanks! Will I have to wait long?'

'About another twenty years at your present rate of progress.'

'That long!'

'Be glad. Most of your sex never grow out of being little boys.'

'Don't you like men?'

'When I can find any. There aren't that many around.'

NIK'S NOTEBOOK: She's not butch, I don't mean that. Just tough-minded. You wouldn't think so to look at her. And she's poker-voiced but not poker-faced. So just to hear her, you'd think she was as hard as nails. When you look at her, you know she's a kidder.

Her car is a prehistoric Mini she claims she maintains herself with a little help from her brother who just happens to be a motor mechanic. She treats it like she was ignoring it. Drives like that too. Functional precision.

I said: She goes well.

She, she said, refers to human beings. This is a machine and hasn't a soul.

I said: You don't like machines?

She said: They're all right. Very useful. But machines are machines. If you treat them like people you end up treating people like machines. Which I'm against.

I didn't argue about that because I don't know if she's right, but I shall have a think about it and when I've decided it'll make a nice subject for another day. And that's something else I like about her. Two things in fact. She makes me think. And she likes a good argument.

Selah.

Being such a Christian nation, the great British public was still fervently worshipping the lord between the sheets so, of course, the common was the way I like it. I.e.: Empty of the human animal. Except inevitably for one or two compulsive underwear flashers. It's amazing. It doesn't matter where you go or what time it is there's always at least one panting and puffing middle-aged duffer lolloping across the landscape like a lost soul everlastingly on the hunt for the way out.

Note for film: If Christ came back today, he'd have to turn up as a body-building health-freak jogging fanatic with a regular programme on TV. Otherwise, none of the great proletarian masses would pay him any attention at all. So I suggest we start the film with a TV ad in which our recycled Christ performs his first miracle: turning a titchy chickenwhite wimp of a man into a bronzed Tarzan by one application of New Messiah suntan oil and then telling him to take up his metal and pump. That done, he says, Follow me, and they go off together, jogging into an explosive sunrise, as the title CHRIST COMES AGAIN appears on the screen.

Selah.

We parked at the far end, near the cattle grid, and walked to the edge. The usual great view, clear enough today to see Wales and the Black Mountains. In the valley, the glint of the Severn snaking; the twin towers of Berkeley nuke power station, square tombs picked out by the sun; the bluff of the scarp fluffed with trees gloomy in shadow close by on the bend, hiding Bristol; in the other direction Haresfield Beacon blocking the view to Gloucester. And through the upriver gap, the Malvern hills breasting up from the plain. A sharp blue sky edging on the horizon to pale grey.

We were standing side by side taking it all in when a strange thing happened.

In a field steeply below us was a man. He was bending over, his hands in the grass. As we watched, he suddenly sprang up, a rabbit grasped in one hand by its back legs. As he rose, he swung the rabbit up into the air, caught its head in his other hand and brought it down, across his raised leg, snapping its neck sharply across his knee. Then he held the rabbit out at arm's length by the back legs.

The animal gave a number of convulsive kicks that made its body jerk and its loose head flop about. And the man, waiting for the death to end, looked up the hillside, where he saw us watching. He grinned, and raised his empty hand and waved, and when we didn't wave or move at all, he held the dying rabbit high above his head and shook it at us in triumph, making its head flip-flap again. Then he turned and set off down the field in a bounding kind of run, the rabbit jigging about in his hand, till he reached a gate in the hedge, vaulted over, and disappeared from sight.

For a while neither of us, so stunned, even blinked. Then Julie let out a painful, bitten cry and slumped to the ground, where she sat cross-legged, staring across the valley, stonefaced, but her eyes pleading.

I waited, not knowing what to do or to say. What I wanted, just like yesterday, was to touch her, take hold of her. Yesterday I didn't. Couldn't. Today, seeing the bleakness of her, frozen there, a kind of grieving, I couldn't not. So I crouched down and put my arms round her.

STOCKSHOT: . . . *by history and parables we are nourished; by allegory we grow; by morality we are perfected* . . .

†

Something niggled at the back of Tom's mind. A hunch.

His sense of smell was as acute as Nik's sense of touch. And

73

the old man at the scene-of-crime had smoked roll-your-owns. Had reeked of it, even in the open air, a musky-sweet acidy stench coming off his mucky sweater. Tom had disliked him at once, and not only because of the stink of tobacco. More because of the cheery pretence of being co-operative that didn't hide well enough a suspicious attitude.

One of the first things Tom had learned to recognize after joining the force was the prejudice, the mistrust, the dislike, that many people harboured against the police. For a while this had upset him; after all, he only wanted to uphold the law; and people were pretty quick to call the police when they were in trouble. But soon he had grown a skin thick enough to protect himself. 'As a copper,' the sarge had told him one day when Tom was beefing about the way someone had treated him, 'you're on your own. Don't ever expect anybody to help you. Then all you'll get are nice surprises.'

Besides, in criminal investigation the first rule is that nobody's above suspicion; not even yourself. So why care what people think? Mugs or villains, they're all the same because anybody can break the law. Some do more often than others, and some worse than others, that's all. Nobody's honest, everybody's a villain, and his job was to stop them if he could and catch them if he couldn't. As he enjoyed the excitement of running a villain to earth more than the steady plod of prevention, he'd always wanted to be a detective. Now he had an unexpected early chance to prove he was up to the job. And he was damned if he was going to balls it up.

What he needed was to know the chat. That was what all the CID bods started with. Straight on the blower to their snouts, thus saving themselves time and leg work. But not being a CID man yet, Tom didn't have any snouts to bell. Never mind, everybody had to begin sometime, and there was no time like the present.

At this present time of day there was only one place where the juvenile scum would be. Though eleven-thirty was early for the best mouths. They'd still be festering in their pits, giving themselves hand jobs over page three while waiting for their mums to nag them downstairs for mid-day fish and chips. But you never knew your luck.

Tom parked in the multi-storey and walked through the shopping precinct to the snooker hall.

†

'My arm's going to sleep,' Julie said, easing away.

'Pity,' Nik said, 'I was enjoying that.'

'Let's walk a bit. The breeze is cool.'

They got up and sauntered. A few more people were about by now. A pair of early teenage girls on podgy ponies cantered by. Further along, two young men, all togged up, eye-catching, prepared a hang-glider for flight, fitting together the jigsaw of the glider's bits and pieces.

'This job you do,' Nik said. 'What is it?'

'Nothing special. I'm a dogsbody in reception at a health centre in Gloucester. I see the patients in, type letters, keep records, run errands for the doctors—that kind of thing.'

'You're going to be a doctor?'

Julie laughed. 'No no! I'm not clever enough for that. It's just a job. Not that I'd want to be a doctor, even if I could. Too squeamish. As you saw just now.'

Nik, not smiling, said, 'Was that really squeamishness?'

Julie, glancing at him, shook her head. 'Not just.' Her mouth was drawn tight. 'Can't bear wanton cruelty.'

They walked a few paces in silence, letting the after-image fade. The cantering girls went galloping heavily by close enough to smell the animals' body heat and feel the earth shudder beneath their feet.

'Do you ride?' Nik asked.

'No. I did go through the phase of wanting to, though. Desperately. But the nearest I got was riding a bike, which I gather,' laughing, 'doesn't provide quite the same thrill.'

Nik, laughing too, said, 'They say it's all sex really.'

'Some people say everything is all sex really.'

'Do you?'

'Do you?'

'Well—'

'Come on, be honest.'

'Can't say. Haven't enough experience to know.'

Julie snorted. 'Ha! There's a cop-out for you.'

'But it's true! I don't have enough experience to know.'

'Will you ever?'

'What's this—sixth-form phil. and psych.?'

Julie, mocking, said, 'Fill and sike!'

'Philosophy and psychology,' Nik said, not taking the bait.

'Nothing so grand,' Julie said. 'Only just managed fifth-form English and maths. Didn't even get as far as the sixth form, never mind fill and sike.'

'You don't seem to do badly without.'

'Common sense, that's all.'

'So do you think it's all sex really?'

'I'm not quite that out of date.' There was self-defensive sharpness in her voice.

'And,' Nik said, enjoying this sign of weakness, 'you've enough experience to know?'

'No one can ever have enough experience to know. I mean, to know the answer to a question like that. Though some people pretend to.'

'So?'

'You're teasing.'

'No, I'm not.'

'But it's obvious.'

Nik shrugged. 'Then tell me.'

'Some things you know from your own experience, yes? Some you know because other people you trust tell you about them from their experience, yes?'

'Okay so far.'

'But no matter how much you set out to experience, you can't ever experience everything. Not in one lifetime.'

Nik thought a moment before saying, 'Agreed.'

'And no matter how much you trust other people, you can't know for certain they're telling the truth about the things you can't experience for yourself.'

'True.'

'But you *believe* them because you trust them. So some things you only know because of belief. Because of faith. Yes?'

Nik pretended to puke at having fallen into Julie's trap. 'Okay, yes, put like that.'

Julie pulled a face at his vulgarity. 'How else can you put it?'

Their path was taking them close by the hang-glider. It was fitted together now, a large, neat, kite-like toy, hard to imagine carrying anyone safely into the air. A challenge to courage. The pilot, however, was preparing to take off. Nik and Julie stopped to watch as he harnessed himself to the frame, helped by his friend, gathered himself, ran, and launched into the air.

'Would you like to do that?' Julie asked.

'Not a lot,' Nik said, shading his eyes from the glare of the sky with a hand the better to see the pilot's progress. 'Would you?'

'Yes. Must be fun. Think he'll make it?'

'Probably. There's a good breeze now, and he looks as if he knows what he's doing.'

'But you don't know he will.'

''Course not. Do you?'

'No. But I believe he will. So do you.'

Nik grinned, eyes still on the glider fluttering a few metres above the scarp. 'Does it matter whether I do or not? It's his funeral.'

Julie gave him a doubting glance. 'You say that, but you don't really mean it.'

'I don't?'

'You're not that callous. Least, I hope you aren't, or I've misread you. You're just avoiding the argument.'

Nik grinned at her. 'Sure? How do you know?'

Julie shrugged. 'What would you do if you knew he couldn't manage, and would fall and kill himself?'

'But I don't know that.'

'But if you did? Really *knew*.'

'All right, what you want me to say is that I'd try and stop him.'

'Yes. But *would you*?'

They were eye to eye now.

'You're being serious,' Nik said.

'I'm being serious.'

'Okay, yes, I'd try and stop him.'

The glider, sails smacking, wobbled, dipped, slewed, steadied, hung for a moment between up and down, and at last soared, slipping and pawing, out and up and away over the valley, rising into the absorbing sky.

'You believed he could,' Julie said, sitting on a bench, 'or you wouldn't have stood by watching him try.'

INTERCUT: *Long shot of a lake in northern Sweden. Late summer. Evening. The sun has just set. The lake, shaped like a Y, is surrounded by undulating low hills, some covered in fir and birch, a few with fields of grass and ripe corn. The water is mirror flat, reflecting in its darkness a cloud-cushioned sky.*

A small rowing boat sits in the middle of the lake, at the elbow of the Y. A figure in the boat rests on oars, very still. The only movement comes from a dabble of ducks feeding and larking along the edge of the water nearest our view, and from a finger of white smoke rising unruffled from the chimney of a wooden cabin painted rust-red which is set on the brow of a hill at the edge of a wheat-blond cornfield that runs down to the lake near the foot of the Y. The only sounds are from the cackling ducks and the occasional echoing calls of a searching water bird.

Nik and Julie sat for a moment taking in the view.

'Why didn't you want to talk on the way to the church?' Nik asked when they had looked their fill. 'You said you'd explain.'

'Do I have to?'

'Yes. Research: Believers, behaviour of.'

'In that case, did you make a note of your own behaviour just ᵤow?'

'I'm not a trustworthy specimen.'

'Can't say I like being thought of as a specimen.'

'That's what we all are, us animals, didn't you know?' Nik said. 'We're all each other's specimens. We're all observed and we're all observers of everybody else. You even believe Big Brother God—sorry, Big Sister God—is watching us all, all the time. The spy in the sky.'

'Do I?'

'What then?'

'Another day perhaps.'

'I've annoyed you.'

'No.'

'Irritated you.'

'You're a smarty-pants sometimes.'

'Only meant in fun. Self-protection even, if I'm honest. I want to know. Really.'

'If you're that keen.'

'I'm that keen. Cross my heart and hope to die.'

A young mother with a toddler hooked by its podgy hand to one of her fingers went strolling by at baby pace, mother-and-child a confession of pride.

When they'd passed out of earshot Julie said, 'I was concentrating, that's all.'

'What on?'

'The service.' She looked at him, testing his seriousness. 'On God.'

'You mean you were praying,' Nik said.

To their left the second hang-glider took off, a more confident launch than the first, and laddered its way into the sky.

'The thing is,' Nik said, 'I'm not sure exactly what you were concentrating on.'

'The Gospel for the day.'

'What does that mean?'

'If you'd kept your mind on the service,' Julie said, smiling at him, 'instead of making fun of poor old Sister Ann, you wouldn't have had to leave in disgrace, and would know what the Gospel for the day was.'

'But I didn't, I did, and I don't.'

'Every time the Eucharist—the Holy Communion, the mass, whatever you want to call it—is celebrated, a passage from one of the Gospels is read out. I was thinking about the one set for today.'

'Which was?'

'The Feeding of the Four Thousand.'

'You mean the Five Thousand.'

'No, I mean the Four Thousand. If you'd done your research better you'd know there are two stories.'

'It happened twice?'

'According to Mark and Matthew. Luke and John

only mention the Five Thousand. That story comes up in November. On the twenty-fifth Sunday after Trinity to be exact.'

'It all seems pretty unlikely to me. But what were you thinking about?'

'Not about whether it happened, anyway. I'm not very bothered whether it did or didn't. Seems to me the literal truth about most things is never very interesting. What I was thinking about was what the story means. That's the important thing. Jesus gave the four thousand food and after they'd shared it there were seven basketsful left over.'

'Twelve after the Five Thousand.'

'You've done some research!'

'And what were you thinking?'

'I was thinking how odd it is that supposedly Christian countries like ours and the USA and France and Germany and Italy have so much food we let it go to waste or hoard it, while non-Christian countries like India and most African nations are starving. And how both the story of the four thousand and the one about the five thousand are about sharing. They're about Christ giving everybody who was there enough to eat so that they could stay and hear what she wanted to tell them.'

'She!' Nik laughed.

'Leave that for now, till we've done with the loaves and fishes. It's pretty shaming when you think of it like that. We hang on to the spare food we've got, while other people starve. No wonder they don't want to listen to us. Never mind that it's a sin, a real disgrace, that we behave so selfishly. So murderously, in fact. Because keeping food from a starving person, when you've got enough food to keep her alive, really is murder, isn't it? There's no other word you can honestly use for it, and nothing can excuse it, either.'

Julie drew breath.

Nik said, 'But if you think that, why do you stay a Christian?'

'Because I am a Christian. I believe in Christ. It isn't Christ's fault that we murder other people. It's ours.'

'Okay, I suppose what I mean is, why do you stay a member of the church?'

'I didn't say it was the church's fault, either. I said it was what the so-called Christian countries did. That's different.'

'You mean most of the people in the Christian countries aren't really Christians?'

'Isn't that obvious? But even if it were all the church's fault—and, sure, the church is partly to blame—I'd still remain a member for all sorts of reasons.'

'Like?'

'One of them is that Christ is the image of God getting her hands dirty and I'm one of God's people. You can't put anything right by abandoning it. You only abandon something if you think it's finished, or so far gone it's beyond redemption. Sometimes, I'll be honest, I do feel as if the world, or people anyway, have had it and might as well be dumped. But then I remember I'm a person myself, no better than anybody else, and that I'd rather not be dumped, if you don't mind. Besides, God didn't think we were beyond redemption so she got stuck in and dirtied her hands in order to help put things right. That's what the story of Christ is about. And so that's the least I can do.'

She paused.

'Anyway, that's what I was thinking on the way to church. Since you asked!'

Nik said, 'You should be a priest.'

Julie laughed. 'The thought had occurred!'

'Your sermons would be a lot better than most, that's for sure.'

NIK'S NOTEBOOK: She wasn't preachy, though. I mean, she wasn't trying to make me accept what she was saying. Wasn't trying to convince me or convert me. More like she was thinking aloud. Trying to sort something out for herself. The kind of thinking aloud that makes you interested, even if before that you were bored stiff with the subject.

It's strange. She's convinced, but unsure. I can't think how to express it. It isn't that she doubts, but that she isn't satisfied that she's got it right yet. She's a believer who you feel won't be happy—no, that's wrong . . . Who won't be *content* till she's solved a vast, complicated mystery. And she's working at it all the time.

Selah.

So she made me think about the Feeding of the Four/Five Thousand. Afterwards, I tried doing what she said she'd been doing. Concentrating on the story. Just to see what doing that felt like. And to see if the same sort of things came into my mind as came into hers.

They didn't. What struck me wasn't that there turned out to be enough food for everybody to eat all they wanted and leave great basketsful behind (so litterbugs are biblical as well). That's fairly predictable when you think about it. I mean, if everybody shared what they had with them, because this guy they admired started them off by sharing the loaves and fishes he and his mates had brought with them, then naturally there'd be more than enough. That's what happens at bring-your-own parties. They always end up drowned in drink and buried in food.

No, the really interesting thing, I think, is that four and/or five thousand people came all that way to be with him. (*They've been with me three days now . . . some of them have come from a distance.*: Mark 8, vv. 2,3.) Nobody yomps across miles of rugged country in scorching hot weather just to be with a schlunk. And in those days in that area there can't have been a big population. So a high percentage of the locals must have turned out for the jaunt. Which means there must have been quite a lot of something about him.

If it happened at all, of course. The whole thing might be just a fiction. I.e.: all cod.

Is God a cod?

Were the loaves fishy?

Have we used our loaves about the five thousand?

Were the five thousand only bait on a hook in a crook's book?

If so, who was shooting the line? Jesus of Nazareth?

Didn't he have better fish to fry than a few thousand poverty-stricken peasants from an outback area of one of the third-world outposts of the Roman Empire?

In brief: Was Jesus a con-man?

Seems to me a good con has to be (1) easy to set up, (2) simple in design so that there's as little as possible that can go wrong and give the game away, (3) that it's quick in yielding results, and (4) that it's hard to detect.

If the Loaves and Fishes a con:

+ It didn't yield anything except twelve and/or seven baskets-ful of leftovers that must have already started ponging badly in the hot sun, and that the conman and his gang had to pick up off the ground after the punters had gone home.

Whoever heard of a conman who stayed around to pick up rotting litter after the show?

+ It was far from simple in design or organization. For example, where would you hide the loaves and fishes to feed five thousand hungry people when you were stuck in the middle of nowhere? How would you cart all the stuff there unnoticed, when transport was by man or donkey power? How would you keep all that fish from going off without freezers to keep it in? And how could you know beforehand how many people would turn up and so be sure you had enough for all?

Anybody who tried a dodge like that in the middle of nowhere would have to be an idiot. And anybody taken in by it would have to be a jerk. Was Jesus an idiot? Were all his fans jerks?

Or is the story a fraud? And does it matter? Julie doesn't think it does. So how can she believe in something that's supposed to be historically true while thinking that it probably never happened?

Selah.

That's as far as I got before I gave up. More questions at the end than when I started. I quite enjoyed it, but I'm not sure it did anything for me.

†

The local snooker hall was no prettier than an old lag at the best of times. That morning, a couple of blacked-out windows had been opened, allowing in thin daylight that made the neons above the tables look like they couldn't get it on for yawning, and letting out too little of the stale stink of cold fag. Tom's nose twitched.

Burleigh the bouncer was there, as usual, banging away as if a snooker table was a pinball machine. At another table, In-off Jones was playing a spotty-faced youth. Tom didn't know the name. Thirteen? World champion before fourteen. Didn't anyone ever ask why he wasn't in school? He was already three up and it looked like In-off wouldn't visit the table.

None of these any use. But lounging against the wall as far from the grey stream of daylight as he could get, a sour smirk on his designer-stubble face, was Tom's lucky strike.

He sidled up with suitably nonchalant deference so as not to spook his quarry.

'Morning, Sharkey,' he muttered in the required bored and offhand manner.

'It is?' Sharkey said, flat as last week's beer.

'Early for you.'

'Late, more like.'

'All-night job, was it?'

Sharkey sniffed. 'Job? Don't know about no job.'

Tom chuckled. 'Bird, I mean, Sharkey. Nothing nasty.'

Sharkey gave Tom an appraising glance. 'Never talk sex before the pubs open. Bad for the heart.'

'First I knew you had one.'

Sharkey spat at his feet. 'Jokes is even worse. Give me violent headaches. Specially bad ones.'

'No sex, no jokes! What's left to talk about?'

Sharkey's body showed signs of coming alive. 'Honest, Tommy, I wish you wouldn't. Does terrible things to my reputation just bein seen with you.'

'In here! Come on, Sharkey! Bouncer can't remember where his backside is when he wants to wipe it, never mind who he's seen together. In-off is one of your own. That spotty kid has cue balls for eyes. Why be anti-social?'

'Pimpin for the super is it?'

'You're not to his taste, Sharkey, you'll be happy to know. Anyway, I'm not on duty, am I?'

'Not on duty! When are you lot ever off? Listen, Tommy, I'll tell you. It give me a horrible shock when I see you geared in blue. You was always all right at school. A bit on the swatty side, I admit, but a knockout at the footer and generally speakin on the right side. I quite liked you then. But when you come out in blue I thought, my God, you can't trust nobody no more if a nice straight guy like Tommy goes and does the dirty. So do us a favour, eh?'

'Just what I am doing.' Tom turned his back to the room and spoke with befitting secrecy. 'There's some damage on hand.'

'Oh, yes? Your bike had its tyres let down?'

Tom waited a tolerant pause. 'Listen, Sharkey, I'm putting myself on the line to help you a bit. Okay?'

Sharkey stuck a greasy-nailed finger into his ear and wobbled it about. 'Am I hearin right? You're helpin me?'

'This is very nasty damage I'm talking about, Sharkey. And the super has you down for the villain. He's thinking of having a fatherly chat.'

'Need to send more than you to bring me in.'

'I told you, I'm off duty. Here to help. In my own time. Don't know where you are, do I? Haven't seen you for days.'

'Your boss wants me, and you come warnin me off. What do you want, Tommy?'

'Last night a young bloke was hung on a cross by person or persons unknown.'

Sharkey gave a noiseless whistle. 'Very nasty!'

Tom nodded. 'As I said. He was found this morning but disappeared before we got to him.'

'I can see why your boss might be a touch off colour.'

'And why he's acting supersonic.'

Sharkey tutted. 'A supersonic super! Very good, Tommy. You're comin on.'

'And you'll be coming in, Sharkey, unless a few answers are found smartish. Like who did it.'

'Not me, that's for sure. I'm a Catholic. I wouldn't go round crucifying people, for God's sake!'

'Didn't know you were religious.'

'I'm not.'

'You just said you're Catholic.'

'That don't mean I'm religious, though, do it? I mean, I'm

not one of them fanatics, always prayin and goin on about God and bein saved. That's obscene.'

'But you go to mass and make your confession and get forgiven and all that caper?'

'Now and then. Not a lot, but enough.'

'Well, how much is enough?'

Sharkey shifted uneasily. 'Enough, that's all! How the hell do I know, I'm not a priest. And I'm no saint, neither, I know that. I go when I feel like it and that's enough for me.'

'But you believe in it, all that about God and Christ?'

'You have to believe in somethin, don't you? Any idiot knows that. Anyway, I was brought up that way. All my family goes. Even my old man goes a couple of times a year so there must be somethin in it cos he don't believe nothin till it stands up and hits him.'

'Pity he doesn't go a bit more often. Might have kept him out of the nick.'

'Yeah, well, him bein in the nick doesn't have nothin to do with God. That was your lot did that.'

'What, putting him away because he couldn't resist climbing through other people's windows and carting off a few items of their property? Thou shalt not steal. Isn't that what it says?'

'He was out of a job and doin the best he could for the family. Not that a rozzer like you would understand family loyalty. You'd shop your own grandmother if it helped your record.'

'That's a bit unfair, Sharkey, seeing I'm standing here trying to help you so you don't get any aggro for something you didn't do.'

'Sure you are, Tommy, and I'm still waitin to hear what you're gettin out of it.'

'Enlightened self-interest, Sharkey. That's what keeps the world turning, didn't your dad tell you? You scratch my back and I'll scratch yours. I'm tipping you the wink about my super having the hots for you. If I can tell him some interesting news, like I've got a lead on the villains, I reckon I can hold him off for today while he checks it out. That'll give you time to use your considerable powers of persuasion among your friends and come up with a whisper. Somebody has to know something.

Shouldn't be too hard for you to give us a pointer that I can pass on to my guv. The culprit or culprits get collared and you get left alone. I get in good with the super, and that'll do me for now.'

'Very neat,' Sharkey said with undisguised distaste. 'You'll make nice pork.'

'Thanks for the compliment.'

'Any time.'

Tom sighed. 'So don't bother. Let the super talk to you himself. I don't care. You're clean, you know that. You can prove you were somewhere else at the time in question. Why should you worry?'

Sharkey took a deep breath. 'Yeah, yeah.'

''Course, you'll be held on suspicion for a day or two. Till we check out your alibi. And while the super is concentrating on you and your mates, whoever strung the kid up will be spoiling the scent.'

Sharkey pushed himself from the wall and took an agitated couple of steps away and back again. 'All right, all right!' he said. 'I don't like what happened no more than you. But I don't like bein fitted up neither. Which is what this is. I know what you're up to, Tommy, and I tell you, it's worse than anythin I ever do. Next thing, if I don't do what you want, you'll plant something evil as evidence against me.'

Tom looked suitably aggrieved. 'Come on, Sharkey, you've got me all wrong! I'd never do a thing like that!'

'Not right this minute, you wouldn't. Not this time. But you will, one day when you want a villain bad enough you'll do it. And you'll tell yourself, what the hell, he's a villain anyway; if he didn't do this he did some other job we didn't catch him for, so what's the odds. That's your sort of thinkin, Tommy. You always did act innocent, even at school, but underneath you're as evil-minded as all your mob.'

Tom looked Sharkey eye to eye, heated himself now. 'It won't happen, I tell you!' he said through his anger.

Sharkey grinned his bright teeth.

Tom looked away first. The room was unchanged from a few moments ago, the click of colliding balls echoing as in a dismal cave. He hitched his jeans and composed himself.

'Up to you,' he said, his voice still not relaxed, and shrugged, thinking he had lost.

But Sharkey spat and moved towards an empty table. He picked up a white ball from the baize and bowled it with a twist of his wrist that sent it bouncing off the opposite cushion, another and another, before returning precisely to his waiting fist.

'The car park behind Hill Pauls at half-one,' he said.

Tom couldn't help smiling. 'I knew you'd see sense.'

Sharkey sent the ball careering round the table again.

'Piss off,' he said. 'You bog the place up.'

INTERCUT: *The Swedish lake in longshot, as before. Hold the scene: the dying sun's rays glancing on hilltops, the hut in dusk-time shadow with the white ribbon of smoke rising, the little boat utterly still on the water. Five seconds. Then pull a steady, unhurried, soft-focus zoom towards the boat and its occupant.*

'Now it's my turn,' Julie said as they walked back to her car.

'For what?'

'Research. You've been investigating me. Now it's my turn to investigate you.'

The hang-glider came swooping to earth a hundred metres ahead of them, the pilot planting his feet neatly on the ground in a fine judgement of speed and height and moment of stall.

'It's all very well,' Julie said, 'being superior and snooty about religion and other people's beliefs—'

'I'm not!'

'Yes, you are. But are you really telling me you've never wondered about God?'

'Naturally. Doesn't everybody?'

'All right then, not just wondered but—I don't know—experienced anything?'

Nik gave her an uneasy side-glance. 'What sort of thing?'

They strolled past the hang-glider, now again a lifeless kit of spars and stretched sailcloth which the pilot was dismantling for transport in a bag you'd have thought far too small to hold a flying machine that could carry a man into the air.

'I don't know,' Julie said. 'Something that made you sure, even for just a minute, that there's more to all this—' she waved a hand at the view—'than some sort of meaningless accident with meaningless ingredients inside the meaningless stewpot of a meaningless universe.'

Nik smiled at her. 'Do you always talk like that or only on Sundays?'

Julie grinned back. 'Depends on the company I keep.'

They walked a few paces in silence.

'Yes,' Nik said, forcing himself. 'Something happened once.'

When he didn't go on, Julie said, 'Are you going to tell me or leave me in suspense?'

'I haven't told anybody before.'

'If you don't want to—'

'No, it's not that. Not with you, anyway.'

'Was it embarrassing?'

Nik laughed. 'Not embarrassing. A bit silly maybe.'

It was last summer. Grandad took me to Sweden. I live with my grandad, did I tell you? He was in the merchant navy for a long time and made friends with some Swedes then. That was quite a long time ago but they've kept in touch. Christmas cards, a letter now and then.

When he retired last year he decided he'd have a holiday, go to Sweden, and look up his old mates. He took me with him for company, and because he thought it would do me good. He's always going on about me seeing more of life instead of getting it out of books. He's not a big reader, isn't Grandad. Not a reader at all, as a matter of fact. For him, books are a last resort.

Anyway, he took me with him and I enjoyed myself most of the time. We ended up in northern Sweden, not far from the Arctic Circle, and Grandad met his old mates, three of them, and they all got high on the excitement of being together again.

'Come to the forest,' they said, which apparently is the big thing with Swedes when they want to let their hair down and have a good time and be specially friendly. So they bought a car-load of food and booze and drove us off for miles into the country to a little wooden house, more a hut really, all by itself in a field beside a lake surrounded by hills.

That was quite interesting because the cottage had been the farmhouse where one of the men had been born and where his father had been born and where his parents had lived all their lives. The place was pretty well unchanged. There were only two rooms. The biggest had an open fire with a huge brick oven behind that you could sleep on top of in winter to keep warm. There was no electricity and no running water. And an outside dry lav that stank. We had to use Gaz lamps and carry water in plastic containers from a modern house a quarter of an hour's walk away.

We camped there for four days. Most of the time the men spent sitting around remembering the old days, telling stories about life on the rolling road in tramp steamers and grumbling about how dreadful it all is now with modern tankers and ships that just about sail themselves automatically and crews that are pampered and don't know anything about real seamanship.

I got fed up with that fairly soon. There was a small rowing boat belonging to the house so I started going off in that and exploring the lake and the shore around it. And I would land somewhere and walk through the forest. The Swedes have a law that allows you to go where you like because the land is supposed to be for everybody. So you don't have to worry about trespassing or tetchy farmers like you have to here. There was masses of wildlife to see as well.

Well, one evening I was walking through a wood when I saw a bull elk. It came looming out of the trees into a clearing. I nearly panicked. I'd no idea they're so big. So strong and bulky. They've huge flattened antlers, really amazing in size, that grow out of their heads like the branches of a tree and make them look top heavy. And they've overpowering hind quarters that squash the breath out of you just to look at. Fearsome. But magnificent. Lordly. They really are. Proud. Regal. I could see why people use words like that.

He mesmerized me. I couldn't move, just stood there staring at him and feeling like an idiot. He looked me up and down and sniffed and then stalked off quite slowly as if I was beneath contempt.

When he was gone I felt so weak I had to sit down till I was calm and got my strength back again. I felt like I'd had a shock. I was shaking all over, my heart was beating fast, I was panting, the bones had gone out of my legs, and I couldn't think at all, never mind think straight. And all the time I was grinning inanely. If anybody had seen me they'd have thought I was mad.

As soon as I recovered, all I wanted to do was get back to the cottage and tell Grandad what I'd seen. But when I arrived they were already three sheets to the wind, as Grandad says, and at the stage of laughing loudly and singing bawdy seamen's songs in raucous voices. That made me spitting angry. I was desperate to tell Grandad about the elk and there he was, that stupid with booze he couldn't have understood even if he'd have listened.

There was nowhere I could get away from them in the cottage. And nobody else for miles, except the local farmer and his family where we got the water, but they hardly spoke any English even if I'd felt like going to them, which I didn't. I didn't fancy wandering about in the forest again either. I did think of sitting like a spare part in the car listening to music on the radio till they were all so blotto they collapsed. But they might have taken it into their heads to drive off somewhere, and I'd have been trapped with them, which didn't appeal at all. The only thing left was to take the boat out on the lake. At least I'd be well away from them, and I thought a good stiff row might do me good.

So I ran down the field and pushed off in the boat and rowed like crazy up and down the lake till I was drenched in sweat and was choking for breath and could hardly see for blood pumping in my eyes and my arms couldn't pull another stroke. I felt like those guys look at the end of the boat race every year, the ones who lose. You know—the way their bodies slump over their oars and their faces are twisted in agony and they're gasping. And somehow I felt I'd failed too.

I sat like that, letting the boat drift in the middle of the lake till I got my breath back and my muscles stopped snapping like overstretched elastic, and my mind settled down to being as normal as it ever is, and my ears stopped popping, and my eyes were seeing properly again.

INTERCUT: *The shot of the lake. Zoom in to a close-up of the figure in the boat till he fills the screen, head to middle: Nik. We watch as he does what he describes in a voice-over:*

And it was then the thing I'm trying to tell you about happened.

As I came to my senses, everything suddenly seemed clearer. There were some birds, some ducks, dabbling about on the edge of the lake and their calls seemed sharper than I could ever remember hearing any noise before. They were all I could hear. Everywhere else was complete silence which the noise of the ducks seemed to make intense, so that the silence was like a noise itself.

My hands were resting on the oars and I could feel the grain of the wood, though up till then they'd seemed smooth. The sun had set, there wasn't a breath of wind. It was the time when you can almost see the dusk creeping in. But that evening every-thing stood out sharply as I looked, and the colours, though they weren't bright like in sunlight, seemed to glow with a sort of purity I'd never seen before.

And as I looked a deep sense of peace came over me, a calmness that wasn't at all like feeling relaxed, but made me feel full of energy while being quite still inside. And it was as if time was . . . not stopped . . . but waiting. Hanging in the air. I felt I was looking into eternity and that nothing mattered any more because everything was in harmony, like a marvellous tune. Nothing mattered and yet everything mattered, every smallest detail, and all was well at last.

I sat there in the middle of the lake expecting that this strange sensation would pass. But it didn't. I didn't move, just stared and stared in a sort of happiness I didn't want to break. I watched the sky slowly change as dusk turned to night and stars came out, needle-sharp points of light in a darkening, deepening blueblack vastness that made me feel I was shrinking smaller and smaller till a sort of pain came over me, a mixture of joy because of the beauty of it all and sadness because of my insignificance compared with all that unendingness. But I was part of it, however unimportant I was. And I wanted to be totally in it. Absorbed into it, not separate.

And then, when the stars were fully out and it was night, even though there was still light on the horizon because of how far north we were, the strangest thing of all happened.

I started getting a hard-on. Honest! I'm not just being rude. I had an erection! And I wanted it—all that out there, I mean. I wanted all that—I don't know . . . nature. Peace. Eternity. Whatever it was. Like wanting a girl. I wanted to be in it and to possess it. Wanted to belong to it and wanted it to belong to me. And I wanted to hold it in my hands and feel it with my body. And . . . honest . . . I wanted to come in it!

I know this must sound mad. But it didn't seem like that at the time. It seemed natural. I wasn't surprised or ashamed or anything like that. I just felt this overpowering desire. Stronger than anything I've ever felt before.

I didn't think about it. I just stood up in the boat, and quite deliberately, as if I was performing a sacred act, a ritual ceremony, I took off my clothes, one thing after another, folded them up neatly, which I never do usually, and laid them in the stern.

Then, when I was completely naked, I stood erect, everything erect!, and looked around, all around, part of me still expecting this strange mood to pass, but it didn't. The air was cold by then, northern cold, the cold that comes off snow. And the cold of the air felt as sharp and alive to my skin as the colours and shapes of everything were to my eyes and the sounds and silence, the silence most of all, were to my ears.

And I loved it. Desired it. Was randy for it. Wanted to be in it. And there was only one way. I put a foot on the gunwale, pushed up, and jumped.

I went in feet first, straight down into the dark water. The air felt cold, but the water was freezing. God, it was cold! Knocked the breath out of me like a punch. And knocked down what was standing up as well. Like a fist of ice grabbing the goolies!

As soon as I surfaced I started laughing. And the air felt warm so I splashed about a bit just for the fun of it. Then hauled myself into the boat, shivering, all passion spent!

And I tell you, I shall never forget that evening. Never. It's as clear to me now as it was then. And I know it will be all my life.

'That must sound pretty ridiculous,' Nik said.

'No, it doesn't,' Julie said.

'Every detail,' Nik said, 'still sharp. Especially the feeling of happiness and peace and wanting to be part of the vastness. Whatever the vastness was . . . Is.'

'God,' Julie said.

Nik snorted. 'I knew you'd say that.'

'Sorry I'm so predictable.'

They had arrived at Julie's car. She unlocked the passenger door. As Nik stooped to climb in, she kissed him lightly on his passing cheek. Nik checked himself and turned his head, hoping for more. But Julie was already on her way to the driver's seat.

†

Tom waited. After his talk with Sharkey he'd felt pleased, spending the time since then running and rerunning his performance, rewriting the script where he felt he had done badly, storing away the better moments for use again in future. What excited him most was the prospect of hooking Sharkey as a regular snout. His first, and quite a catch. As ageing leader of the town's least prissy teen squad, Sharkey knew everybody that mattered among the juves, and was well placed with the grown-up pros. He'd be a prime source of hot gossip.

A wary predator, was Sharkey, and, true to his name, always on the move. But, thought Tom, predators can be preyed on. Kept alive, given enough time, enough rope, they led you to more tasty fish. Already there were the makings of a useful relationship. Act the clever weakling, Tom told himself. Let Sharkey snap and bite and play the big man all he wants. Make him believe he can break free whenever he likes, and flatter him. But every now and then give the line a jerk. Then he would spit out the juicy gobbets he'd swallowed, no trouble at all.

There was one thing all sharks and all pack leaders feared: that the rest of the pack would find out their weakness and turn on them. Back-bite time.

As he stared at the view from the Hill Pauls car park, Tom decided that Sharkey's weakness was that he was a romantic.

For people like Sharkey, being a leader, and believing they were champion of a cause, mattered almost more than anything. They didn't really care who they led, or what the cause. Those things were often as much a matter of accident as of choice. Sharkey led the Sharks because that was the best of the gangs that played around the streets where he lived. And he was a villain who thought he was Robin Hood because he'd been born into villainy and taught the Robin Hood garbage by his petty criminal dad. If he'd been born in the plusher parts of town he'd maybe have organized the lads into a computer club and been a gospel Tory. It wouldn't have mattered so long as he was the leader and believed himself in the right, fighting against the odds.

Take away their self-righteous confidence and people like Sharkey were lost. Undermine their position as a leader, or better still, disillusion them about their cause, and they were finished. Not just in the eyes of their pathetic followers, but in their own eyes. Take away their belief in themselves and their destiny and they self-destructed. Romantics love failure as much as—even sometimes more than—success, so long as they fail as martyrs.

Take Sharkey in, send him down for his petty crimes as martyr to the cause of the ordinary bloke against an oppressive system, and he'd survive his porridge proudly, come out a bigger hero than he went in, and be all the better prepared for villainy because of what he'd learned inside. But show him how you can leave him on the streets a reject with no following and he would do anything you want to prevent it. Sure, he would twist and turn and snap a lot, and you would have to slip him some nicely laundered reasons why he should do the dirty on himself and his kind, but in the end he'd give.

And you know what the really chuffing thing is, Tom thought, smiling to himself as the game became clear. The really chuffing thing is you get him anyway. Because in the end he gives himself up. Play him long enough, make him do the dirty often enough, and finally he goes to pieces because the disillusionment about himself gradually corrodes his self-respect. And his romantic soul can't stand that! Then there's nothing left except the humdrum boredom of self-disgust, or the romantic's last resort: a nasty little romantic death. Suicide. The Roman way of getting your own back—on a world entirely against you, and on yourself for being a weak twittish human being like everybody else.

I don't like romantics, Tom thought. Don't just dislike them, I despise them. They're just as dangerous as psychos and worse than straightforward, out-and-out villains whose only motives are excitement and greed.

At which moment Sharkey appeared, his heavy frame hunched, his pasty face puckered, reminding Tom of a nocturnal animal, used to the cover of darkness and tangled undergrowth, that's been flushed out into open country in bright sunlight. Though in fact this was one of those moist grey days that make slugs happy. So, thought Tom, why not Sharkey?

'Good news?' Tom asked.

'Sommat funny goin on,' Sharkey said, eyes busy for overseers.

'Don't look like you're dying of laughter.'

'Everybody's heard but nobody knows nothin.'

'Come on, Sharkey, you can do better than that.'

'No, honest. Nothin. Can't understand it myself.'

Tom said with deliberate whining scorn, 'All your connections and you can't come up with *anything*?'

Irritation flickered round Sharkey's eyes. For a moment Tom was sure he was going to hit him. But instead he slouched against the wall and said, 'You're full of shit, Tommy.'

Tom grinned. 'And you'll be full of porridge before long.'

Sharkey sniffed. 'Yeah, well, I need more time. Nobody who'd really know is around yet. Too early.'

They stood side by side in silence, Sharkey waiting for Tom, Tom turning over his next move. Was Sharkey testing him? Trying him out for size? Or maybe he'd heard something and was holding back till he was certain he really did need to give it away? Should he push him hard now, or play him along?

While they stood there the sun found a break in the cloud and, like a theatre spot, cast a beam that fell on a window in a house across the valley, which reflected a brief flash of light at

Tom's thought-glazed eyes, making him blink and attracting his attention.

As if the sunflash was a heliographed message, the event perked up his senses, sharpening his mind. Not that he knew at once what the message was. But he knew something important had come to him. A clue to the answer he wanted, if not the answer itself.

Natural instinct—the instinct that would make him a talented cop—as well as his yet unfinished training told him to stay silent for a minute till he could act without betraying any of this to Sharkey.

Then he said, 'Look, suppose I can keep the super happy, how long do you want?'

Sharkey shrugged. 'Dunno, do I? Till tonight when there's more of the lads around. Half-seven? How about then?'

Tom pretended doubt. 'Risky. Not sure I can hold him off that long. I'm putting myself on the line for you, Sharkey, if I do this. You'll have to turn up something. Okay?'

'Yeah, yeah, sure, you're a big mate, Tommy. All ready to go down with me, aren't you.'

'Best I can do.'

'Best I can do as well. And I don't like meetin like this neither. Can't you think of nowhere better?'

'How about the nick?'

'Very comic!'

'Seven-thirty sharp, bottom end of the railway car park, back of the old goods shed. Nobody'll spot you there. Okay?'

'I must be a proper mug,' Sharkey said, and slouched off, leaving Tom to nod at his back unseen, and grin to himself with satisfaction. Hooked or not as a regular, Sharkey was damn good practice, a useful rehearsal for bigger shows.

ADVANCES

JULIE: Dear Nik: Today they took the bandages off my chest. Not the ones round my eyes or hands, though. So I still can't see or do anything for myself. But isn't this good news?

They drugged me beforehand, of course, and clucked and cooed, trying to reassure me, like midwives at a rebirth. And it did feel like a kind of resurrection.

Afterwards, I asked Simmo to tell me honestly how I look. She said the wounds are healing very well but that it's too early to tell how bad the scars will be.

At first I was so glad to be rid of the bandages I wanted to shout for joy. I can't tell you how good it was to feel air on my skin again, and to move my arms and legs without being fettered by those suffocating wrappings.

But this afternoon I slept for a while and woke up feeling very low. Depressed about everything again. A kind of emotional relapse, I suppose, or perhaps just a hangover from the drugs. Whatever it was, I began to loathe myself. I kept imagining my body covered in repulsive scars and gashes, and my face disfigured, and my hands paralysed like claws, and my skin all scaly like a reptile's. I was sure I'd turned into a freak, something hideous that people wouldn't be able to look at without feeling ill. It seemed as if I'd been bandaged up a reasonably normal human being, and had somehow changed, like a caterpillar in its chrysalis, but instead of coming out a beautiful butterfly, I'd come out a monster.

After going on like that for a while, I began to hate myself all the more for being so defeatist.

Mother arrived just then. She'd come over because she knew about the unveiling. They'd told her yesterday, apparently, when she rang as usual to ask about me. They didn't tell me they were going to do it until they were ready to start this morning. Mum had thought they might take the bandages off my eyes as well and wanted to be here so I could see her if they did. That's what she said. But I know that really she was worried I might be blind, and wanted to help me through the ordeal.

[*Pause.*]

Well, I still don't know. And I can't use my hands because they're covered in what feel like boxing gloves. Now I know what it's like to be incapable, and totally dependent on other people for even the simplest things. Worst of all is that they have to do all your most private things for you. Everything from wiping your bum to picking your nose.

Don't laugh!

[*Chuckles.*]

You'll think it a bigger joke than Sister Ann in church, but they do! Even pick your nose, I mean. They use those little sticks with cotton wool on the ends. Though, to be honest, they aren't entirely successful. When Simmo does it, she gets on with it, using her own finger! 'Let's see what we can find up here,' she says, matter-of-fact as always, just as if she were clearing out a cupboard. But I can't tell you what a relief it is. I never thought picking your nose is so important. But if you don't do it . . . well, I suppose you'd clog up and always have to breathe through your mouth, which would be awful.

At school there was a girl who always seemed to breathe through her mouth. We used to hate her sitting beside us. Though, I have to say it was more usually boys than girls who did it. And then we made fun of them. Used to call them Gobgasper. How rotten we were! Perhaps they'd never discovered about picking your nose. Because it's one of those silly things that everybody must do but nobody talks about.

Well . . . I'm talking to you about it now, I know. But that's different somehow. I'm allowed to because of the state I'm in. Sick people—or very sick people anyway—are allowed to break the rules a bit, aren't they? They are in here. You can tell how sick people really are, no matter what the doctors tell them, by how much they're allowed to get away with, like being rude to nurses or messing the bed or shouting all night long and keeping everybody awake. If you aren't very sick, you're soon told off.

Just as dying people can tell the truth about themselves no matter how bad they've been, and everybody thinks they're

99

wonderful for confessing, and forgive them at once. Whereas if they'd stood up in a crowded room and confessed when they were healthy and strong they'd have been arrested. Or else become one of those sordid people who appear on TV talk shows and tell about their criminal or wicked private lives while the audience ogles and gasps and thinks how daring they are.

[*Pause.*]

I've lost myself, as usual. Where was I . . . ? Oh yes—picking my nose, and what an affliction it is not to be able to do it.

I keep thinking about affliction. Only natural I suppose. And I did say I'd try and make it into my God-work, because I couldn't do anything much else.

Actually, I said I'd think about pain. And affliction isn't the same thing. One of my discoveries. I might as well tell you about it because talking to you is raising my spirits again, and talking about what I've been thinking might help me sort it out better than just keeping it in my head. I've found I can only get so far thinking to myself. The thoughts start going round and round, getting nowhere and confusing me more than I was before I started.

As a matter of fact, I found that out before. And I used to write my thoughts down, which helped make me sort them out so that I could think clearly in my head again. But as I can't write in my present blind and boxing-gloved state, perhaps saying what I've been thinking will have the same effect. If you don't want to be bothered with it, just switch off. I'll never know if you do, so you won't upset me.

Usually I give my written thoughts a title in the book I use to write them in. I'd better do the same now. So let's see . . .

[*Pause. Then in a more formal, thoughtful voice*:]

Meditation on the Nature of Affliction

The best example of affliction I know of is Christ nailed to the cross.

She wasn't ill. She hadn't committed any crime. She didn't nail herself up. She was put there by other people. Not because of anything dreadful that she'd done, but because of what she was.

She was Christ, just as a man is a man, a woman is a woman, a black person has black skin. These are not choices people make for themselves. They are accidents of birth. Inescapable facts.

You can rejoice in being what you are. But you can suffer for it too. So what you are can be an affliction. An affliction is not something you bring upon yourself. It's something visited upon you over which you have no control. As being black can be an affliction in a country of white, prejudiced people. And being a woman can be an affliction in a society ruled by men.

That's why Christ can be for everyone, because she came to earth as a man and was herself afflicted by the men who ruled at that time. So she is an ally of all the afflicted, who are the touchstone of human frailty. Not because of themselves, but because of what they reveal about everyone else. As a black person walking into a room full of whites very quickly reveals the real attitudes of the majority.

My suffering here is an affliction. I know now it's the first real affliction that's come upon me in my life. And like all the afflicted, I'm a victim of the actions of others. Actions of which I was innocent. I mean, I lacked knowledge of them, and was given no choice about them. Being afflicted is therefore like being a slave. You have no choice about what happens to you.

When affliction comes upon you, it always brings with it two consequences. The first is physical pain. The second is an uprooting change in your life.

Physical pain can often be lessened or even ended by someone taking action—yourself perhaps or a doctor, for example. Just as Simmo gave me drugs this morning to dull the pain of my unveiling, or the pain of hunger can be ended by eating a meal. Then happiness returns. The pain is forgotten. So physical pain is not the same thing as affliction. I used to think toothache was an affliction. But now I know it isn't. It's simply a pain. I can do something about it.

[*Pause.*]

The real pain of affliction isn't physical. It's the pain of knowing you can't escape the disaster that's befallen you. This pain isn't physical, and it isn't emotional, though both can be part of it. No. It's a spiritual pain. It's like sorrow, which is the pain of separation. The affliction separates you from the life around you—the life you would prefer. It separates you from other people. But worst of all it separates you from the fulfilment of your self. Of your *being*.

I'd prefer to be walking, seeing, doing things with my hands. This affliction that's come upon me has changed my life. Stretched out on this bed, shut up in this room where others are not allowed unless they're tending me, I'm separated from people. From everyday, ordinary life. Often, I feel I'm not even a member of the human race any more. And it prevents me from fulfilling myself in the work I chose.

So my body, my mind, my life with others are all nailed to a cross of affliction that removes me from my true self.

No wonder Christ, nailed to her cross, cried out against God. Now I know what 'My God, my God, why have you forsaken me?' really means. For I have heard myself cry out those same words in the most painful time of my affliction when there seemed to be no one out there. Not even God. But only an absence. A hell made of nothing. A place alone, for myself alone.

Then I felt accursed. Marked for ever as a reject. Abandoned. Prevented by the evil of my affliction from helping myself.

And no one else can help. Not even the afflicted can help each other. Their afflictions prevent it. Christ, nailed to her cross, couldn't climb down and help those hanging on either side of her. And I can't get up and go next door when I hear my neighbour's alarm call sounding in the night.

And people who are not afflicted can't help—can't remove the affliction—because they don't, they can't, *know* what it is like. For affliction can't be described. Other people might be able to relieve the physical pain but they can't remove the deep soul-strangling knowledge of separation that an affliction gives you.

[*Pause.*]

Affliction makes you into a thing. An object. Something like a machine that needs attention now and then to keep it going, and makes noises, and sometimes causes trouble. An object that can be kept ticking over if it's given the right fuel and maintenance. And that can be switched off and even dumped if you get fed up with it.

Affliction makes you anonymous. It takes away your personality. Just as happens when one person thinks of another as only an object for sex, or as a slave. Or as a racist will say of those he dislikes, 'They all look the same to me'. Or as a pagan will say, 'The trouble with Christians is . . .', as if all Christians were one kind, one thing that lacks any individuality.

[*Pause.*]

Looking on the bright side, not all afflictions are for ever, thank goodness. Christ came down from the cross. But the wounds were still there, of the nails and the spear, and the crown of thorns. Even in her glorified body, when she wasn't flesh and blood any more. So, though affliction may not be for ever, it leaves its mark on you for ever. Its name is engraved on your soul if not on your body.

I don't know yet if my affliction will pass. I don't know what scars it will leave on my soul. I don't even know yet what good I can make of this evil.

[*Pause.*]

That's the hardest part. Something I can't think out yet. How to turn such crushing evil into something good.

[*Pause.*]

Except . . .

[*Pause.*]

I don't know . . .

Even while I'm saying these thoughts to you, Nik, something keeps coming back into my mind. Your hand. Remember? That awful time when they were sure I would die and they brought you here because I was calling your name?

Your hand was like a thought . . .

Like a message.

[*Pause.*]

Didn't I tell you the touch of your hand made it possible for me to believe I could live again? I can't remember exactly because I was still in a bad way and heavily drugged when I recorded the first tape.

Whatever I said, what I *meant*, I know now, was . . . What? . . . Well, here I am trapped in this bed like a creature in a zoo, having to live quite unnaturally, not at all the way I used to or want to, living a kind of horror, struggling against it, and I keep remembering the touch of your hand . . . And what it did . . . what it *does* . . . is make me want to love.

[*Pause.*]

The words fail. I'm tiring I expect. No wonder!

But that's the nearest I can get just now to what I mean. Your hand . . . *you* . . . made me want to love. And there is nothing my affliction can do to stop that. It can't kill that part of me. The part that can love.

[*Pause.*]

Which means something very very important. I think. Or is it just sentimental rubbish? You'll tell me. But I can't say any more now. I've worn my thoughts out. The tape must be nearly full anyway. So I'll rest and think about what it means later and tell you about it another time.

†

Tom waited till Sharkey was well clear before leaving the car park. While he waited he considered the sun's heliographed message. Why should that bright flash of reflected light have so caught his mind as well as his eye?

He studied the houses across the valley, searching for the one with the swinging window. It wasn't easy for him to find at that distance because now they were all bathed in sunlight, anonymous boxes with few distinguishing marks. But then he saw it, an upstairs window swinging on its hinges like a lazy weather vane. And as he watched, a woman appeared and pulled it closed. As the window turned, it flashed another brief message from the sun.

At once Tom realized what it was telling him. Standish, the insurance agent, had said that his attention had been attracted by the early morning sun flashing on the boy's face. But does the sun *flash* on faces? It hadn't flashed on the face of the woman at the window. Light only flashes from hard shiny surfaces. Like glass.

He needed to make a phone call.

The nearest box was outside the railway station. He couldn't prevent himself sprinting across the car park into the back of the station, had to restrain himself from getting to the front by crossing the line instead of using the pedestrian bridge, and felt the omens were good when he found the phone box empty and in working order.

Stay cool, he told himself while he dialled. Don't let on.

The secretary connected him to Standish as soon as he said who he was.

'Just another question, if you don't mind, sir. I wonder, can you remember, was the boy wearing glasses?'

'Spectacles, you mean?'

'Yes, sir. Specs.'

'Wait a minute . . . Goodness! . . . Yes, I think he was. Fancy not remembering a thing like that.'

'No matter, sir. But you're sure?'

'Positive, now you mention it. How do you know? Found him, have you?'

'Not yet. Just an idea, that's all. We'll let you know when there's any news, sir.'

Tom's next call was to the duty sergeant.

'Sherlock Holmes is it?'

'Maigret, sarge, no less.'

'Margaret who? Is there something you haven't told me, laddie?'

'Very witty, sarge. Listen, would you have a squint at the scene-of-crime report for the crucifiction and see if a pair of specs is listed.'

'Wait.'

Tom heard pages being riffled. Then silence except for the sarge's habitual clicking of his tongue in a tuneless tattoo.

'No, lad, no specs.'

'Sure, sarge?'

'Looked through twice.'

'Damn.'

'Onto something, are we?'

'No. A dead end.'

'Pity. But never mind, Margaret old girl. Even real detectives have their off days.'

'Sarge, you're always so supportive. Like an old truss.'

'You mind your manners, boy, or you'll be back in the blue and on the plod double quick instead of poncing about on the loose.'

'How could you, sarge! That's professionally insulting as well as sexist!'

He put down the phone before there was time for reply.

†

LETTERS:

Dear Nik: Thursday is my birthday. I'm taking the day off so that I can go to Norwich, as a treat, and visit the place where someone used to live who I admire. A kind of pilgrimage. Her name was Dame Julian. She had visions on the day of my birthday, 8th May, but a few years before I was born. In 1373 to be exact. Afterwards she wrote a book about them. She called it *Revelations of Divine Love*. You should read it. Good for your research. Might get a surprise as well. She called Christ Mother Jesus. 'Jesus Christ, who sets good against evil, is our real Mother,' is what she actually wrote. Here's some more:

> *I came to know there are three ways of looking at God's motherhood. The first is that our human nature is made. The second is that God took our nature, which is the beginning of the grace of motherhood. The third is the work of motherhood which God spreads out over everyone—the length and breadth and height of it is without end. And all this is one Love . . . In essence, motherhood means kindness, wisdom, knowledge, goodness, love . . . By the skill and wisdom of Jesus Christ we are sustained, restored, and saved with regard to our sensual nature, for he is our Mother, Brother, and Saviour.*

Interesting? Interested? There's lots more.

I thought I'd drive over after work on Wednesday evening, slum it overnight somewhere nearby, leaving all Thursday for sight-seeing. Drive back Thursday evening. Late back but

106

worth it. For me anyway. How about you? Would you like to come? Would they let you off school? Be good for your education.

Let me know. *Julie*

Dear Julie: I can resist everything except temptation. Sure I'd like to come.

But I thought I'd better check up about Thursday before saying yes. Especially as I'll be mucking about with dames who have visions. Dead and alive. Dangerous stuff that.

So I've been doing some runic arithmetic. The results:

This old dame had her 'visions' (really?) on the eighth day of the fifth month of the year one thousand three hundred and seventy-three. That is:

8   5   1373

Reduced to their fundamental number (because I know you like getting down to fundamentals) this becomes:

$8 + 5 + 1 + 3 + 7 + 3 = 27 = 9$

Let's do the same with your birth date, which, if you are nineteen this year, must be:

$8 \quad 5 \quad 1967 = 36 = 9$

Each of you reduce to nine!

The figure nine is a cardinal number composed of the prime number three, three times repeated:

$3 + 3 + 3 = 9$

I don't need tell you that three is a mystical number, and so is nine. According to your lot, God is 3-in-1. In your birthday and the date of the old girl's visions the three-in-one is three times repeated, making the religious magic even stronger because that makes nine.

Now take your age and reduce it to a single number as before:

$19 = 10 = 1$

Similarly, your birthday this year:

$$8 \quad 5 \quad 1986 = 37 = 10 = 1$$

Also, find the difference between the year of the old dame's 'visions' and your birthday year:

$$1986 - 1373 = 613 = 10 = 1$$

Three ones! And:

$$1 + 1 + 1 = 3$$

How about the difference between the old dame's vision year and your birth year?

$$1967 - 1373 = 594 = 18 = 9$$

Glory! Now we have three nines. 999. The emergency number.

And the three-in-one thrice repeated and thrice repeated. Strong magic this!

Let's get a grand total. Add up all the reduced figures and reduce them to one final all-inclusive Big Deal number.

Old dame's 'vision' year:	9
Your birth year:	9
Diff bn old dame's vision yr & yr b. yr:	9
Yr age:	1
Yr birthday this yr:	1
Diff bn OD's vision yr & yr birthday this yr:	1
TOTAL:	30
REDUCTION (3 + 0):	3

BINGO!!! The mystic trinity: three-in-one!

Your God is in all the figures. How can I not go with you? Something stupendous is bound to happen.

But what about the day?

This year 8th May is a Thursday.

What do we know about Thursday?

1) Thursday's child has far to go.

This sounds okay. You plan a journey that day. (Well, you

start on Wednesday, but after six, because you have to work till about then, don't you? And in ye olden tymes, the day always began the evening before, right?)

2) Thursday is the fifth day of the week, as defined in Collins English Dictionary.

What happened on the fifth day? Quote:

And God said, 'Let the waters bring forth swarms of living creatures, and let birds fly above the earth across the firmament of the heavens.' So God created the great sea monsters and every living creature that moves, with which the waters swam, according to their kinds, and every winged bird according to its kind. And God saw that it was good. And God said, 'Be fruitful and multiply and fill the waters in the seas, and let birds multiply on the earth.' And there was evening and morning, a fifth day.
[First Book of Moses, commonly called Genesis, Chap. 1, vv. 20–3, Revised Standard Version.]

So on Thursday life got started. A bit of the old how's your father sounds all right to me. Can't miss out on that.

Trouble is, there's all that stuff about how Thursday got its name. You know: Thor's Day. Quote (Collins E.D. again):

Thor: Norse myth: the God of thunder, depicted as wielding a hammer, emblematic of the thunder bolt.

Wowee: Thunderbolt Day. Could be exciting.

Further: Funk and Wagnall (don't you just love the name?) tell much more about old Thor in their *Standard Dictionary of Folklore, Mythology and Myth*, which your 'umble researcher naturally consulted:

Such as Thor being *one of the greatest of the Gods; God of yeomen and peasants and opposed to Odin, God of the nobility*. Which makes him a hammer of the people and an okay guy as far as I'm concerned.

Added to which, he was *large, strong* and *capable of epic rages* so bad even his own mother, bless her, couldn't stand them, so she gave him away to foster parents, motivated of course by that caring, supportive concern for their offspring's welfare we all expect from doting, selfless progenitors.

He was such a Jack-the-Lad among ye gods that, Fun-Wag report, *In many localities no work was done on this day*. Great. I'll tell them at school that I've joined the Thorians and can't come Thursday because it's our day off. Thursday's Thor's day, folks. Lay-about day. Bring your own hammers and rages and lay about all you want. Epic eppies are all the rage. Rage, rage against the dying of the light, etc.

STOCKSHOT: *There is only one definition of God: the freedom that allows other freedoms to exist.*

More about Thursday, because there's more to Thursday than Thor, would you believe:

Apart from saying it is the fifth day of creation, your lot add:

a) *Maundy Thursday*: Christ washed the feet of his disciples the day before he died, right? The day before he died is supposed to be Thursday. So Thursday is the day your lot remember this.

I got all confused by the 'maundy' bit. So I looked it up. Derivation: 13th century Old French: *mande*, meaning 'commandment', which you'll know but I didn't came from JC's words: *Mandatum novem do vobis*: i.e., 'A new commandment I give unto you'. The new one being, I guess, that they must love one another. (You see, I really was paying attention during RE, after all.)

b) Thursday is also supposed to be the day JC ascended into heaven. My grandad says they used to have Ascension Day off when he was a kid. They all did something together, as a school, like a seaside outing to Weston or a walk from Berkeley Castle to Quedgeley, all along the Severn, with picnics on the way and a bonfire and bangers and a singsong at the end, then buses home dead tired and filthy but happy. He says they were the nicest days he can remember, and they sound pretty good to me too. We don't do things like that now because Ascension Day isn't a holiday any more. Nobody thinks of celebrating somebody rising up into the sky by having a jolly jaunt. Not even astronauts any more.

Maybe there's some use in religion after all, even if it's just that you get a good time once a year as a kid. Well, and Christmas Day as well. And Easter, come to think of it—they used to have nice times then too, like rolling hard-boiled eggs down hillsides, which sounds wild. And, my grandad says, they always had off the patron saint's day of their local church, and Whit week. I'll make sure us Thorians have lots of pi-holidays. (Hey, I've just realized that 'holiday' comes from 'holy-day': a day off for a religious reason. Yes, I know, I'm thick.)

My last bit of research:

8th May: you were born under the sign of Taurus, the bull. You are therefore supposed to be EARTHY, MELAN-CHOLY, and STRONG-WILLED. I should have known after the CND demo. That day you were certainly earthy (covered in it, in fact), melancholy (very fed up, if you ask me), and strong-willed (stubborn is the word I'd use). But you don't look like a bull, I'll grant you that. Quite nice, actually, in an un-bullish way. Just shows how appearances can deceive.

Taurus and *Thor, the thunderbolt* and threes and nines and footwashings and ascensions into the sky!

When added up, what does this mean?

Answer: I am invited to accompany a wilful, moody, sensual but religious female, whose life is dominated that day by the power of one (the self: one is one and ever more shall be so), three times repeated (a triangle, strongest of all shapes and signs), adding up to 999 (an alarm call with spiritual/magical properties), on a birthday pilgrimage (something I don't be-lieve in) to a place where an old woman who died over six hundred years ago (a herstory) saw what *she* thought were visions of God (but which I think must have been hallucina-tions because I don't believe in visions).

This trip is to be made in an ancient chariot, and we are to spend a night together in uncertain circumstances, before a day when the female's God ordered that we love one another and on which s/he/it rose up into Paradise, but which is also the day of the hammering thunderbolt wielded by a rival God, champion of the peasants, he of the epi-temper.

If I had any sense I'd stay at home. There's bound to be trouble.

and no one came to inquire. Which struck him as odd even then. Surely there was someone around in the middle of a working day?

Thirty-five minutes passed. Tom had spread the circle as wide as he felt was worth it so he started back towards the middle, but tracking counter, viewing things contrarily.

A pyramid of used tyres lay on the edge of his circle. First time, he had skirted it, paying only a cursory glance, not fancying a climb on its treacherous rubbery mess. This time, he gave it more attention, decided a close inspection was necessary, and began goat-stepping his way up, prying only with his eyes into the jumbled cavities.

As he climbed he felt himself tensing with excitement. He was warmer, he was sure, as in a game of hide-and-seek. His blood pulsed. There *was* something here, he knew it.

But he reached the top without success. Began to doubt himself, his hunches, his rozzer's instincts.

Then saw.

A glint, a miniature of the flashing window.

On a side of the pyramid from that facing the scene-of-crime, two steps below him, clinging to the rim of a tyre by a bent arm, its one remaining but cracked lens catching the light, hung a pair of granny specs.

He almost let out a whoop.

ASSAULT

NIK'S NOTEBOOK: Four days after.
They say I'm still shocked. Shouldn't I be?
They say I should rest. Not think about it.

How can I not think about it, with the press and photographers still sniffing round all the time and interviewers trying to talk to me, and people pretending to be friendly when all they really are is curious, and the police asking questions?

Anyway, I WANT to think about it, damn them. But my own way. Not their way. And how can I with them all rabbiting on and confusing me?

Treat it as research. Hold it away so I can look at it, get it in focus, think about it.

It might be the most important thing of all.
IS.

But couldn't hold it away from me without my wp. Hands keep having spasms when they shake uncontrollably. And my legs, when I stand, will suddenly give way, as if all the bones had melted. But can prop myself up in my chair and tap away without too much trouble, watching the green fingertip write words, words that glow like green jewels quarried from the depths of the VDU.

Words on the VDU are different from words you write on paper. Not so much your own. Not anyone's. Removed. So less dangerous, less upsetting.

Anyway, whatever they say, I'm going to think about it, and the only way I can think about it without breaking into a sweat and having my hands shake or my legs melt, or even, dammit, bursting into tears, is to record it, look at it in words held away from me, not mine, but themselves—OTHER.

Words words words. I like words. Begin to like words more than people. Not like: LOVE.

LOVE: that which cannot be done without; wish always to

be with, be part of, belong to, know intimately inside and out, entirely, WHOLE-LY, for ever and ever amen.

Shining bright words in amazing patterns of endless variety. Drawings of the inside of my head.

Selah bloody selah.

STOCKSHOT: *People like you must* look *at everything and* think *about it and communicate with the heaven that dwells deep within them and listen for a word to come.*

Chapter One   THE JOURNEY

We drove via Cirencester ring road, through Bibury to Burford, on along the Witney bypass, left at north Oxford for Bicester and Buckingham, then Stoney Stratford and the Newport Pagnell bypass to slow and awkward, in-the-way Bedford. After that St Neot's and the flat, straight A45 towards Cambridge. Outside of which she stopped just off the main road on the edge of a parcel of trees.

Driving the way she drove in her ancient car and mostly in the dark with me navigating, using a flashlight to see her AA map and never having been further east than Witney and nearly losing us in rotten Bedford because I missed one of the signs, took three hours and ten minutes.

She said: We can make Norwich in an hour or so tomorrow and here's as good a place as any to bed down.

I said: Why not push on?

Because I'm too tired, she said. I've been working since seven this morning, unlike you coddled school kids. Besides, I thought you might like to see a bit of Cambridge tomorrow. It's supposed to be beautiful, and you ought to give it the once over as you're the sort who'll end up at university there.

She laughed. Me too, but from surprise, not humour. Never considered it. Would I want to?

And what sort end up there? I asked.

The clever, curious and uncommitted, she said, and laughed again.

Julie said: There's a small tent. One of us can use that, the other can sleep in the car. I don't mind.

I said: You choose.

She said: You take the tent. You'll be able to stretch out. I've dossed down in the car before and it doesn't bother me.

When we'd prepared for the night, we sat outside the tent drinking coffee from a flask I'd brought. Half eleven by then. A still night. I remember: An owl hooting over the fields. The warm air. A clear sky like a vast VDU with bright full stops scattered over it—the hundreds of trillions of millions of stars and galaxies, sucking black holes and popping white holes, and quasars with their red shifts and pulsars bleeping their radio call signs, and how many other unknown universes beyond? And smaller than all, bigger than all, a beaming moon. And us here on earth, a speck of sand floating in the unthinkable ocean of endless space.

This seemed the right romantic moment to spring her birthday surprise. I reached into the tent and produced the parcel like a magician from under my sleeping bag, and laid it in her lap.

What's this? she said, lighting the Gaz lamp to see.

I said happy birthday.

A present! she said. And reached over and kissed me. On the lips. Not passionately. But not just sisterly either. Which I misread.

Selah.

She delicately undressed the parcel.

A book, she said, fingering the cover. You shouldn't have!

People always say that, I said, full of witlessness at the sight of her glowing.

Well you shouldn't, she said. *A Humourment*, she said, misreading the title the same as I did when I first saw it.

A Hum-U-ment, I said.

By Tom Phillips, she said. Never heard of him before.

She began flipping pages, making surprised noises of pleasure at what she found.

Strange, she said. Unusual. Pictures with words in them. What's it about? How's it done?

I said: He explains at the end. One of my favourite books. A sort of vision but a bit different from old Dame Juliana's.

Thanks, Nik, she said. I'll read it properly when I get back home. It's a lovely gift.

And she reached over and gave me another unsisterly kiss and a hug as well this time. Which I misread even worse than before.

Chapter Three   COUNTRY MATTERS

I said: If you want, we could, I mean . . . if you like, we could . . . you could sleep with . . . in the tent . . .

She smiled and at once looked down to hide her face.

I laughed, not exactly voluntarily. More a spasm of nerves.

She said: Another birthday present?

I said: Well, no, well I mean, if you like . . . well yes, I wouldn't mind . . . Or put that another way—I would mind, I'd like it a lot, to be honest.

Pause.

Are you, she said, making a pass at me?

Pause for controlling of breath.

Yes.

Silence, her head up, eye-balling.

Julie: Did you think I expected something like this?

I shrugged, not knowing then what I'd expected, but knowing now that I'd hoped for it.

She looked down, hiding her face again.

The longest pause so far.

Then, almost whispered: I'm sorry.

I spluttered: Hey, look, it's okay, it's all right, I . . .

No no!, she cut in. I don't mean, I'm sorry I don't want to sleep with you. I mean, I'm sorry, I should have known, I should have thought . . . inviting you, you know, like this, you'd expect . . . it's only natural . . .

She looked up, her expression pained. The first time I'd seen her unsure of herself in the face of me. Vulnerable is the word.

She had seemed so utterly strong till then, so unshakeable and knowing.

I couldn't speak. Didn't know what to say. Confused about myself and her and what I'd just done, which already, then, seemed twittish, and now seems worse than grubby and makes me cringe. How could I be so crass?

But instead of letting it go, trying to apologize and forget, I sat there, staring at her, even letting myself feel angry, as if she had done something wrong to me.

She said, shaking her head: I'm stupid, I'm really stupid!

I shook my head, meaning: No you're not.

I don't know, she said, perhaps . . .

What? I said, wanting to know, but the word came out like a rebuke.

Just . . . !

Her turn to stammer and fluff. She looked away, a blank stare into the night blackened by the glare of the fizzing lamp.

. . . Perhaps I wanted you to try.

I said, cloddishly puzzled: Wanted me to try?

A sort of test, she said.

A test, I said, and now the anger took hold: Great! Well, I failed. Asked too soon, did I?

She laughed, which didn't help, misreading her again.

Just like a man! she said.

Not surprisingly, I said.

Thinking you're the only one who can fail. I can fail too, you know.

You're the one who set the test, I said.

Look, she said, you've got it wrong. What I mean is, I think perhaps . . . She sighed . . . Perhaps I asked you to come with me hoping you'd try something, but not admitting it to myself.

Why would you do that?

So as to test myself. To find out if I'd let you . . . If I'd sleep with you.

But you haven't. Not yet!

No.

So you haven't failed yet.

Not with *you*, she said, glaring at me. But with *myself*.

Selah.

Moths were buffeting the lamp, burning themselves, fluttering away in maddened circles, but coming back for more. Julie turned it off, plunging us into star-pricked night again.

What she was telling me didn't sink in. I still felt I'd been rejected, and was at fault for even trying. But I was thinking, why shouldn't I? I was only letting her know what I wanted, how I felt about her. What was wrong with that? And I really did think she had given me a hint, that her birthday-present kisses were more than thank-yous.

I couldn't help asking: Is it that you don't fancy me?

No no! she said, sounding now as irritated as I felt. Just the opposite if you must know!

Then why? Is it religion? Sex before marriage, all that stuff?

Yes! . . . No! . . . Yes, of course it's got something to do with religion. How could it not? My religion is about all of my life, not just about the bits of it that don't matter. But no, it hasn't got anything to do with sex before marriage and what you call all that stuff. It isn't like that any more—God, I mean, religion, Christianity. Not for me. It's only like that for you because you haven't thought about it enough, haven't *lived* it, but only assumed things . . .

There was anger between us now.

Selah.

Rows are stupid. That's why they seem so funny afterwards. Not always. But often. We laughed about this one next morning, while we were driving into Cambridge.

But the real joke about rows is that they're futile. I'm no expert on girls or how to deal with them, and I'm no expert on sex. But I am expert on rows, thanks to years of training by my row-loving parents.

When I felt anger bubbling up between us I thought: This is just the way it used to be at home! The thing would boil up, like a kettle full of water, until it boiled over and we'd all get scalded.

I thought: I'm even sounding like my dad. Like I'd caught a disease from him. Verbal cancer. Why don't I just shut up!

Switch off, goon! I thought. Or make it different, make it *sane!*

Selah.

Look, she said, I'll try and explain. About the sex, I mean.

Don't bother, I said, like a sulky boy who's been refused an ice-cream.

For my own sake, as much as yours!

Pause. The night echoing its deadness.

She shuffled closer, as if crossing a boundary.

She said: It isn't that I don't fancy you. I do.

There was a change of tone in her voice, a new tune, a caressing sound.

She went on: I didn't admit it before. Not even to myself. I've been pretending, I suppose—that you were just a funny, interesting schoolboy who said he was researching for a half-baked film project but who deep down was really trying to sort out his ideas . . . his relationship . . . with God.

And me, she said, I'd help you, wouldn't I! I was older and more mature, wasn't I! I'd open you to religion, show you the way, bring you to God! I'd convert you!

She laughed, self-mocking.

Isn't that great! I hate it. That I'd even let myself think it, I mean, never mind try and do it. Wanting to make converts, wanting to persuade people to believe what I believe the way I believe it. I can't bear it when I see other people trying to do that. Like those creepy evangelists on television, with their glossy suits, and their big rallies, and their stage-managed fervour, and their packaged sincerity, and their sanctimonious humility that somehow always makes you feel they possess a God-given superiority over the rest of us.

She heaved a sigh and rubbed a hand across her eyes.

One of the reasons I like Philip Ruscombe is that he's hopeless at conversion. If you had to make converts in order to qualify for Heaven, he'd fail. Not because he doesn't know how, but because he can't bring himself to do it.

It's one of the great temptations, you see—wanting to prove the strength of your own faith by making others believe what you believe. It shows you're right.

She huffed.

But it doesn't prove anything of the sort. All it proves is that you're condescending and arrogant and good at doing what half-decent actors can do, or advertising agents, or pop stars, or politicians, or con men, or any of the professional persuaders. They sell illusions. And that's all they do. And they feel good when they succeed. That's what their lives depend on.

Which isn't true about religion. Or shouldn't be. Your belief shouldn't depend on what other people think about it. And it certainly should not depend on whether other people believe the same as you.

She laughed.

But there I was, she said, falling into the trap. Wanting to make a convert! And the funny thing is that I was only *pretending* I was trying to do that. What I was really doing was falling into a different trap—fancying you and not admitting it to myself.

I said: Sounds as if wanting to convert me was a substitute for having it off with me.

Could be.

So you admit you fancy me?

Yes.

And you don't have any worries about sex?

Not the way you mean.

And I fancy you and certainly don't have any hang-ups about sex, so why don't we—

Because, she said firmly, for me there's a bit more to it than that!

Selah.

Can't remember word-for-word what she said then, but do remember her reasons. They went something like this:

Sex is a maker of life, as food is a sustainer of life.

Sex can also be an appetite, as eating is an appetite.

Just as you can eat for the sake of eating, so you can enjoy sex for the sake of it.

There is necessity in sex for making life. There is no necessity in sex for the sake of it.

One of the illusions that the Big Persuaders have sold us is that sex for the sake of it is necessary—that we've failed or lost out or somehow actually damaged ourselves if we don't have sex for the sake of it.

Julie doesn't want to make a new life, just for the sake of becoming a mother. And her appetites are all for God. She wanted to know more about God—wherever that took her, whatever it demanded, whatever God meant. She wanted to know more about herself as she looked through God's eyes, as she put it. She wasn't denying herself anything so that she could have something else. She was using all she had for one main purpose that meant more to her than all the other things on offer in life.

She laughed a lot about all this. She knew, she said, that most other people would think her weird, which is why she didn't talk about it. She also knew what she said sounded old-fashioned, just about extinct in fact. But it was the way she was and she just accepted it.

She wasn't saying everybody should be like her, or that she even thought she was right. She knew most people thought that sex was there to be enjoyed any time you liked, so long as you didn't force yourself on anyone and didn't do anything that hurt the other person. And she didn't disagree. But for her, she said, her sex, having sex, was such an important part of *her*, of her*self*, that she couldn't treat it as if she was just having an enjoyable meal with a friend.

Anyway, she said, it was wrong to compare sex and food. They weren't the same. When you share food, you share something from outside both of you. Each person takes part of the whole and enjoys it in the company of the other. When you consume food you consume something of the world about you and so you make yourself part of that world. But when you have sex you give part of yourself, part of your own interior being, and take a part of the other person, part of their inner being.

Something more is involved than simply keeping yourself physically alive, or enjoying yourself with someone you like. Food keeps you alive and binds you to the world we live in. But sex has to do with making life itself, and binds you to the life that's greater than any of us, and greater than the world we live in—the life that Julie calls God.

Sex has something directly to do with God. And as God fascinates her, is the most exciting, most important Event (her word, her capital E), she wanted to use her sex (her sexuality, her womanhood) to help her get to know God. Even though she

123

doesn't understand yet how to use it that way, and fails sometimes to resist the temptations that confuse her.

But no giving in to temptation tonight? I said.

Not tonight!

We both laughed.

I told her I thought I understood but that I'd never be able to do it myself, even if I thought it was right.

She said: Because you don't believe yet. You want to know what belief feels like, don't you? Well, I'm telling you what it feels like. Belief makes it possible for you to do crazy things other people who don't believe can't do.

Not even if they want to?

Not even then.

So you could sleep in the tent and you'd be okay after all?

Now I can.

Now but not before?

Because, she said, now I know that I was unconsciously testing myself I'll be okay. Knowing that, I can resist temptation.

I said, laughing: But what about me? I'm just a weak unbeliever! Maybe I won't be able to keep myself under control.

Then you'll get a good strong believing tweak where the temptation hurts most, and I'll evacuate to the sanctuary of the car.

Selah.

We spent the rest of the night talking. Or most of it.

And it was the happiest night of my life.

I'm wondering why.

Because we shared without demanding?

Because we gave without taking?

Because we received without expecting?

That's what Julie would say, I think.

But then the next day happened.

Dear God, if you are there, WHY?

Chapter Four   THOR'S DAY

When we finally went to bed I lay awake, mind frying fat after our talk.

Whenever Julie turned over I felt the shifting shape of her against me, but muffled through two layers of cloth, an echo of a body.

Mind frying fat, body hungry.

I sweated.

My bare arm outside to cool me, my hand on bare ground. Soil like flesh. Stones beneath my fingers like bones. Naked earth.

Remembering Sweden. The huge magnificent elk, the lake, the boat, myself starkers in the sky, in the water, knowing as never before never since how everything is part of the same beyond-everything life. Remembering the timelessness of it, how I seemed to see into the heart of things and understand the mystery of the universe. Remembering the randy longing to be absorbed into it, to come into it, to lose myself in it.

All that feeling swept over me again as I lay there, and is so impossible to put into words. The words contradict each other:
a joy that hurts with sadness
a sadness that is pleasurable
a pleasure full of terror
a terror that excites
an excitement that calms
a calmness that frightens.

And I feel I am just about to make sense of it when it fades away and is gone, leaving behind a longing for it to come again, to feel the power of it, the awe.

Now in the tent my nakedness was wrapped in an imprisoning envelope, like the body of a maggot imprisoned in its cocoon while it is changed into a butterfly. Was I being changed like a maggot? And if so, into what? Does the maggot know what it will be when the time comes to break out? And who is performing the trick? Or am I my own magician and don't know it?

The fat sizzled, burning thoughts to a frazzle.

And then the birds burst into their dawn chorus and blazed away, obliterating my thoughts and making me feel so exhausted at the sound of such wide-awake energy that I fell asleep at last.

But not for long.

Julie's morning cold hand woke me, searching out my face hidden in the warm depths of my cocoon. She was dressed, her stuff cleared away, all ready for off.

We'll stop, she said, somewhere along the road to wash and eat. Have this to get you going.

She stuck a slice of apple in my mouth.

Eve! I tried to say through her juicy gag.

If you're playing that game, she said laughing, just remember that the nasty little serpent who caused the trouble by lying to Eve about the apple was a he.

Pax, I said, holding up crossed fingers, pax!

How about unpaxing yourself so we can get moving?

Groan groan.

Best I can do this early, she said, and left me to slough my cocoon.

Selah.

Forget the damp morning, the grey clouds, the soggy grass, the geriatric car coughing and wheezing before it would start. Forget the shivery trip down the road to the nearest caff. Forget the caff's tired washroom and the pongy loo. Forget the half-asleep waitress and the spongy toast. Forget our silence because I still hadn't come to and Julie was miles away like Sunday mornings and for the same reason. Forget the drive into Cambridge, both of us perked up now and warm and the grey clouds letting through shafts of sunlight, brightening our spirits. Forget our chatter and jokes about last night.

Forget parking the car. Forget the explosion we heard as we walked away, heading for the centre of town, where the noise came from. Forget the worn-out joke I made, that the revolution had started at last. Forget the screaming sirens we heard soon afterwards, and the crowd we saw as we turned a corner, and more people running to join it. Forget us wondering what was going on, and edging our way to the front. Forget the policemen holding the crowd back.

Forget the scene down the empty street. Forget the blackened, crumpled, smoking remains of the exploded car. Forget the shattered windows of the buildings all around, the junkyard rubbish littering the road.

Forget the man lying splattered in the road. Forget his ripped clothes, his blackened body. Forget the draining blood. Forget his tortured, torturing cries.

Forget Julie asking the policeman what was happening. Forget her distress, her outrage, that nothing was being done to help the wounded man. Forget the policeman saying they were afraid the man might be the bomber himself, that he might be boobytrapped. Forget the bullhorn announcement that we should all clear the district in case of a second explosion.

Forget Julie flaring into anger. Forget her suddenly slipping past the policeman and sprinting towards the stricken man. Forget the policeman yelling after her. Forget my own shouts, screaming her name: Julie, Julie, come back, come back! Forget the awful gut-sick sense of doom. Forget my own desperate unthinking wild dash after her, the policeman beside me springing off at the same second.

Forget, as I pounded with leaden feet, seeing her reach the splattered man. Forget, forget seeing her bend over him. Forget her hands outstretched as if towards a lover. Forget, forget.

And then there is nothing to forget because my mind was blown and there is nothing to remember.

Only the breathtaking shock of Thor's thunderbolt.

The explosion lifts him up,
hurls him down,
a crotch-hold and body-slam.
Out.
Conditioning him for death.

RETREAT

NIK'S NOTEBOOK: Now I know I must be calm.

Now I know I must write clearly.

Now I know my life has taken a new direction, and I must map it.

I know this because I've just got back from the hospital. What I saw there taught me.

They sent Old Vic for me. Julie's mother phoned him. Julie was asking for me, calling for me from her deep unconscious. They asked Old Vic to take me to her, hoping my presence would help somehow.

We drove there in his down-at-wheel Volvo, big enough for his bigness, big enough for Old Chum collapsed on the grubby crumpled rugs in the back. Not big enough though to lose Old Chum's decaying pong. But I hardly noticed after the first few throat-grabbing minutes.

We followed the same route we drove five days ago. Then in the dark, now in the light. Stared at the things I hadn't seen then but couldn't *see* now. Couldn't think about them. My brain was stalled. Couldn't move it from Julie.

I'm trying hard to write this the best I can. For Julie.

Because of her, the sight of her, a different voice speaks in my head now. But finding the right words, putting them in their best order, is taking ages. The green fingertip deletes and inserts and repositions time and again, and with long pauses, while I listen in the silence for the new voice, which comes like a faint radio signal from far away.

But writing—doing the writing—also soothes me.

Going through Banbury we passed a funeral.

I thought: I am seventeen and have not yet died.

A mother with a baby in her arms stood watching the coffin being loaded into the hearse.

I thought: I am seventeen and I am still being born.

Writing this now I think: The green fingertip writes my birth.

I have not had such thoughts before. Where do they come from?

This is also how I know that I have changed direction. Have changed.

I do not like hospitals. I do not like their barracked look, their clean metalled clatter, their disinfected smell, their contained air of calamity, of pain bravely concealed behind forced smiles. I do not like the way they make illness and suffering a public spectacle.

For years and years you can be healthy and live your life in private. But when you get ill, seriously ill, you are put into a public room with strangers and there must perform the most intimate details of your life in full view of everyone. And this happens at a time when, because you are so ill, you need privacy the most. A double suffering. Organized torture.

But I feel uneasy writing this. Because another thing I do not like about hospitals is that they always make me feel I should be eternally grateful for them. The slightest criticism seems like a blasphemy, a sin, for which I might be struck down by some ugly and revengeful disease. But this is superstition.

INTERCUT: *Julie in her hospital bed in an intensive care ward. Her eyes are bandaged but the rest of her face shows, scorched. Her hair burned away from the forehead, she is grotesquely bald. Her arms lie by her sides, covered in bandages encased in transparent polythene and ending in what look like swollen stumps. The rest of her body is covered by a single sheet and looks barrel-shaped because a wire cage over it keeps the sheet from touching. Nik stands at the side of the bed between a nurse, Simmo, and Old Vic, with a middle-aged woman, Julie's mother, behind them.*

Nik is staring at Julie, appalled. Her head twists slowly, side to side. She tries to raise a hand but it flops back onto the bed heavily, as if weighted. She moans, an agonized, anguishing sound only just decipherable as Nik's name.

Nik's face buckles. Instinctively, he stretches out a hand towards Julie's, but hesitates when hers falls back. Then, slowly, he gently places his hand against her cheek.

Julie's moaning stops. And the twisting of her head.

For a moment the whole room is tense, waiting.
Slowly pull focus into a big close-up of Julie's face. Nik's
hand on her cheek.
Silence, except for the sound of clinical machines and of
Julie's breathing, which gradually settles into a calm, quiet
rhythm.
Then, with a just discernible movement, Julie's head presses
against Nik's hand, snuggling.
Julie sighs.

In the car, coming back, the world was torn.

I have never seen anything that shattered me as much as the sight of Julie.

Yes, I have seen worse things, more terrible. TV pictures of thousands of people starving to death in the African drought. Old film clips from the second world war of the Nazis' death camps with heaps of naked and emaciated bodies rotting outside the gas chambers round which the survivors shuffled like ghosts. Those are two of the very worst. They stick in the gullet of my memory. Just thinking of them upsets me. But not in the same way, not as crushingly somehow, as the sight of Julie and thinking of her now.

For I have felt her charred flesh on my hand and heard her pain through my bones.

Those other, greater horrors someone else saw for me. Camera men, reporters. Professional peeping Toms. Their pictures come between me and those famished Africans dying now, those humiliated men and women and children herded to their deaths before I was born.

Knowing about famished Africans and murdered Jews sickens me, angers me, saddens me, but does not change me.

Knowing about Julie has already changed me only hours after seeing her. Even though I am not yet sure exactly how.

But being there, putting my hand on her suffering, is what caused this.

These are two different ways of knowing. Now I know this too. Two different kinds of knowledge. One is the knowledge of history. The other is the knowledge of my own life, my own being.

And now I also know why the man they called Doubting Thomas insisted that, until he placed his finger into the holes made by the nails in Christ's hands, he would not believe. They should not have called him Doubting Thomas but Knowing Thomas.

Every I is a You; every you is an I.

We were through Bedford before either of us said anything. I couldn't have done before then. Too screwed up. Too near to tears. I think Old Vic was too.

How do you speak about such things? How do you write about them, come to that? Without diminishing them, I mean. Without *insulting* them.

How do you tell such truths?

I don't know.

Why do I try?

I don't know.

I only know that I want to try. Must try.

Not speak about them. Write about them.

So I must try and find out how to write the truth.

Not for Len Stanley. Not for the stupid film.

For Julie. For me.

Vic broke the silence after Bedford's bottleneck, which seemed to put a wedge between me and Julie.

It wasn't up to him to advise me, he said, but didn't I think it would be a good idea if I went away for a while, had a change, did something different away from news reporters and over-kind friends? There was nothing more I could do to help Julie just now, he said, and I would be better able to help her later on, when she was on the mend, if I was fit and well myself.

I said I didn't know where I could go or what I could do, and didn't have any cash anyway.

Vic said he didn't want to press me on the point but I might consider going to stay with the monks he mentioned before. He'd be happy to take me there and fetch me back and the monks didn't charge anything for staying with them so I wouldn't need any money for travel or accommodation. And there was always plenty to do around their house or in their garden if I wanted to repay them and keep busy. Besides, he said, trying to make light of it, I'd get some more material for my research.

I said I'd think about it, talk it over with Grandad, and let him know. Vic said: I've come across people before who say they'll let me know. They often don't. So, if you don't mind, I'll call in now and hear what your grandfather thinks.

And he did. Grandad was keen, surprise, surprise. I thought he'd pooh-pooh the idea. He can't stand anything to do with the church usually. But he said: Go, get out from under my feet, better than drooling round here all day.

I'm not sure. Going there seems a betrayal of Julie. Like going on holiday while she is sweating it out. I want to be here, ready, in case. But Grandad says there's no point. They can fetch me from the monastery as easily as they can from home.

They both went on at me. I argued, but then Vic said we should take the doctor's advice, and he phoned him. Much matey chat; they obviously know each other. The doc said if I felt up to it, it was a good idea.

So in the end I said yes, and Old Vic phoned his monk pal and arranged to take me.

†

'Could be anybody's,' the sergeant said.

'But might be his,' Tom said.

'Could have been there for months.'

'Don't look it. Forensic will tell.'

'Up to their eyes. Take a day or two.'

Tom thought, then said, 'Suppose our chappie lives round here. And suppose he gets his specs from a local optician. And suppose the optician can fit specs to customer. We'd have a trace, wouldn't we, sarge?'

'That's a lot of supposes.'

'Can't be many opticians in town,' Tom said, reaching for the yellow pages. 'Worth asking. If nothing comes up, the specs can still go to forensic today.'

He found the place, ran a finger down the list.

'Four. One optician—dispensing. Three opticians—
ophthalmic, whatever the difference. All in the centre. No
sweat.'

He scribbled names and addresses into his notebook, carefully replaced the specs into their protective bag, winked at the
sergeant, said, 'Worth a try,' and made for the door.

†

NIK'S LETTERS:

Dear Julie:
I'm in the monastery Old Vic wanted me to visit. He brought
me here today. They think I should have a change after what's
happened.

At least you've come out of the coma. That's great.

I know you won't be able to read this yourself. Maybe one of
the nurses will read it to you. Anyway, I wanted you to know
where I am. They've said I can telephone every day for news of
how you are, and I'll smuggle out these messages from a spy in a
foreign land every day too.

This place isn't anything like I thought it would be. And as I
know you're a fan of monasteries, I'll describe it for you, so
you've another—and a male one!—to add to your collection.

The house is largish, a square stone building in a public park
on the edge of town. Downstairs there are four big rooms and a
big central hall with three tall windows, Regency style, looking
out over the park, and a wide stone staircase with an ironwork
banister curling up from it. Quite grand really. The house dates
from the sixteenth century, but what you see now is early
nineteenth, when some rich exploiter thought it would be nice
to have as a country cottage. Some cottage! He also landscaped
the grounds. Now the whole thing belongs to the local council,
who rent the house to the monks because nobody else wants it,
apparently. The public use the park for walking their dogs,
jogging, etc., and of course for nefarious activities that must be
educative for monks!

One of the rooms is a dining room. The monks call it the
refectory. One is a sitting room, with squashy second-hand

133

chairs and tatty scatter rugs on a polished wood floor. They call this the visitors' room. It's where they see people who have just dropped in for a short visit. One is the kitchen. Big enough for all the usual mod cons plus a table that will seat eight. And one room, near the front door, is the chapel. Everywhere, except the visitors' room, is sparely furnished. White walls. Bare polished wood floors.

The chapel is panelled in dark oak from the days of the rich gent. A modern altar made of a square slab of light oak supported by a single up-swelling pedestal, so the whole thing is like a fountain of wood. Grandad would like it: good craftsmanship. More like a piece of sculpture in wood than an ordinary altar. It's set in the middle of the room, diagonally, so it's like a diamond in the cube of the room. A lamp made of stainless steel shaped like a crown hangs above it. Round three walls are long prayer benches, also light oak, and standing on stainless steel legs, with bench seats behind for about six people each. Above the three-quarter panelling, the walls and ceiling are painted white. White-globed lights hang down above the prayer benches, three lights to each bench. The windows are casements and look out over the park. Polished floor. No religious images except for a plain wooden cross, light oak again, set on the wall without prayer bench. Under it there's a lectern made of slatted strips of light oak, holding a Bible for readings during the services (which the monks call 'offices' —but I suppose you know that). It's quite an austere place, but feels very peaceful and smells of incense, which I liked, a kind of sweet, woody smell that reminded me a bit of Grandad's workshop when he's cutting certain kinds of pine.

I like the chapel very much. Not all the usual churchy clutter or fusty atmosphere. It's odd in an interesting way as well. The combination of old and new, dark and light, clean lines and uncluttered space. I feel I want to stay in it you'll be surprised to know!

Upstairs, there are ten or maybe twelve small bedrooms. Some of them have been made by partitioning rooms as big as the ones below. The monks call them cells. Each has a single bed (I guess they'd have to be single, come to think of it!), a chest of drawers, a desk or table, and a sit-up chair. Bare polished floors again. Almost everything white, except for the desk and chair. A wooden cross on one wall.

There are two bathrooms. There's a larger room packed to bursting with bookshelves—they call it the library. And there's another larger room with some easy chairs in it, a table with magazines and newspapers on it, a couple of small desks, a record player, a bookcase in a corner, and a TV set. And a carpet, but an old threadbare thing. The monks call this the common room.

The upstairs is called Enclosure, because only the monks and male guests (ahem!) who are staying in the house are allowed there. Something to do with the monks' vow of celibacy and keeping silence.

Behind the house there's an area that used to be a tennis court. The monks have fenced it off so they can't be seen by people in the park, and have converted it into a vegetable garden, with a small greenhouse and a bit of lawn where they can sit. They hang out their laundry there too. (I don't know why, but I was surprised by the washing. Somehow, I never thought of monks having washing. As if they were permanently clean! But I suppose they get their underpants dirty, like everybody else.)

We arrived about an hour and a half ago, at 3.30. The only person here was a man I thought must be an odd job labourer. He was dressed in mucky old shirt and jeans and a pair of battered trainers. He was scrubbing the kitchen floor. Old Vic didn't bother to ring the door bell or anything. Just walked in, went straight into the chapel, did a quick prayer, then led me into the kitchen, where this bloke was on the floor, scrubbing the boards. As soon as he saw us, he jumped up, all smiles and hello-o-o-s. Brother Kit.

Didn't know what to make of him at first. He's very small. Not stunted or anything grotesque, but nearly a miniature person. His head is quite big, though, with sticking-up brown hair cut short, almost a crew, which makes him look top-heavy, and he wears glasses with thick frames. But he is quite different from the leptonic OBD. He and Vic were a sight: Laurel and Hardy. Old Vic loomed and boomed, Bro. K. squeaked and chuckled.

Couldn't believe this funny little bloke in mucky gear was a monk. Not just a monk but a priest as well. He put a kettle on a vast Aga stove, shifted us into the visitors' room, said, I'll be back in a jiff, disappeared for five minutes, then returned carrying a tray with mugs of tea and a plate of cake on it. But now he was dressed in a very light grey, very loose and floppy sort of down-to-the-ground frock with a hood on the back, and a black leather belt buckled round his middle with a plain wooden cross hanging from it at the side. His habit of course.

He said: Thought I'd better look the part, and grinned.

I felt peculiar, the way you feel when you're fully clothed in a sitting room with someone dressed only in their undies. One of you is out of place. And you never know what to do with your eyes because you can't help staring at the other person, especially at the private parts. Only, in Bro. K.'s case, the private parts were his chunky wooden cross and his mucky cuffs sticking out from his habit's big-mouthed sleeves, and his trainers poking from under his skirt.

All a bit comic, like he was an actor dressed for a play who had strayed among the audience instead of waiting back stage. But somehow fascinating as well.

While we were drinking our tea and eating the cake (Old Vic put it away like he hadn't eaten for months) Bro. K. chatted ten to the dozen with Vic about things I could only half understand, and made jokes they laughed at like naughty schoolkids. Very unholy, both of them. Didn't think Old Vic could be so lively. He really enjoyed himself.

All sorts of questions kept coming into my head I could hardly stop myself asking. Like how Bro. K. got to be here, and what he did about sex and not having any money, and where were the other monks? And ridiculous things like did he lift his skirts when he went for a pee or was there a secret opening?

After tea he showed me round, then took me to my cell. I felt like a condemned sinner being locked up. He left me to get settled in while he has a private session with Old Vic. I expect Vic is telling him about you and me.

Soon as I unpacked (not that I brought much, just a change of clothes and toilet stuff and a book), I sat at my desk by the window, which looks out across the park that slopes down to a small lake (a large pond really, with a few ducks on it) and across to some trees that mask the main road. And suddenly I felt very lonely, even a bit panicked, knowing I'm to be left here on my own.

I expect you think this is pretty much a laugh, considering what you're putting up with. But it just occurred to me that I've never ever been anywhere on my own before. I've always been with someone I knew—my mum or dad when I was little, Grandad since the breakup, teachers and friends on trips from school—and you to Cambridge.

Makes me feel scared, would you believe! Like I was when I was still a kid, and even a little like I felt at the worst time during the breakup, not knowing what's going to happen next.

And I'm nervous about whether I'll do the right thing, or make an idiot of myself. I mean, how *should* you behave in a monastery?

Why did I agree to come? What am I doing here? It was a goofy idea. And why should I have a 'rest' while you . . .

Footsteps along the landing. Bro. K., I expect, coming for the condemned man.

Love, *Nik.*

†

JULIE: Dear Nik: I got your tape. Thanks for visiting Mum. I know she likes to see you. She can talk to you about it in a way she can't to anybody else, because you were there, and that helps.

Yesterday, they said they were so pleased with my progress that they're hoping to take the bandages off in about two weeks. Then they'll know whether my sight is okay or not.

Today's Thursday. Thor's day! Every Thursday I spend some time praying about what happened, and for all the times when bombs are set off and hurt people. I heard on the radio there was another today, in Beirut again.

I was thinking this morning about my bomber. He must have known he'd die. Probably thought of his death as a martyrdom. Dying for his cause. But they never found out who he was, or what his cause was. The police told me nobody claimed responsibility. They thought he was probably acting alone.

They said there is more and more danger from individuals or very small groups who nobody knows anything about but who are determined to use violence, and use it without warning, unpredictably, and don't mind if they die, in fact they want to die, as if their own death were part of their protest.

Perhaps my bomber was like that. And when I think about him, I wonder if he was trying to say something about the way we live, the sort of society we live in. That's what most terrorists seem to be doing. They want us to change, and live differently—in some way they believe would be better for most people. And I want that too, so why wouldn't I ever let off bombs?

People who set bombs off must have a very strong belief that they're right and they want to change things as quickly as possible, even if achieving it means they die doing it. I can understand that. I can even understand why they're often admired and made into heroes. Everybody with any goodness in them wants to change our way of life for the better of poor people, and the sick, and the oppressed, and are against those who keep all the power and wealth to themselves. And it seems so hard to make things change that I can understand why some people get frustrated and go to extremes to try and bring about even a small difference. And letting off bombs is dramatic and satisfying, I imagine, like making big banging noises when you're little, and startling the grown-ups so that they pay attention to you.

Perhaps one of the reasons I'm not keen on that sort of protest is that it always does seem to me a bit childish.

But that's not the main reason I don't go along with it.

People who bomb and shoot want change now, this minute. They want the world of our lives—the world they can see and touch—to be different at once. And they believe this is possible. All their belief is concentrated on their lives—their physical, bodily lives—here and now. Even if they believe in God and a life beyond what we can see and touch, they want Heaven on earth, and they want it immediately. And if they can't have it, they prefer to die. So they're ready to suffer and sacrifice themselves, and other people too, in order to bring it about.

Perhaps they're right and it is possible. To make changes

quickly, I mean. I suppose in theory it is. I just don't agree with them. I love the world I can see and touch. I long to see and touch it again. Not being able to has taught me just how much I love it. But it's also made me realize something else I was only half aware of before. Which is that, however much I love the life I know, I've never really felt that I belong here. I mean, I've never felt that the world is my home. To me, it's like a waiting room at a railway station or the departure lounge at an airport. I'm on the way from somewhere I can't now remember to a destination I know very little about yet.

This particular waiting room, our world, is quite nice to be in. Most of the people are considerate and thoughtful. But some, it's true, aren't too pleasant, and have bagged the best seats and behave a bit as if they owned the place and push their way to the head of the queue for the food and drink. Quite a lot of people have even forgotten they're on a journey at all, and have started settling in as if they expect to stay here for ever. And they cause quarrels and even fights, because they're afraid of losing their place, or they want more space, or more than their fair share of what's on offer.

So what do I do? Make a bomb and blow the nasty people up? One bomb in a Cambridge street isn't world-shattering. But to my mind, one bomb in a Cambridge street means just the same as letting off all the nuclear bombs in the world and blowing us all to bits.

I don't just want to ban The Bomb. I want to ban all bombs, whatever, and all bombers, whoever, and all bombings, whyever. There have to be better ways of saying no and making changes.

Anyway, being a stranger away from home my mind is more fixed on my journey and on my destination than it is on this waiting room, even though the place is very beautiful and full of interesting things that help me pass the time without getting bored.

But for the bombers, I think, all there is is the waiting room. And if they can't run it the way they want to, they'd rather destroy it and themselves too. The only future they've got is here. And if they can't have it the way they want then nothing else matters.

For me, because I believe my future lies somewhere else, somewhere beyond the waiting room, I'm not so keen to cause chaos now or to blow myself up. Getting on with my journey, reaching my destination, depends on staying alive now and keeping myself fit for the rest of the journey. So I concentrate on that. I'd like to be comfortable, of course, and have a pleasant time, and get along with the other travellers. But I don't put all my store on that.

Death doesn't worry me. Not death itself. But suffering does, my own or anybody else's. Because suffering is an impediment. It gets in the way. All that stuff about it strengthening our character and refining our will, and teaching us that we're only human and must put our faith in God. No. Suffering is bad for us because it makes pain a substitute for thought. The way religious fanatics talk about suffering is the way people used to talk about bringing up children. Spare the rod and spoil the child. Beat the evil out of them. Make them fear punishment and then they'll learn to do good.

I don't believe in a God of fear. And I don't believe that we only learn that we're human by being made to suffer. If we can't think out for ourselves what we are, and if we can't make decisions about ourselves and the way we want to live and the way we want to die without being tortured into them, then we aren't worth anything. The people who put their faith in bombs, in killing and in violence, all belong to those inadequate people all down the ages who believed in fear and torture. They may not have begun that way, they may have begun by acting from the best of motives. But in the end, the only cause they truly believe in and live for is torture itself.

I expect that seems pretty simple-minded to you. Full of holes! But it helps me, because it tells me that whenever I'm faced with doing something, there'll probably be two ways of going about it. One that'll make things worse for somebody else and one that might help make them at least no worse off.

[*Pause. Clatter of metal utensils and indecipherable chatter.*]

Got to stop. Simmo's just come to change the bandages on my eyes. My daily squirm when I'm supposed to have my character refined and realize just how human I am.

Isn't it funny how pain is easier to bear if you can grip

something with your hands. Because I can't I groan and moan instead, and feel foolish and ashamed afterwards for giving in like that. But Simmo is terrific. All the time I'm moaning she says, 'Go on, let it out, have a good yell!' And that helps.

†

NIK'S LETTERS:

Dear Julie: 9.50 p.m. The end of my first day as a Spy in a Foreign Land.

I'm in my cell. I'm bushed. What a day! But don't want to go to bed yet. Brain too busy sawing wood. Writing to you might calm me down.

I hate not being able to see you. Couldn't, I guess, even if I was at home because of the distance. Damn distance. Damn money that makes distance no problem. And, also, I feel a bit locked up here. Not that I am. Just the way I feel.

When I phoned the hospital this evening, they said you're improving. You had a comfortable night last night, and are 'as comfortable as can be expected'. Did you know that? I hate the coolspeak of hospital people. They wouldn't let me talk to the ward. Too busy, they said. Huh!

I think of you all the time. You'll laugh when I tell you I even prayed for you tonight. Must be the religious atmosphere. Well, not prayed exactly. The monks included your name in the list of people they prayed for after Compline. (I always thought Compline was that milk powder stuff they give geriatrics who can't eat proper food. Maybe it's spelt differently?) Anyway, the last office of the day. (I'm picking up the jargon, you see.)

I admit I asked them to add your name to the prayer list, and I did say it to myself when they read it out, and willed you to get well. That's nearly praying, isn't it? But not quite. My idea about prayers is that they have to be addressed to someone—to a God—before they're really prayers. And I wasn't addressing anybody. No, that's wrong. I was speaking to you.

But I'd better start from where I left off yesterday.

Old Vic stayed for Evensong and for supper afterwards, which we have at 7.00 p.m. I was glad he did because he

141

showed me the ropes in chapel and during the meal. (Meals are strange. There's a funny routine about passing things, for instance. At the start of the meal everything goes round the table, passed to the left from one to the next. It's bad manners not to pass things. And you're supposed to keep an eye on the blokes next to you to see if they need anything and pass it before they have to ask for it. This doesn't matter so much at talking meals, like supper. But at silent meals, like breakfast, it matters a lot, otherwise you might never get the marmalade.)

Old Vic also explained about Silence. Silence is when the monks (and their visitors!) are not allowed to talk AT ALL, except in the visitors' room on special business. Silence happens from 8.30 p.m. till 9.30 a.m. the next day (the Greater Silence) and from 12.00 till 1.00 mid-day, and from 5.00 till 6.30 in the evening (the Lesser Silences). During those times you're supposed to pray and concentrate your mind on God, etc. Reminded me of you and your Sunday morning silences on the way to church. When it's time for Silence a little bell is rung in the hall by the monk whose turn it is, and all the talking stops. It's peculiar at first, everybody suddenly going dumb on you, like they've suddenly taken agin you. They even go distant; their eyes don't see you any more, as though you didn't exist for them. Least, that's how it is with Bro. K. I haven't had much chance to talk to any of the others yet.

But I already like Silence. Whatever is happening you know there's soon going to be this pool of quietness. Bro. K. says they all look forward to it. All the real monks, anyway. He says Silence is a true monk's natural state, part of what he is born for. When someone comes to try the life, the others watch to see if he takes to Silence, because it's a good sign of whether or not he's suitable. Apparently, some people can't stand it and go to pieces and have to get out quick.

By the time Vic left it was Greater Silence. Bro. K. had already asked me if I wanted to live the kind of day the monks do or just please myself. Out of curiosity, and because I thought he would like it (creep creep), I said I'd follow their day. Little did I know! This place is a slave camp.

He gave me a folder and said everything I needed to know to start with was in there and we'd talk tomorrow. Tinkle-tinkle little bell and Bob's your uncle: no more chat. I went to my cell and did my homework. Here is my timetable:

5.30 a.m.: Get up. (Couldn't believe my eyes!)
6.00—8.00 a.m. Chapel:

Matins (i.e. Morning service. 20 mins)	Whatever am I
Eucharist (20 mins)	going to do in
Silent Bible reading (20 mins)	chapel for all
Meditation (60 mins)	this time?!

8.00 Breakfast (Usually cornflakes, egg, toast, honey or marm., tea. But today is Friday, a 'fast' day, so tea and toast only!)
8.30—9.00 Housework (This morning I had to clean my room, one of the bathrooms, and dust and tidy the visitors' room. I didn't get properly finished, which for some reason amused the others.)
9.00 Work starts. (Wasn't all this other stuff work? Today I weeded the garden. By now I was beginning to think this was getting too much like home.)
10.30 Coffee break. (Thank goodness! Coffee and biscuits.)
10.45 Work again. (I peeled spuds & prepared peas & salad stuff for lunch & supper, and washed up the breakfast things, etc., in the kitchen.)
12.00—1.00 Silence. (Hurray! Private prayer & meditation. I sat in the chapel because I like it there, and nearly fell asleep.)
12.45 Mid-day office. (Some prayers said aloud together, a psalm, a bit from the Bible.)
1.00 Lunch. (Bread, fruit, tea, because it's a fast day. I'll starve at this rate. At least Grandad doesn't stint on the food. Usually there's cheese as well.)
1.30—2.00 Rest. (Lay on my bed and wondered what I was doing here.)
2.00—4.00 Work. (Given a book to read about the monastery. Then sent for a walk round the park, which is just as well because I was nodding off again.)
4.00—4.30 Tea. (Tea. Usually cake as well but not on fast days.)
4.30—5.30 Reading Time. (But for me today a session with Bro. K. until Silence put a stop to the chat. See below.)

5.00—6.30 Silence. Private prayer. Did mine in chapel.

6.00 Evensong.

7.00—7.45 Supper. (Cauliflower cheese, pots, peas, salad. Rice pud. Coffee. Fast over because it is officially tomorrow after 6.00 p.m.)

7.45—8.30 Recreation. (All the monks and live-in visitors meet in the common room and talk about their day's work, etc., plus gossip and jokes. A kind of family get-together. I was nervous at first but am getting used to it. It's meant to be a relaxing social time. On special days they have treats —drinks and sweets or whatever they've been given. Vic had left them a bottle of whisky so they opened that to celebrate me staying with them, which I thought was a pretty lame excuse to have a booze-up, especially as I wasn't given any and had to have Bro. K.'s home-brew beer instead.)

8.30 Silence.

9.30 Compline.

12 midnight. Lights out, except with special permission from Kit.

See why I'm bushed? Haven't worked as hard in my life, not even when Grandad is in one of his slave-driver moods.

The hardest work of all is in chapel. At first, I thought that would be the easiest—a doddle just sitting there in that nice room watching the monks do their stuff. But to start with, it's very hard to concentrate at six o'clock in the morning, and when the offices are happening you have to bob up and down, kneeling and sitting and standing, and find the right place in the office books. You feel an idiot if you don't join in or do the wrong thing—kneel when you should stand, etc. So you have to keep your wits about you. And unless you're just going to slump like a pudding in your seat during the private patches you have to decide how to spend the time 'meditating'.

In fact Meditation is the most difficult of all. I've heard people talking about it like it's a spiritual happy hour when you float inside your head in a kind of cosy limbo. Well, it wasn't anything like that for me. I hadn't a clue what to do, so I tried thinking about what monasteries are supposed to stand for and why people want to be monks and nuns and whether Jesus

Christ would be a monk if he came back. But I hadn't been at it long before my mind started wandering all over the place, thinking about anything but what I wanted to think about. The harder I tried to keep it on the subject, the more it wanted to think about something else. Like an itch: the more you try to ignore it the itchier it gets. I got to wondering, for example, how Grandad was doing on his own, and how you were feeling and if you were awake at this unGodly (?) hour. (I guessed you would be, knowing how keen hospitals are to wake everybody up before anybody in his right mind would want to wake up. Hospitals and monasteries are alike in this respect, I guess. Which isn't surprising when I come to think about it, as hospitals were first started by monasteries! Maybe that's why nurses still look a bit like super-efficient nuns.) After that I started thinking about breakfast. I was famished and kept having visions of luscious bacon and fried bread sandwiches and lashings of marmalade and toast.

This had a dramatic effect on my innards. They started rumbling and gurgling, and generally making a lot of lavatory noise. I was certain everybody in the room could hear. Could feel myself blushing. I had a quick glance at my watch because I was sure it must be nearly eight. It was nine minutes past seven. I'd been meditating for eight minutes. Couldn't believe it! Looked up, and caught Bro. K. watching me, a grin all over his face. He looked away as soon as our eyes met, which is just as well because I'm sure I'd have had the giggles if he hadn't. It all reminded me of Sister Ann at St James's. Remember? How could you forget! Luckily, the others kept their eyes to themselves. But they've been calling me Rumbletum ever since.

I'd better tell you about the others. There are six of them. Kit, David, Mark, Dominic, John and William. I'm the only visitor. A novice, Adam, is expected tomorrow. He's been with them eight months and is coming here from their main house to stay for three months to experience life in a 'working' house.

Kit is in charge. Which he says means being the dogsbody who does what they all decide should be done when they meet at their weekly 'chapter'. They vote for their 'prior' every two years and nobody can be prior more than twice. Kit's on his second jag. He looks after the house, sees to visitors, and because he's a priest, celebrates the Eucharist every morning.

The others have ordinary jobs outside, except for William, who is the youngest, twenty-four, and only recently made a full member. He came to the house two months ago and is still looking for a job, so at present he helps Kit when he isn't job-hunting. David is an electrician working with a building firm in the town. Mark is a teacher in a local primary school. Dominic I'm not sure about yet but he seems to have something to do with social work among unemployed teenagers. John is a gardener with the council and works in the park and local cemetery.

What happens is that they all go off to their jobs like ordinary people at whatever times they have to. Dominic, for instance, has irregular hours sometimes. At home, they do their monk work and keep the daily timetable as best they can. They don't put themselves out to convert people. They think of themselves as representing Christ in ordinary life, and they only talk about their faith if someone asks them about it. They believe what they are and the way they live is what matters, not how many converts they make or whether people even know they are monks. When they're outside they wear ordinary clothes exactly like the people they work with. In the house, during Silence and for chapel, and when they are being monkish, they put on habits like the one I described Kit wearing.

Whatever they earn they pool. And they allow themselves a certain amount of pocket money each week so that they don't have to cadge from their workmates. They don't believe in begging or living off other people's charity. They think that working for their living is part of being like other people and not becoming somehow special. At the end of the year, what's left over from their earnings, if anything, they give away so that they never have anything to rely on or ever get cosy and lazy and right-wing.

There's a lot more to tell, but later . . .

Anyway, they aren't a bit like I expected. Not pompous or devout in a stuffy way. You don't feel they're going to pin you in a corner and give you the holy third degree. Which somehow only makes you keen to talk to them about what they believe.

I'm quite impressed in fact. When they're together during Recreation and meals, they're lively and quite funny—they're always making ghastly jokes. So I'm beginning to enjoy myself, if I'm honest.

The way they behave in chapel is the most interesting of all. They do everything in a kind of routine way, but somehow they make it seem special as well. Can't explain it yet. But I quite look forward to the offices already, just to watch them and be part of the ritual. It's like a play or a very serious game, yet it's also private and—I don't know—*essential*. If they didn't do their chapel work, they wouldn't be anything, just a bunch of reasonably nice blokes living in the same house and pooling their pay. What they do in the chapel seems to make them into what they are outside chapel. As individuals as well as a group, I mean.

This is all confused. I'm too tired to explain properly.

I'll just tell you about what Bro. K. said to me this afternoon, then I'm off to bed. He explained about the community, then asked me how I'd like to spend my time here. All depends on how long I'm staying. Said I could just treat it like a holiday. Or I could go on like today, helping out and joining in with as much of their life as I like. (You needn't suffer all of Medi tation! he said, laughing.) Or I could do a proper Retreat, which he would 'direct'—i.e. guide me about what to do. This is a kind of organized three or four days when I try and think seriously about myself and what I believe and my attitude to religion, etc.

I didn't know what to decide so Bro. K. suggested I think about it over night and tell him tomorrow. I made this the thing I concentrated on during the Silence this evening. I've almost decided I'd like to do the Retreat. Might as well, as I'm here, and it's something I've never done before. And you've made me think about spiritual things. Though, the only result so far is that I don't know where I stand at all now, whereas I was quite sure before.

I told Bro. K. that I think I'm an atheist.

He said: At least we can try and help you to be a good one.

I said: What's a good atheist?

He said: The same as a good Christian—one who doubts.

147

I said: Do you doubt?

Sure, he said, thank God!

I said: Why thank God? Don't you want to be sure?

He said: There's a line in a book by Graham Greene: 'The believer will fight another believer over a shade of difference. The doubter fights only with himself.'

I quite like that line, too.

Love, *Nik.*

    †

The first three opticians on Tom's list were of little help. There was no quick way, they said, to trace the owner of the specs, even if he did happen to be a customer. With enough time and trouble they would be able to work out from the remaining, cracked lens what the prescription was; then, if they searched their records, they might be able to match prescription to customer. But only *might.* Besides, it would all take days not hours, and was a long shot because the likelihood was that the owner wasn't a customer.

The fourth optician wasn't at first any more keen to get involved.

'We do traces for the police sometimes,' he said, 'but frankly, it costs so much time and effort I'd only be willing if the case is really serious.'

'Serious?' Tom asked.

'Murder, rape, something of that order.'

Tom smiled. 'Would crucifiction count?'

The optician cocked his head. 'You're kidding.'

'Confidential info, sir.'

'Grief!'

The optician bent his head to inspect the twisted spectacles lying on his desk where Tom had delicately placed them.

'All right to touch?'

'Carefully, sir.'

The optician shifted them with the end of his pen, bent closer, and used a small magnifying glass to inspect the inside edge of one of the arms near where it hinged to the frame.

'Could be in luck,' he said, straightening. He was a tall man, thin, grey-haired with a bald patch on the crown that Tom thought looked like a monk's tonsure. Grey-suited, rugby club tie, rotary club badge in his lapel, flushed complexion, very precise manner. Probably near retirement. One of the town's pillars. Would know everybody. Worth keeping on his right side; never know when he'd come in useful. Like now, maybe.

Tom gave the optician his best schoolboy grin of excitement.

'For a time,' the optician said, warming to the work, 'we stamped a small mark on our frames. Thought it might prove useful, save time in other ways. Turned out not to be the case, so we gave up the practice about a year ago.'

'And there's a mark on these?'

'Must have been among the last pairs we did.'

'So you know who the owner is?'

'When we gave it up, the records were stored in the basement. Almost threw them away, but somehow, records being records—'

'When do you think you might know?'

'Let's see . . .' The optician consulted his appointment diary. 'Busy the rest of the day. Won't be free till after we close. Then time for the search. Say seven. How will that do?'

Tom, champing at the bit of his impatience, said, 'Okay, sir, if that's the soonest you can manage. I'll call back then.'

'I'll do my best.'

The optician inspected the frames with his magnifying glass again, jotted down the mark. Tom carefully retrieved the evidence.

'Seven o'clock, then,' he said and left, feeling at once excited by his success and irritated by the enforced delay before he could get his hands on the reward for playing his hunch.

†

NIK'S LETTERS:

Dear Julie: Meditation this morning was no better than yesterday. Is my mind always this slapdash and all over the place? After Silence, when I had to polish the upstairs landing (hands and knees and old fashioned gluey wax you have to buff up, which takes ages if you put too much on—sweat, sweat), I had a session with Bro. K. I told him I thought I'd like to do a Retreat but that I didn't think I'd manage.

Bro. K.: Why?

Me: Because I've discovered I can't concentrate for more than two minutes, never mind for three days.

Bro. K.: We all have trouble with distractions. It's normal. Most people never notice how much their minds jump from one thing to another. They can't concentrate for long on one thing. One of the things Meditation teaches you is how to focus your attention, all your being, on one thing, one idea.

I said: But apart from that, I don't see how I can spend three days meditating and what you call praying when I don't believe.

He said: I thought you didn't know what you believe?

I said: I don't.

He said: Then this is as good a time as any to start finding out. Use your Retreat for that. You've got to start somewhere. Start there.

I said: But how?

Bro. K.: How does anybody do anything? Take something obvious. For example, how does somebody who wants to be a football player become a football player?

Me: Practice?

Before that. How does he know he wants to be a football player?

Probably because he saw football being played and thought he'd like to do it.

Right. Then what?

Gets a ball and kicks it about?

And?

Gradually learns to control it.

Watches good players playing?

And learns from them. And joins a team. He'd have to do that because football is something you have to be in a team to play.

Bro. K.: So he slowly gets better and better and if he really likes the game and is good enough at it, he might end up playing with a major side.

Me: Yes. But belief isn't a game, is it?

Bro. K. laughed. No, he said, but it's something you have to decide you want. Like you begin by deciding you want to be a footballer. At first you don't know anything about it. But you find a ball and play with it. And—this is the important thing—you copy what real footballers do—the people who already know how to play well. The same with belief. You learn about it by doing it. And you learn what to do by copying what believers do. You want to know about belief? Behave like a believer. But the first thing is deciding you want to believe. Deciding to play football is an act of will, isn't it? So is belief.

Me: Julie—the girl we're praying for—says that belief is a gift. She means a gift from God.

Bro. K.: Doesn't she ever doubt?

Never asked her.

Ask her then. I think what she might really be talking about is conviction—a kind of *knowing*—rather than about belief. Most people who believe in God have times when they doubt. When they lose their sense of conviction. But they go on believing. They make a decision to accept the idea of God, even though they're doubtful, rather than the idea that there's nothing. In other words, they make a conscious act of will to believe. There's no other way.

But that seems hypocritical to me.

It's only hypocritical if you pass yourself off as someone who *knows*. You only have to say you *believe* but don't *know*. A true believer is someone who's searching for knowledge. That must be true, mustn't it? Because as soon as you *know* something, you're not a believer any more. You're a *knower*. You've found out the truth and can prove it. But first you have to be a believer. So a believer is simply someone who's decided what kind of knowledge he's searching for. Not just any knowledge, but knowledge of what he calls God. Just like a biologist searches for knowledge about animals and how they live, and a medical doctor searches for knowledge about human sickness and how to cure it. They can be those things—biologist or medical doctor—and be a believer as well—a searcher after knowledge of the ultimate, the above all, the source of all knowledge. See?

I see what you mean. Don't know if I accept it!

Sounds to me like what you want to be is an academic, God help you!

It's just that I don't have any strong feeling I want to believe. All I think I want is to know about belief.

Bro. K. sucked in his breath. Then you're on dangerous ground, he said. Because where belief is concerned, you can't find out about it without taking the risk of accepting it—of becoming a believer. So watch out!

Why?

Look, Nik, the problem is that you're trying to behave like a biologist studying the behaviour of an animal, when the subject you're studying isn't an animal and can't be investigated like that. You've made the classic mistake of using the wrong tools for the job. Like wanting to know what the air around you is made of and trying to cut it open with a hammer and chisel to find out.

With belief, he said, you have to live it if you want to know about it. You have to be your own laboratory, your own set of tools, your own specimen. You have to observe belief at work in yourself, if you really want to understand it. That's why some people say belief is a mystery. You can't take it out and examine it. You can't cut it open on a dissecting table. You can't even describe it very successfully. And you can't explain it to someone else. Plenty of people have tried, and they've all failed. You can only experience it and know what it is by living it.

I said: But you have to will yourself to believe first?

No other way, I'm afraid, Bro. K. said.

By the time we'd got this far, it was coffee break.

After coffee I told Bro. K. I'd stay till the end of the week, and do a Retreat, and that during the Retreat I'd think about what he'd said about belief and try and behave as if I believed. I mean, what had I to lose?

He said that was okay so long as I agreed to follow his guidance. I said I would, unless he asked me to do anything I thought was wrong.

He said: Right, you start now. Between now and lunchtime I want you to write your Confession.

I said: What! My confession! I don't have anything to confess! I don't feel guilty about anything.

He laughed his funny squeaky chuckle and said he was very glad I was already fit for Heaven. But guilty or not, he wanted me to write whatever came into my head under the title *The Confession of Nik Frome.*

I said I didn't know where to start.

He said: Start at the beginning, with your birth.

But why? I said.

Explanation later, he said.

I said: This is too much like school.

He said: So why are you complaining? School is where you should be right this minute!

So I said I would try but he wasn't to be surprised if all I had by lunchtime was a blank page.

He said: If your life has been nothing more than a blank page so far then at least there's nothing you want to cross out, lucky chap!

Anyway, I did it. You won't believe what came out! And because you won't believe it, I'm sending you a photocopy. I had it done when I was sent for my afternoon exercise in the park. Walked into town instead and had the copy made at a quick-print shop. (I'm not supposed to go into the town. Too much of a distraction! But as far as I can see the place is a dump with about as much to distract you as there is in a morgue. I.e.: only dead bodies.)

I'm not really telling the truth. The real reason I'm sending you what I wrote is that it tells you about something I want you to know about but never told you.

The Confession of Nik Frome

(or as much as he could manage in an hour-and-a-half)

I was born seventeen years and four months ago. This is not really a confession, as it is not a secret and I do not feel guilty about it. The guilt belongs to my parents. I did not ask to be born. They caused it to happen. I do not know if they decided to create me or if I was an accident. I never asked them. All I know is that, judging by what happened afterwards, I feel like an accident.

I can't ask them now because my parents aren't around to ask. They were divorced seven years ago, when I was ten. Since then I have lived with my grandfather (my mother's father). He was a ship's carpenter who set up his own woodwork business when he gave up the sea because he wanted to spend more time with my grandmother. She died the year before I came to live with Grandad. He is now officially retired, but he still has a workshop which he goes to every day as if he were still working. He does odd jobs for people. He says a person is the size of his work. I think he means that people need their work to give their lives a purpose and to make them feel useful. He can be cantankerous sometimes and difficult to live with. Everything has to be just right and ship-shape, and he hates clutter. But he is mostly fun and I love living with him. He has been very good to me, and has taught me many things. One of the things he has taught me is to be sceptical.

My parents divorced after many rows. And now I come to think of it, I do feel guilty because of something I *didn't* do during the last and worst row. I will confess this.

The problem was that my father couldn't, as my mother put it, 'keep his hands off other women'. And my mother's problem was that she was nearly insane with jealousy. (This may explain why, ever since that time, I have disliked people who sleep around, especially when they boast a lot about it. And I have disliked even more people who are possessive. So I guess I think jealousy is a worse sin/crime than lust. Another thing I like about Grandad is that he doesn't try to own me, or coddle me, but wants me to be my own independent self.)

On the night when the last great row happened, my father arrived home late from work. My mother had already hyped herself into a state, convinced he was with 'one of his whores'. She was stomping around the house, banging things, tidying and dusting, as if making the house ultra-clean would somehow show my father up, be an affront to him—his uncleanness against her cleanliness, like it was a competition.

This is what usually happened, and was one of the signs that told me there would be a mighty row soon. During the rows she often shouted at him that he was 'a filthy beast'. At the time I didn't realize exactly what she meant. I was only eight, remember. I used to think she meant Dad didn't wash himself enough, because Mum had a thing about being properly washed and used to say my hands were filthy if I came in with them even slightly grubby from playing in the garden.

Mum had laid the table ready for supper and the food was overcooking in the oven. I was hungry but didn't dare ask for anything. When Mum was in a pre-row mood she made a big production of getting anything for me and I had learned that it was best at these times to keep out of the way. That night I sat in a chair in the corner pretending to read a comic.

Dad arrived two hours late. By then Mum was going at full throttle. She let him have it as soon as he got inside the back door. (I should mention that Dad was a big man. He worked as a fitter in a local factory and used to do body-building. Mum was thin and not very tall. When Dad had had a couple of pints of beer and was feeling in a good mood he used to call her his little sparrow.)

Whenever Dad could get a word in he kept repeating that he'd only been kept on at work for an emergency job. But Mum wouldn't listen. She rampaged on. Usually, Dad rode out these storms by letting Mum shout herself to a standstill and then wheedling himself into her good books again during the next day or two. But he didn't do that this time. Mum started listing off his previous misdemeanours. Dad said what a good memory she had. Mum opened a drawer, took out a pocket diary, and said she didn't need a good memory because she'd been keeping track of his 'filthy habits' for two years.

This sent Dad into orbit. Now he started ranting and raving and stomping round the room, accusing Mum of spying and having a cesspit for a mind, and all sorts of stuff I couldn't understand the meaning of and can only half remember now. I got so scared I hid behind the armchair I'd been sitting in. I could feel that the row was turning into a fight.

They were standing either side of the table, yelling across it at each other. Mum shouted at Dad that he was a coward. This made him speechless with rage. His face turned red, his eyes almost popped out. I was sure he would burst. Instead, he grabbed the tablecloth and gave it an almighty heave that sent everything on the table flying off in all directions.

There was a terrible clatter. Crockery smashed onto the floor. Cutlery flew into pictures that fell off the wall and shattered. A knife stabbed the chair I was hiding behind as if it had been thrown at my head. Salt and sugar and mustard and milk sprayed everywhere. A bottle of tomato ketchup burst against a wall, spreading a splat like blood across it. The room was a mess.

After the crash there was a tense silence. I think we were all stunned by what had happened, even Dad. Then Mum let out a piercing scream, and the next thing I knew they were almost locked together. Mum was banging away at Dad's face and body with her hands, and kicking his legs with her feet. Dad was trying to smother Mum's attack while keeping his legs out of range. And they were bellowing and cursing at each other enough to bring the ceiling down. They looked like they were doing a very violent (and when I think about it now, comic) dance.

At this sight I broke into terrified tears. I thought Dad was going to smash up the entire house, including Mum and myself, and that Mum was aiming to murder Dad. Such a prospect crossed all my wires and I became hysterical. I ran from my hiding place and tried to hurl myself between them. Dad tried to push me away, but succeeded only in punching me in the face. Mum, aiming a foot at Dad's shin, hit my knee instead. That made me scream and claw at them all the harder. Dad yelled at me to get away. Mum yelled at Dad that hitting children was all he was good for. In the ensuing struggle, with me less than half Dad's height, the only result was that my head finally rammed into Dad's groin.

Dad doubled up, his hands grabbing his crotch. At that same instant, Mum's feet got tangled in my legs. She tripped and went sprawling among the broken dishes on the floor. As for me, suddenly left flailing at empty air, I slipped and fell on top of Mum.

Then began the worst part of all. Mum struggled upright and hugged me to her. Seeing what had happened, Dad came for me and tried to pull me to my feet with one of his hands while the other held his still no doubt painful goolies. Each of them tried to grab me from the other. So a furious tug of war got going. Accompanied by me screaming blue murder and them shouting at each other again. The frightening thing to me was that I felt like I was a parcel that two people wanted only because they hated each other. After that, even if they had patched it up and stayed together, I don't think I would have trusted either of them ever again.

As it turned out, Mum won the parcel. She was always more determined and stubborn than Dad. When he gave up, she clutched me to her till her grip was so tight it hurt. Dad stood, snorting and cursing, and glaring thunderously at Mum.

Get out! she hissed at him. Get out and never come back!

He stood his ground for what seemed to me like hours. Then, without a word, he turned and went out through the front door, which he rarely used. He shut the door behind him very quietly, I remember that clearly. It seemed somehow more frightening, more ominous than the noise there'd been. Right now, as I think of it, it echoes in my memory like an unfinished sound.

I've only seen my father four times since then. Our meetings have always been awkward and have left me feeling unhappy. I haven't seen him for two years now, and I don't want to.

I stayed with Mum for six months after Dad left. Then she made friends with an Australian working near where we lived. Soon he came to stay with us. I was nearly ten by that time and reacted badly. I went through a patch of throwing tantrums and stealing things—money from Mum's purse, even shoplifting in the end. I was never caught, but Mum found out and we had a row of our own that was a mini-version of her rows with Dad.

After that I deliberately made myself as unpleasant as I could, finding ways to annoy them both and smashing things accidentally on purpose, and especially spoiling any occasion when they were enjoying themselves. I won't go into details. Maybe I do feel a bit guilty and ashamed of this.

It was during one of these upsets that Grandad suggested I go and live with him for a while to give us all a chance to sort ourselves out. Three months later, Mum announced she was going to Australia with Bill, her friend, to live, and said I could go with them if I wanted. I said no, and she didn't try to persuade me. I still think she was pleased and didn't want to change my mind. Grandad said he was happy to have me go on living with him. And that was that. Mum went and I haven't seen her since. For a time, she wrote every month. Now less and less often. I stopped writing to her ages ago.

End of story. Except that I haven't said what it is I feel guilty about *not* doing. I feel guilty that I didn't ask for my supper before Dad got in on the night of the Big Row. If I had, I would have been sitting at the table when he came in. They would have had their row, but he would never have pulled the cloth off the table with me sitting there. And if he hadn't done that, they would never have fought as they did, between themselves and over me, which is the most demeaning, painful thing that has ever happened to me in my life. And if they hadn't fought like that, they would probably have stayed together.

What I mean, I suppose, is that somehow I feel responsible for their breakup. That's ridiculous, I know. But, it seems to me, that's the truth about guilt. It's irrational, ridiculous, a terrible waste of yourself, like a kind of sickness. It's a contamination. We should discover how to get rid of it, as we would if it were an evil disease.

I've only a few minutes of my hour-and-a-half left. I didn't intend going on so long about this one event in my life. Usually, I try not to tell people what happened. It embarrasses me. And compared with what some kids have had to put up with it isn't anything, so who cares?

I guess I should also confess that I've done pretty much the sort of things everybody else seems to do. I've told lies, all of them pathetic. I've hated people and wished that ghastly things would happen to them. I've felt superior to some people and secretly envied others. I had a sexy pash on a friend when I was about fourteen, then decided I preferred girls, lusted after various ones, who just thinking about would make me masturbate in desperation at not being able to have them, till a girl called Melissa did a sort of routine job on me one evening when I think she couldn't find anybody better to make out with.

But I don't feel any guilt about these things. They seem so

pitifully ordinary. I think what a lot of people call guilt is just fear of the consequences when they've done something they shouldn't. They're guilty in the sense that they did it. But they don't feel remorse. Which is what I think guilt really means: remorse that you've done something, whether it's 'officially' wrong or not. Remorse means regret for doing it and being determined not to do it again. Not because of what other people might think, but because you feel what you've done has diminished you in your own eyes, made you feel less and worse than you want to be.

So I guess my worst confession—my *only* confession really —is that I feel less than I *want* to be. Not some of the time, but most of the time. And I regret that. Want to do something about it.

End of time.

†

Notes on the crucifiction

Background

1) There was nothing unusual about crucifiction. It was used for almost a thousand years, first by the Phoenicians, then by the Romans. It was abolished by the Emperor Constantine, first 'Christian' emperor of Rome (there's a laugh!) in AD 337.

2) The Romans were the real experts. They improved the method until they could cause the maximum of pain, and could regulate the time it took for the victim to die—shorter or longer.

3) After the defeat of the Spartacus rebellion in 71 BC, six and a half thousand crosses lined the Appian Way from Cappadocia to Rome, each bearing a rebel.

4) So wearing a cross round your neck to show you are a Christian, or just as a nice piece of jewellery, is like wearing a gallows or a guillotine or an electric chair or, more likely these

days, a hypodermic needle. You're wearing an instrument of torture and death.

How was it done?

5) Christ's cross was T shaped (called *crux commissa*), not like the one usually shown in churches and paintings.

6) After his interrogation he did not carry all the cross to the rubbish tip of Golgotha, but only the cross-piece (*patibulum*) made of cypress wood, weighing 75–125 lb. Carrying this for approx. 750 m. through narrow, crowded streets from Pontius Pilate's praetorium, where he was tried, to the execution site on Golgotha was torture. He was also flogged at the same time, just to make life more fun for him.

7) The nails used to pin him to the cross were not driven through his palms, but through his wrists. The palms would not have supported the weight of the body. The nails would have torn the hands in two down through the fingers. 20 cm. nails with blunt ends were hammered into the wrist through the gap between the wrist-bones. This was extremely painful. When going through, the nails impaled the median nerve. This caused the thumb to bend across the hand so strongly that it cut into the flesh of the palm, causing worse pain still.

8) The cross-piece, with the victim's hands nailed to it, was then hoisted up and attached to the upright (*stipes*), which was already waiting, planted in the ground.

9) The victim's knees were then bent upwards. The sole of one foot was pressed flat against the upright. A 20 cm. blunt-ended nail was hammered through the foot, between the second and third toe-bones (*metatarsals*). When the nail came out, the other leg was bent until the nail could be hammered through the second foot and on into the wood.

10) The victim was left to hang from the three nails. There was very little loss of blood, but the pain was unendurable.

11) To prolong the death struggle, the executioners could:
   a) tie the arms with ropes, thus easing the weight on the wrists and reducing the pain;

b) a 'saddle' or seat could be fixed to the upright where the victim could rest on it, thus easing the strain on the feet, allowing the death to take up to three days.

12) To shorten the struggle they smashed the victim's legs so that he could not push up on his feet and ease the strain on the wrists and arms.

13) The downward strain on the arms and shoulders and chest prevented the victim from breathing properly. He began to stifle, and the muscles therefore suffered agonizing cramp from lack of oxygen. If this was unrelieved, the victim suffocated in less than an hour.

14) But with his legs bent and his feet nailed, he could push up and relieve the pain in his chest. For a while he could breathe more easily. But the pain of his full weight resting on the nails in his feet was so fierce that he soon slumped down again.

15) The victim's temperature rose rapidly and very high because of the pain and exertion. Sweat poured from his body. This caused excruciating thirst.

16) The victim went on alternately hanging down from his wrists and pushing up on his feet until he could take no more, gave up and died. In Christ's case this took six hours.

17) Crucifiction is thought to be the cruellest form of torture and death known to the human race.

†

NIK'S LETTERS:

Dear Julie: It's afternoon Reading Time. I'm supposed to be reading a book by Simone Weil that Bro. K. gave me. She's good. You ought to try her when you're fit again. But I'm breaking the rules—sin, sin!—in order to write this because I want to post it when I go out later on.

I'm in my cell, looking over the park. It's a lovely sunny evening. There's a weird old woman standing on the other side of the pond feeding the ducks. She's dressed in layers and layers of clothes that are all too big for her, and wrinkled woollen stockings and old football boots. And she's singing. My window's half open and I can just hear her. I think she's singing *Over the Rainbow*.

My job this morning was helping Bro. K. paint the woodwork at the back of the house—kitchen window frames, back door, etc. While we worked, he talked to me about my Confession. I've noticed he usually tries to find a manual job to do while we talk. He says it makes it easier for people to say things that might be embarrassing if you're sitting in chairs with nothing else to do but look at each other. I guess this is the monastic equivalent of the psychiatrist's couch. Maybe shrinks ought to take their patients gardening while they bare their psyches. Weeding the garden while weeding their minds.

Anyway, Bro. K.'s technique helps me. Not that either of us did any psyche or soul-baring. I'm beginning to see that what matters is not *how much* is said, but *what* is said.

Kit quizzed me about my parents, and told me a bit about his own. (His dad was a shop assistant all his life and lived for his family—two sons and a daughter—and for his fishing—fanatical, apparently. His mum was a home help. Used to take Kit with her sometimes when he was little. He told some creasingly funny stories of things that had happened on these visits. His mum was also devoted to the church in what Kit called an 'Oh my God!' sort of way. He said it was from his mum that he caught the religious bug and learned not to take it too seriously.)

But what he really wanted to say to me was that he thinks that what happened with my parents caused me to lose my trust in people, especially people who get close to me. And not just my trust in other people, but in myself as well. Belief, he said, is partly to do with trust. For a start, you have to trust your inner instincts, your 'inner faith', that there's more to life than meets the eye, if you're going to decide *for* belief rather than *against* it. If you don't even trust yourself, never mind others, you find it hard to 'put your faith in' anyone or anything. You tend to believe only in what you can know through your senses—what you can see, touch, taste, smell, hear. And even then you doubt, because so often your senses mislead you. Poison fruit can look beautiful and taste sweet but . . .

He didn't make a song and dance out of saying this, just said it and then chatted on about something else. But I knew he was right. I didn't realize till I wrote about it yesterday how hurt I still feel about the breakup. And that hurt does invade my life still. I guess everybody has a deep hurt inside them. Most people probably have much worse hurts than mine. But I guess, whatever your hurt is, you have to heal it somehow.

Kit has been giving me passages from the Gospels about the crucifiction to meditate on. I objected at first, but he told me to think of them simply as a story of what happened to an ordinary man, and to try and sort out what it meant and how it had happened and why, and what he did about his hurt. Simone Weil is interesting about this, though not easy. So my Silence times today have been spent trying to concentrate on that.

Which reminds me to tell you that I'm really hooked on Silence. Can't wait for the bell! And I'm gradually learning how to control my mind then. If I start by going straight to chapel and spend the first half hour there, working myself in, then I can go to my cell or the library or even into the park and keep myself concentrated. Like I was enclosed in a Silence capsule. A Silence Support Vessel—an SSV! I still get plenty of distractions, of course. In fact, I'm more often distracted than concentrated. But I'm slowly getting my mind organized *towards* concentration, rather than *away* from it.

Does this make sense? Which is another thing I'm discovering, by the way. That the usual way of explaining things doesn't seem to work when you're talking about what goes on in your mind when you're in the SSV. The words don't seem right. Inadequate, ridiculous. Banal was Kit's word, when I tried to explain this to him. They don't have enough meaning. Enough *go*. Enough energy.

During Silence, especially in chapel in the early morning, when it's very beautiful with the rising sun streaming into the room from the end window, I don't find myself thinking in words like these I'm writing now. I'd think of them as a distraction. They'd irritate me and I'd try and shut them up.

The words I think in when I'm in Silence come—I'm not sure how to put this—in 'clusters'. More like they were objects than individual words. Or, maybe it's better to say the words in the clusters seem to make an object, something three-dimensional, and mobile. They come out of the Silence and go into the Silence and are made of the Silence.

Does that make sense? I think it might to you because I think you must have experienced it. I'd not dare say it to anyone else because they'd think I was crackers. I did say it to Kit, though. As my Retreat director, I have to describe to him what I think is happening to me. He says what I'm describing is what he calls prayer. I haven't agreed to this yet because I still think of prayer as being addressed to another person like myself only more powerful—a God. Kit says I've got to grow out of being crude.

After telling him this, Kit set me another writing job. He asked me to try and write down a 'cluster' so we could look at it and discuss it together. I didn't think I could do this, because words on paper aren't three-dimensional and don't 'make' an object, do they? And apart from this, the clusters slip away as soon as my mind is distracted. Trying to write them down would certainly be a distraction. It's almost as if Silence Thoughts are so elusive that they vanish the split second I take the eyes of my mind off them. Just a slight movement of my body, a blink even, and they're gone.

Which is something else Kit is helping me think about: how I use my body during Meditation. He's making me attend to my posture and position and the effect these have on my concentration and the thoughts that happen.

I start by sitting relaxed but squarely and upright. Not rigid or uncomfortable, but not slumped. When I've got myself settled and going—quiet inside and ready—I kneel, supporting myself with my forearms on the prayer bench in front of me. Upright but relaxed again. I keep my eyes closed, or look at the words of the text I'm meditating on. But I'm finding that when you're concentrated, your eyes go blind even though you're looking at something or even someone, which I now realize explains that funny absent stare I noticed when I first came here and Silence was rung. People who've learned the trick, like Kit, can kind of switch off from seeing what's around them and switch on to seeing their interior Silence Thoughts in one go.

When my knees tire of kneeling, which is fairly soon compared with the experts, I either sit back on my haunches for a while or sit up in my seat again.

It's when I'm kneeling upright that I'm finding the clusters appear. One came this evening so I made an effort to remember it so I could write it down later. It didn't quite work. I lost the 'essence' of it—the *energy* of it. But maybe it's a start, like learning how to make a photograph with a poor camera and doing your own processing when you've never done any before and don't really know how. You're bound to get a hopeless picture. And it *is* only a picture, not the real thing.

So here's my badly shot, badly processed picture of today's Cluster smuggled from the S S V!

This is how it happened. I was feeling tired by the time the 5.30 Silence started. I sat in chapel, not able to concentrate very well, my mind drifting. I tried kneeling, but wasn't getting far, mostly just enjoying the quiet and the calm and the view of the park through the window. After a while I looked at my watch, because I was feeling hungry and hoping that Evensong and supper weren't too far off. But not as much time had passed as I expected, so I held my watch to my ear to make sure it was still going. It was. I tried giving myself up to Silence again, and after a minute or so, the Cluster came.

Tick-Tock

(or: Death as a Way of Life)

Clocks tick
regularly turning   time is intensity
Earth time   of experience
                       short or long   in density

How time seems   I am
for me
now fast
now slow
is not clock-
time never changes   I am that
                       I have been
For me
yesterday is sometimes

165

further off than
last year
and sometimes
ten years ago
is more present
than last week

Yet there is death
death in time
conspires
but death
is not me

Time is what I am

That which I
have been most
not
that which clocks
regularly ticking
tell
I must be

Hell is time
unending endings
everlasting deaths

What God is

waits in time
for an end

Time is all   God is   in eternity
Now   heaven
where else   being timeless
can I live

in these words

†

Notes on the crucifiction

On Good Friday 1983 three people were nailed to wooden crosses in Manila as their way of celebrating the Crucifiction.

Manio Castro, aged 31, and Bob Velez, aged 41, remained on their crosses for five minutes after the nails had been hammered through their hands.

Luciana Reyes, aged 24, was nailed to her cross for the eighth year running in Bulcana province. 10,000 pilgrims and tourists watched.

These events were reported, with pictures, to newspapers world-wide by the Philippine News Agency.

On Good Friday 1985 in the Manila suburb of Manaluyong, Donald Rexford, aged 38, was crucified for the fifth year running with four-inch stainless steel nails driven through his palms. He was hoisted up for seven seconds, and turned round twice so that one thousand onlookers could view him. Rexford was celebrating his reunion with his American father. When asked how he felt he said: 'It's okay. It's my way of giving thanks.' The event was reported, with pictures, world-wide by the Associated Press.

†

NIK'S LETTERS:

Dear Julie: Just phoned the hospital. They let me talk to Simmo. She said you're on the mend, doing really well, surprising everybody. Hurray! *And* that you've been tape-recording letters to me. Terrific! Can't wait to get home to hear them.

She also told me the first of my letters had arrived and that she read it to you and that you laughed and said it made you feel better. Great! Helping you feel better makes me feel better.

This morning Kit read 'Tick-Tock'. He said it was a poem. I said it wasn't. I don't know how to write poetry. Don't even read it much. He asked if he could use it during his meditation tomorrow. Said I should write some more.

I'd better explain, because you can't see it yet, that it can't be read like prose. You have to read it across as well as down. A bit like a crossword puzzle, Kit said. A Cluster isn't just vertical or horizontal. It's three-dimensional. And the phrases, the lines, are like mobile sculpture: they move around one another, making different patterns and shapes—different meanings but all linked. Or they would if I could write them really well. To write them really well, though, I'd have to make them into a hologram! Can you imagine, words weaving in and out of each other and criss-crossing, moving all the time, always combining and recombining to make new sentences, new meanings. Wouldn't that be great.

That's the way I think of the world. And not just the world but the entire universe. And, if I was forced to say what I think God is, then that is what I think he/she/it is: the whole convoluted, ever-changing, unthinkable cluster of Whatisthere.

We only ever know little bits of it.

But today I have to tell you about how I was a naughty boy. Yesterday evening, Adam, the newly arrived novice, asked me to play tennis with him. I'm not sure I like him. He's a big lumpy bloke, twenty, with a loud confident voice. A rugger-playing type—thick arms, muscly chest, very thick hairy thighs that strain the seams of his shorts. Gross really. Apish but not very monkish. Plays tennis as if he's fighting the third world war.

I lost. Hardly even scored, in fact. Afterwards he said: Well, at least we had a bit of fun! And he patted my bum with his racquet. Have you noticed how sporty types are always patting each other's bums while making hearty remarks?

Let's take the long way back, he said. Don't want to go in till we have to, do we?

He was like a conscript in the army on a night out instead of a volunteer monk. As we were walking along, he asked me if I had any money on me. I had, so he said: Let's have a drink. And he took me into a pub near the park gate. He asked for a pint of beer. He downed his in one go like he hadn't drunk anything in months, banged his glass down, did a lot of lip-smacking and said: Any chance of another? So he had a second pint. Living it up! I have to confess, I did feel at the time a bit like a kid playing truant.

He drank his second pint more slowly and we started talking. I asked him why he joined. You can do a lot worse, he said.

I said: Sure, but being a monk isn't like being other things.

Right, he said. One of the things I like is that it's a bit special. And that it's a good laugh.

I said: A laugh?

Right, he said. (He says Right a lot.)

I said: What's funny about it?

He said: Everything. The way we go on, the things we do, the way other people—lay people like you—treat us. And the brothers, of course. They're the biggest laugh. Take Kit. He's a laugh just to look at.

So he had a good loud laugh to prove it.

I said: What about you? You're one of the brothers. Are you a good laugh?

168

Right, he said, 'course I am.

I said: I don't know what's so funny.

He said: Grown men wandering around in floppy dresses with solemn faces and making a fuss about not talking to each other for hours on end. Doesn't that strike you as funny?

I said: But what about God?

Adam said: What about him?

I said: You do believe?

He laughed like I was some kind of idiot. Naturally, he said.

I said: I don't see what's natural about it.

Right, he said. (I thought: If he says Right once more, I'll throttle him!) Right, that's your problem, but it isn't mine. I've never had any problem about God. Always seemed obvious to me, ever since I was little. That he's there, I mean. Can't say I spend much time thinking about him.

I said: So what do you do during Meditation?

He said: Pray, of course.

I said: What about?

He said: Kit must have explained what monks do, he likes explaining what monks do. (I thought: I'll bet you and Kit don't get on.) I said he had.

Adam said: Well then, you'll know we divide our time between worship, study and work, right? All a monk's life is a kind of prayer. But during meditation I pray for people who need it, and about things going on in the world and stuff like that. Doing that is part of a monk's job. What we're here for. I don't mean just praying for what people need. I mean praying *for* them because they can't pray for themselves. Or won't more likely. I mean, we have people whose job is to generate electricity and people who grow food for us, and suchlike. Well, a monk's job is to generate prayers that help keep the human spirit alive. And the price of that sermon is another pint. The labourer is worthy of his hire.

And he patted my bum again with his racquet.

When he had his third pint, I said: You mean you believe your prayers make a sort of energy that keeps the entire human race going?

Sure, he said.

I said: And if all the praying stopped, we'd all go phutt?

169

Right, he said. Not straight off, of course. Not like us all being shot at the same second. But gradually, like slow poison. I mean, he said, it has to be obvious even to a non-believer that people aren't only bodies and minds. Well, a monk's job is to help keep the other part fit, right? And it's worth doing because most people don't bother. In a way I'm a sort of life saver. So I'm doing a job that's a bit special and is useful and I get plenty of fun out of it. Nobody can ask for more than that. Does that answer your question?

Before I could stop myself, I said: But what about girls? (I'd been dying to ask since I came here, but it isn't the sort of question I could ask Kit.)

Adam laughed extra hard and said: I thought you'd never ask! Look, he said, I can take them or leave them, right? Like God, no problem. Before I joined I had a few hot pashes, naturally. Who doesn't? And I've been a bit hot under the habit a few times since. But you're not really talking about girls, are you? You're really talking about sex. And when it comes down to basics, sex is nothing more than a steamy cuddle that ends in a mucky dribble. To be honest, I'd rather have a good game of tennis myself.

There didn't seem to be any answer to that and anyhow it was time we got back for Compline.

As we approached the house Adam said: You're not thinking of joining us, are you?

I said I wasn't.

He said: Just as well. You'd have a bad time.

I said: Why?

He said: Because you think too much. You'd get hung up on wanting to know the reason for doing everything instead of just getting on with it. You take yourself too seriously. You should relax and enjoy yourself more.

This got up my nose. I said: What do you know? You've only been a novice for a few months. You're not even a proper monk yet. You can't possibly know all about it.

Right, he said laughing and patting my bum again, but anyway, thanks for the game.

And we went inside. The bell was ringing for Silence.

I don't know why he annoyed me so much. Maybe he just

of self-righteous hypocrites, etc. etc. Am I an unpaid char? I was thinking. Did I come here to be treated like a servant while they swan about pretending to be holy? What's scrubbing this floor got to do with me getting well again and finding out about belief?

When I finally got back to my cell, long after the others had finished their jobs, I found an envelope from Kit lying on my bed. Enclosed, a copy of what was inside.

When you've read it, you'll be able to imagine how I felt! I spent the rest of the day thinking about what it says.

I'm beginning to understand what he's driving at.

When the time came to leave I was sorry. Part of me wanted to stay. But another part wanted to be back home. So much has happened in the last few days. I need to sort it out. And I ought to get back to school. I'm missing stacks of work.

This morning I woke very early and felt odd not going down to chapel. How quickly a habit like that gets a hold. I tried meditating in my room but it didn't work. So after a while I gave up and cycled to St James's for Old Vic's early service to see if that helped. The usual six people there, plus the man who always looks nervous when he sees me because he thinks I'm going to have a hissy fit again.

I told Old Vic I'd be writing to you. He said to give you his love and prayers and tell you he plans a visit next week. If I can, I'll come with him. There's so much to talk about.

Love, *Nik.*

Dear Nik: The job I gave you this morning is the one we all dislike doing the most. Unless you are already a saint, you will have grumbled to yourself about it, just as we do. However, I hope you will understand, when I explain, that in an odd way I was paying you the best compliment I could. For we would never usually subject our guests to such a task. We keep its pleasures for ourselves!

But we have enjoyed having you with us. We have admired the courage with which you have thrown yourself into our unnatural life. For unnatural it is, and hard enough for anyone to enter into, even more so when recovering from such a terrible experience as the one you suffered recently. We have all

174

wasn't what I thought a monk (even a trainee monk) should be like. Anyway, I couldn't concentrate at all during Compline and didn't stay in chapel afterwards.

Kit followed me out, waved me into the visitors' room, and gave me a right going over, very coldly polite, for playing tennis with Adam and going to the pub. First off, because, being in Retreat, I should have asked Kit for permission, and then because Adam, being a novice, ought to have asked permission as well but hadn't, and then making it worse by going drinking. Kit made it sound like we had both been very naughty boys and that it was all my fault.

I said I didn't see what all the fuss was about.

Kit said: Didn't you agree to go into Retreat? I'm simply pointing out that you've broken your own agreement. Not a crime, but a neglect of a willingly accepted responsibility. As for Adam, he knows well enough that the hardest part of a monk's life is his vow of obedience. This evening he kicked over the traces and it's my job to help him back into harness. You said you wanted to share our life. This is part of it.

I said I didn't see that any harm had been done.

Kit said he didn't want to argue tonight, but would talk about it tomorrow.

I went to my cell feeling pretty cheesed, had a bath, which calmed me down a bit, and lay on my bed thinking about you.

How do I think of you? As someone I want to be with. As someone as young as me, but 'older', if that makes sense. As someone I like to look at, not just because you're good to look at, but because just looking at you makes me smile and feel happier. As someone who I want to know all about and yet who seems more and more secret the more I get to know her. As someone who knows her mind and who I envy for that. As someone who is strong in herself without seeming to need anyone else to help her. As someone who makes me think and *unsettles* me in a way that makes me feel more alive.

I'd better stop before this list gets too long.

Anyway, it's almost midnight and I'm ready for bed. Tomorrow is the last day of my Retreat.

Love, *Nik.*

†

171

At seven o'clock prompt, Tom was back at the optician's.

'Any luck, sir?' he asked as he was led inside.

The optician was flushed. 'The owner of these glasses was crucified, did you say?'

'It's possible. We aren't sure yet.'

With a touch of melodrama, the optician placed a piece of paper on the desk between them. On it was a name. Nicholas Christopher Frome.

'Mean anything to you?'

Tom thought. 'Rings a bell but I don't know why.'

'The car bombing a few weeks ago?'

Tom looked at him.

'"Pilgrim lovers victims of terror bomb"?'

'Christ!' Tom said.

The optician smiled. 'Glad those old records came in useful after all.'

'You're sure, sir?'

'Most of my patients are as old as I am. I get very few youngsters these days. No trendy frames and no young staff. I remember him. He came to me because I treated his grand-father. Nice boy. Mild myopia. Slight astigmatism in the left eye. I've written his address on the other side.'

Tom's first instinct was to race off. But the optician said: 'Bit of a facer, eh? If he is the chap you're looking for, the press will have a field day.'

The optician was right. Which made Tom think again. One false step now, and goodbye plain clothes.

'Could I use your phone, sir?'

'Help yourself.'

Tom dialled the station. The super was still in his office but not at all pleased to be held up.

'I've an official dinner in half an hour, Tom. This had better be good.'

'I think I've traced the crucified man, sir.'

'Why bother me with what you think? I want certainties.'

'There could be bad publicity. I thought I should check.'

'Who is he?'

'Name of Frome. The boy involved in the car bombing a few weeks ago.'

'Jesus!'

'Yes, sir.'

'Who else knows?'

'Only the optician who helped us trace him. I'm with him now.'

'Right. Listen carefully. Have you any other leads?'

'Might have, sir, in about half an hour.'

'Splendid. Follow that up. We'll check on your info from this end. You've done well. Now, give me the boy's address and then put your optician on so I can gag him. If this gets out, all hell will break loose.'

†

NIK'S LETTERS:

Dear Julie: I'm back home. Old Vic fetched me last night. There's a lot to tell. In future I'll send tapes so you can listen instead of someone having to read my letters to you. But I've just discovered that my Walkman is on the blink and I can't g it fixed till tomorrow, so I'll send this as a stop-gap. The Epistle of Nik the Spy in a Foreign Land. At least I can us wp again, which is a relief. All that writing made my hand and took ages.

Kit kept me at it right to the end. He might be li funny-looking but he's no slouch.

Yesterday, he made me scrub the kitchen floor as work. It's HUGE, that floor. Big as a football fie felt after about five minutes. And the floorboard splintery and full of ridges. All the time I was others kept tramping in and out, messing up th because they wanted hot water or cleaning eq own jobs. Adam was the worst. He was in an times. I'm sure he was doing it deliberately. at me every time with a superior smirk. Co with my floorcloth. I felt humiliated, dov bum in the air, scrubbing like a skivvy.

By the time I was finished I was rea sure Kit had done it to punish me fo was also moaning to myself about

been praying for you and Julie with extra concern, and will go on doing so until we know you are both fully recovered.

When you arrived, I talked to Philip Ruscombe about you. We agreed that offering you the challenge of our life, and all of it, not just the easy parts, would be the best way to help. In your position, some people need rest and comfort. For others, cosseting is a mistake. They become depressed from dwelling too much on their misfortune. Both Philip and I strongly felt that you would thrive best on re-engagement in the business of life. And that this is what you would want. So we weren't surprised when you accepted our offer.

In these few days I think you have discovered at least a hint of what it is that breeds our belief and sustains our faith. Including the surprise of our doubt. I have witnessed with great satisfaction how you have come to understand the place of Silence in our life; and how the *Opus Dei*—the Work of God—which we perform in chapel (the monk's true workshop) is our power base.

Besides this, you have wholeheartedly shared yourself with us in community. I hope what you found helped restore your wounded faith in the ultimate goodness of working people when they live in trust together.

But when I was thinking all this about you last night, I wondered if you had also understood about our holy serfdom! I mean the grinding, tedious aspects of our life—of all working people's lives. Our visitors often miss it, because they are not with us long enough or only have eyes for our obviously religious activities. You have been so inquiring about us that I decided you might even welcome a practical insight into this side of us. And so I gave you the kitchen floor.

Our belief is lived out, is *known* to us through images of action. We pray, we worship, we work manually, we study. We do not live out our belief only in words written down. Indeed, I find it much easier to scrub the kitchen floor than to write this. So when you read it, remember that while you were groaning and grumbling on your knees in the kitchen I was groaning and yes, even grumbling a little, at my desk, writing to you.

I know I shall fail to explain what I mean. But I have learned that in such failure there is a kind of success. For my failure announces the infinity that I call God. It demonstrates God's *unwritableness* (if there is such a word, which I doubt!).

Your 'cluster' seems to me to be the evidence of your own struggle with that truth. God is not to be captured in anyone's prose. Others discovered this before you. The Psalmist, for example, whose words we repeat at every office in chapel, knew that God can only be celebrated, but never captured, in words of *special* worth. So you too were led to speak, to write, in other shapes—in words of special worth to you. You will not allow me to call them poetry. All right! But the Psalms are poetry, and the Sermon on the Mount and much else in the Bible. Poetry seems to me much closer to *writing* God than is any prose. So will you allow me to make one last Retreat leader's plea and ask you to read more of it? I have attached a poem I have long loved and often found useful during meditation, just in case. It may not be to your taste, but I hope you will give it a chance.

Now about the kitchen floor. Let me try saying it this way:

The young men who come here to try their vocations are of two kinds. The first kind are those who are attracted by the trappings. They love the *idea* of being a monk. They like wearing the habit, like feeling special, enjoy the ritual of chapel, and make a great fuss of their vows. Their attention is on themselves and on the drama, the romance, of being a monk. They are like actors playing monks in a never-ending play. They often do not stay long. They get tired of playing the part.

The other kind are in love with the *work*. With the business of our life. They sometimes find the trappings irksome, and ask awkward questions of us older brothers about why we do some things which to them seem out of date or which make us different from other people. Why we wear the habit, for example. This can make them at first more difficult to live with than the other kind. But their attention, their *energy* is given to the slog of prayer, the discipline of worship, the hidden grind of our labour.

The first kind are here to fulfil their fantasies about themselves. Scrubbing the kitchen floor doesn't usually feature in their desires. At first, they may think of it as romantic—an act of humility in the style of St Francis. But they like everybody to know how humble they have been! And after a few months of such drudgery, they begin asking if they have not done it for long enough. They think scrubbing the floor is only for beginners. A job for those on the lowest rung of the ladder. For them, monastic life is like an ordinary profession, with a system of promotion, and a hierarchy of seniority. You start at the bottom doing the worst jobs and work your way up to ease and comfort and power over others. They often have a vocation to be Superiors, in charge of monasteries!

The other kind are here to search for God in the work of God in community. These are the people (and they are the fewest of all) who have a true vocation. Scrubbing the kitchen floor may make them grumble, but in their heart of hearts they know it must be done. It must be done for the practical reason that there is no one else to do it. But more importantly, it must be done for the spiritual reason that in the meanest work, in manual labour, in necessary drudgery, we encounter the disgust of monotony.

Those who give their lives to God, rather than to the elevation of themselves, soon learn that scrubbing the kitchen floor is forever the test of the strength of their givenness to God. They know that their life as a monk is not about climbing ladders of professional success, but about lifelong acceptance of their commonplace equality with their brothers, and, through the community, with men and women living and departed all over the world.

This is what I wanted you to glimpse today, on your last day with us. It offers you another clue, another piece of evidence, about what belief is—what belief 'feels like'.

Belief not only begins as an act of will, but it is sustained by the drudgery of everyday work. My belief is kept alive by the monotony of everyday prayer—which is the same for a monk as daily training sessions are for an athlete, or daily practice is for a musician. It is nothing elevated, you see. It is not usually accompanied by beautiful feelings or holy thoughts. It is not a kind of trip into a spiritual wonderland of pleasure. It is like scrubbing the kitchen floor—a routine necessary chore that helps keep the place clean and in good repair.

When you feel confident in your faith, such work is not difficult. It is even enjoyable. But when you lose your confidence, when you are off form, when the dark night of the soul besets you, and faith seems hollow and ridiculous, such drudgery, though tedious, even disgusting, anchors you to reality. It is all that is left to keep your belief alive. And then, when faith returns, it finds a home fit and ready to inhabit.

In this a monastery is no different from anywhere else. Everywhere in the world there are people who seek only their own elevation—comfort for themselves and power over others. And there are people who give themselves to *the work*.

If you remember us at all when you return home, I hope, Nik, that you will think of us scrubbing the kitchen floor.

I pray for you. *Kit*.

P.S. Here is the poem I promised. It is by George Herbert.

Love

Love bade me welcome; yet my soul drew back,
    Guilty of dust and sin.
But quick-eyed Love, observing me grow slack
    From my first entrance in,
Drew nearer to me, sweetly questioning,
    If I lacked anything.

'A guest,' I answered, 'worthy to be here.'
    Love said, 'You shall be he.'
'I, the unkind, ungrateful? Ah, my dear,
    I cannot look on thee.'
Love took my hand, and smiling did reply,
    'Who made the eyes but I?'

'Truth, Lord, but I have marred them; let my shame
    Go where it doth deserve.'
'And know you not,' says Love, 'who bore the blame?'
    'My dear, then I will serve.'
'You must sit down,' says Love, 'and taste my meat.'
    So I did sit and eat.

ENGAGEMENTS

JULIE:

Dear Nik: I can see! I CAN SEE!
[*Laughs.*]
Isn't that great!
[*More laughter.*]
I expect Mum has let you know.
But I want to tell you about it myself.
[*Heavy breaths.*]
I'll be calm now.
[*Pause.*]
They took the bandages off yesterday. Oh, Nik, I've been sitting up in bed just staring at everything, and grinning like an idiot! Everything looks so new, so . . . *fresh*.

Some things *are* new, of course. I mean, I'm seeing them for the first time. Simmo, for example. Not that she's a *thing*. But, after all this time talking to her and being looked after by her, being dependent on her more than on anyone else, I'd never seen her till yesterday. And there she was! And the other nurses. And the doctors. And this room I'm in.

I'm having to readjust myself. Almost as if I'm a new patient, just arrived.

But the amazing thing was the view out of my window. I still can't get over it. And I just have to tell you about it.

But I've jumped ahead of myself. I should tell you about everything in the right order, the order things happened.
[*Pause.*]
I knew ahead of time when they were going to take the bandages off. They told me a few days ago they thought my eyes were about ready. So I asked them not to tell anybody —Mum or Philip Ruscombe or you or anybody who would worry and want to be here. I wanted to be sure about the result myself first, and have time to cope, whether I was blind or not.

I don't mind telling you now, I was pretty worked up. I prayed about it a lot, and Simmo had talked to me, buoying me up and preparing me for the worst, just in case. She's been really terrific all along.

But even so, I didn't know how I'd take it if the news was bad. And, to be honest, I didn't think I could cope with people who are close to me standing around and being sympathetic at the same time as I found out the truth myself.

Besides, I knew it would be a strange kind of experience. Having taken my sight for granted for nineteen years and then suddenly to be blind, which is something you can never take for granted, not for a single moment, and then after worrying about it for weeks, to face the unveiling, when I'd discover if the gift I'd always taken for granted had been given back to me . . . Well, I wanted that occasion to be as unfussy, as clear and simple as possible. I wanted to give it all my attention.

Anyway, the doctor agreed. No one to know. And just her and Simmo with me.

Before the doctor arrived Simmo prepared me. An extra careful clean-up of my room. Fresh sheets on the bed. A new nightie she'd brought me specially. And the blind on my windows pulled down because my eyes might be damaged by strong light after being covered up for so long.

Humankind cannot bear very much reality. Who said that? It's a line of poetry I read somewhere. Remembered it when Simmo pulled the blinds. My eyes couldn't bear the reality of unshaded sunlight.

What Simmo does, it seems to me, Nik, is exactly what you've been asking about. What she does is what belief *is*. Simmo being faithful day after day to people like me is belief. Nobody proved anything to her that persuaded her to do it. No one promised her much of anything, as a matter of fact. She just decided for herself that she would spend her life this way. I suppose what Brother Kit told you is right after all. Belief is an act of will, as much as it is anything. It's given you, true. But you have to decide to accept it.

[*Pause.*]

There I go again! Another sermon. But you did ask, even if it does seem centuries ago. And you keep on telling me no one knows the answer, and I keep on trying to tell you that they do. It's just that you're blind to it! You don't want to see it yet. You're like someone closing his eyes when he thinks he is going to be hit in the face. You're doing it so as to protect yourself. You know that if you accept the answer you'll have to do something about it. Because belief is about deciding what you mean to yourself. And once you know that, you have to do something about it, and you don't want the trouble this might cause. Not that I blame you. I'm only pointing out what's so.

[*Pause.*]

If you haven't switched off, I'll tell you the rest of the story of my seeing again. And no more sermons today, promise!

[*Pause.*]

Simmo got everything ready, then propped me up in bed in all my laundered glory, and I waited and waited for the doctor, but she didn't come and didn't come. Some emergency. She was two hours late! I was exhausted from keeping myself poised for the big moment. Even Simmo was sounding frayed.

Naturally, as soon as she arrived I felt guilty about grumbling to myself when she'd been attending a patient who really needed her, and so I came on too cheery and offhand, overcompensating like mad. The funny thing is, I've seen this kind of thing happen time and again in the surgery at work, and yet when it happened to me I behaved just like everybody else. But doctors get used to people acting like clowns, and she chatted to me for a few minutes to settle me down before she started the unveiling.

Which didn't take long. I deliberately kept my eyes shut till the bandages were off and the pads were removed and Simmo had cleaned the skin and rubbed in some sort of salve. Then the doctor said that was it, everything was ready and I could look.

I opened my eyes and blinked a few times, like you do after a long sleep, to get them working again, and there in front of me was the room I've been in all these weeks. Smaller than I'd expected, and even the gloom with the blinds down seeming too bright. And there was the doctor standing on one side of my bed and Simmo on the other. And my hands like stumps because of being wrapped up, lying on the bedclothes.

At first all I could do was stare at everything. I don't remember what I felt. Except astonishment and relief. But then I started laughing, giggling really, and the doctor and Simmo started laughing too, and Simmo gave me a hug and a kiss, and the doctor kept saying, 'Well done, well done!' as if I'd just won an Olympic medal, and before any of us knew it we were all streaming with tears, even me, which was somehow marvellous too, because I thought if my eyes could cry they must really be okay. So for a while it was blubbing day in Side Ward Two, and before long Chrissy and Jean, the nurses on duty in the main ward, and all the walking wounded who've been visiting and reading and chatting to me lately, came in to join in the celebration, till Simmo had to put a stop to it in case I got over-excited and tired my eyes their first time out, so to speak. She sent everybody packing, and insisted I wear a blindfold for an hour to rest my eyes before giving them some more exercise.

[*Laughter*.]

Simmo is almost exactly like I imagined her, by the way, only prettier. You've seen her so you know. But the doctor is quite different. From her voice and her manner, I'd thought she must be tall and heavily built, one of those strong older women who are a bit tough from fighting their way up in a male-dominated profession. But in fact she looks like a kindly granny, thin as a fork, not very tall, with bobbed grey hair and a nice face with such amazing skin she doesn't need to wear make-up, and with gold-rimmed half-glasses stuck permanently on her nose. Just to look at her you'd think she wouldn't dare say boo to any kind of goose, never mind the geese she must have to put up with among her colleagues not to mention patients. Some people must get an awful shock if they take advantage of her, thinking she looks a push-over. Which just goes to show how deceptive appearances can be and how you can't always trust your eyes. So after all, seeing isn't enough for believing! [*She chuckles*.] I knew you'd want to know that, Nik!

[*Pause*.]

They wouldn't let me read or watch television, nor put up my window blinds. By night-time I'd got quite used to seeing again. Even the excitement was wearing off. But then this morning . . .

Phew!

It still takes my breath away.

[*Pause.*]

When I'd woken and settled myself for the day, Simmo came in and raised the blind. And that was the moment when I *saw*—really saw again. Simmo raising the blind was like opening my eyes for the first time, and there, through the window, was the scene I've been gazing at all day, and still am as I talk to you now.

Probably, if you were here to see it, you'd wonder what all the fuss is about. Because it's quite ordinary. Nothing to write home about in the normal way of things. Just a field of grass rather roughly cut to keep it trim. And a pond in the middle, not much bigger than a large pool. And a tree, a huge chestnut, to one side of the pool. And beyond a high old mellow brick wall hiding the main road. And above all that the sky. Nothing else. At least, nothing I can see from my bed. And framed by my window, it's like a picture. And I've watched it hour by hour all day, as the light has changed from early morning brightness to the evening glow I'm looking at now. And it's been like taking a long long drink when you're so dry you can't get enough to slake your thirst.

I looked and looked and thought: That was there all the time and I didn't know. I couldn't see it, and no one told me, so I couldn't even believe it was there and hope to see it one day. But it was there, all the time—like a ghost just waiting to show itself.

Which reminded me of a kind of poem, or maybe it's a prayer, I copied into my meditation book ages ago. It's by a Tibetan Buddhist monk from years back, fourteenth century, I think. His name was something like Longchamps—no, Long-chenpa, that's it. I remember it word for word because I've always liked it a lot.

> Since everything is but an apparition
> Perfect in being what it is,
> Having nothing to do with good or bad,
> Acceptance or rejection,
> One may as well burst out in laughter.

And I did—burst out in laughter, I mean—because those words suddenly seemed exactly right in a way I'd not understood before. Partly, I laughed because it is so odd how you can read some words time and again, liking them, and thinking you understand them, but then one day you read them again for the umpteenth time and they suddenly make sense in a way you've never understood before, a way that you know properly and deeply for the very first time is what they really wanted to say to you all along.

You see, as I lay here looking so hard and so long, I began to see everything was perfectly itself. The grass was perfectly grass, and the pond perfectly a pond, and the water in it perfectly water, and the tree so perfectly a tree. And the light! Oh, the light! It was so perfectly itself too, perfectly *light*, and yet also perfectly everything else. Because without the light I couldn't have seen anything. It illuminated everything. Made everything visible. Made everything *there*.

And I thought: Yes, the light made everything visible that is *there*. But it also *made* everything. Without the light nothing would exist. The grass, the pond, the water, the tree are all light, only light. Their perfection is made by the light.

For hours I had the amazing impression that time had stood still—that all the world around had ceased to move. I waited for the sensation to pass, for time to begin again, but the strange feeling persisted. Time seemed suspended. And I cannot forget one detail of the time I lay here watching it all.

As I watched, the sunlight played on the ripples of the water and flickered on the leaves of the tree as they moved in the breeze. And the light broke up into thousands of individual flecks. But I knew they all came from the same source. They were all, each fleck, perfect sunlight, and were also all the same thing, the Sun. They came from the sun and go back to the sun and are the sun now while they are flecks of light on the water.

The light reveals the water so we can see it, and the ripples of water reveal the flecks of sunlight so that we can see in them perfect individual particles of the sun. They don't blind us if we look at them, though we would be blinded if we looked at them all together in the perfect Sun.

And I knew that is how it is with us and how it is with God.

We are perfectly what we are, as the flecks of sunlight are perfectly flecks of sun. And we are individual particles of God who we come from and are already all the time, now, here, every day. The flecks of light don't go looking for the sun. They are the sun. In themselves and all together. And we don't need to go looking for God. We are God, in ourselves and all together.

Perhaps that's why I've always loved St John's Gospel more than all the other books in the Bible—because it starts off by saying just that, and goes on to tell us how it is that we are God.

[*Pause.*]

'In the beginning was the word and the word was with God, and the word was God . . . In him was life; and the life was the light of men.'

[*Pause.*]

As I looked and looked, it was all there, written in front of me, in the grass and the pond and the tree. Like a message written in the earth and left for me to find. Just like it was all there for you, Nik, that evening in Sweden. Only you felt apart from it, shut out from it, and wanted to plunge into it so you could belong to it. Whereas for me, as I lie here in the fading light still looking and still knowing, I feel already part of it. One of it. One with it. Me . . . perfectly me . . . confined to bed and not happy like this, but perfectly unhappily me. And happy at the same time to be me because I know I am part of that which always Is—capital I—all the time for ever. And after today, the great gift of today, I can remember and tell myself about it and try and understand more deeply still. But in my own time and at my own pace. It's all there waiting, simply *being*, like the grass and the pond and the tree were there and waiting when I opened my eyes and the blinds were raised. It won't run away.

Perhaps this is one of the good things to come out of my bomb. And maybe what was being given me in the terrible second of the explosion was time. Time to think at my own speed, I mean, and to see what I saw today.

[*Long pause.*]

It's dark now and I'm tired. I've done nothing today, nothing at all, except look at a pool of water and a tree and the light playing on them. And, dear Nik, dear God, I've been for the first time in weeks perfectly myself and perfectly happy.

†

NIK'S NOTEBOOK: The nightmares have been terrifying. Every night I was away. Julie running. The explosion. Julie in flames, screaming. The fire, like fingers reaching out for me. Then I black out.

Twice I woke up, shouting, with Dominic, whose cell was next door, holding me so that I wouldn't throw myself out of bed, which I did the first night.

Since coming home I haven't been able to sleep much. Maybe I'm afraid of the dreams? But also, a couple of press people are still sniffing around, wanting to talk to me. And that makes me furious. Grandad curses at them now, which only makes things worse. So I have to watch it when I go out. If Grandad is here, he performs diversionary tactics at the front while I skip off at the back. But I'm fed up of this.

The leptonic OBD turned up yesterday, all gush and smarm. The group send their best, etc., *ad nauseam*. Don't know whether he meant it, but he never sounds sincere, just creepy. And he's still sticking it to the holey mints with his reptilian tongue. Asked about the explosion. Everybody asks about that, everybody, and what they really want to hear are the gory details, the blood and guts and mayhem. He even suggested it would be 'a smashing idea' if we included a reconstruction of the bombing in the film.

That'd grab em, says he, rubbing his little hands together like an excited lizard. Really contemporary, that would be, really relevant. Maybe Christ could be the bomber? That's it, he says, getting quite beside himself with excitement, Christ the urban revolutionary. And the bomb he's placing has been tampered with by the CIA so that it blows him up when he's setting it. Instead of being crucified, he'd be blown to kingdom come by the fascist functionaries of the state. He lies in the road, squirming and black and bleeding, and muttering my God, my God, why have you not stood by me, and around him, peering down at him are a soldier, a policeman, a man in a dark suit with a briefcase—representatives of the earthly powers that be —while he dies in agony as a church clock strikes three. I can see it all. Terrif, eh? So the political establishment wins again, just like it did the first time. And with you playing Christ, Nik, there'll be the extra human interest of knowing you went through that, well nearly that, you're still with us, thank goodness. But what a great scene, eh?

Note for school essay: It may be true that the human race is basically religious, but it is also true that it is basically brutal, bloodthirsty, and cruel. Therefore, either religion is to blame for encouraging this or one of its main aims must be to change human nature. When you think of things like burning people at the stake, holy wars, and human sacrifices made to keep in good with some God or other, it doesn't seem like most religions want to do much about changing human nature.

Not to mention the crucifiction. That's a pretty good example of blood and guts and mayhem.

Julie would say I'm being cynical. She'd pray about it. So would Kit. Even Adam. Wish I could. Last week, I might have done. Why can't I now? I feel a bit like when I was a little kid and Mum wanted me to do something, and I knew I should, even wanted to, but wouldn't, so as to assert myself, I suppose. To be me, and *not* do what someone who mattered to me wanted me to do. Is that it? Maybe, as well, if I'm honest, I have to have help. Last week, there were other people who made it seem—not exactly natural, but *possible*.

Thinking about last week, one of the things I now know I learned was how a group of people can live together, even under quite a strict set of rules, and yet not be a crowd. Not a bunch of follow-my-leader robots. I liked that. I felt I was myself, independent, private. But also felt I was one of a group who worked together and made things happen.

Been thinking about these things during the sleepless nights. And when I'm tired of thinking, and feel lonely, I put on Julie's two tapes that were waiting when I got home, and listen with the cans so as not to wake Grandad. Her voice fills my head. Trouble is, I hear her pain. She tries to sound cheerful, but the pain breaks through. Expect she's also not telling me the worst, just as I'm not telling her.

There she is lying in her bed, remembering. Here am I in mine, trying not to remember, and listening to an electronic memory of her. I know she's right, we can't do without memory. But she doesn't say that some memories hurt.

Looked up the poem she couldn't finish. Just as well she couldn't. The last lines wouldn't exactly cheer her up.

> I remember, I remember,
> The fir trees dark and high;
> I used to think their slender tops
> Were close against the sky;
> It was a childish ignorance,
> But now 'tis little joy
> To know I'm further off from Heaven
> Than when I was a boy.

Thomas Hood, b. 1799 d. 1845. He didn't last long, poor bloke. Probably died of depression, judging from his poem.

I'll not read it to her till she's better. Is religion only for kids? Or is he saying life makes you sour? He doesn't say there's no Heaven (and therefore no God). He only says he's further off from Heaven now he's a man than he was when he was a kid. Anyway, it's a bit sad, and Julie doesn't seem to remember it that way. She also seems to think it's about a little girl and by a woman. Wonder what she'll say about that.

Remembering last week is good. I've tried to live the same at home. It doesn't work. I've tried St James's. But it seems—I don't know . . . Optional. Outmoded. A hangover from something finished, done. An antique shop full of wornout nicknacks.

Note for film: If Christ returned today, he'd bulldoze most of the churches. That would make quite a scene too! He hijacks a huge 'dozer and rubbles a church. A crowd gathers. He says: My house shall be called the house of prayer and you have made it a mausoleum.

Nowadays church buildings get in the way. Millstones round the neck of belief. They stand for the wrong things. Heavy, cold, empty, geriatric, cavernous, immovable, inflexible, museum-like, bossy. They're about property not prayer.

Christ said: When two or three are gathered together in my name, there I shall be among them. *Two or three*, not twenty or five hundred or thousands. And nothing about meeting in a draughty old-fashioned barn of a place designer-built for the purpose. Or in expensive posh modern buildings, come to that.

Fact: he used to pray in the open air, or wherever he happened to be. And he held the Last Supper in the upstairs room of an ordinary house. He'd do that again. Why not? Those are the places where ordinary people are and live.

The first time round, he was arrested for claiming to be the messiah and therefore a threat to the establishment. Not this time. This is where the OBD is wrong. Nowadays, nobody would care less if he claimed to be the son of God. People would just laugh and say he was another nutter, and ignore him.

But 'dozing a building would really stir them up. Not because it's a church, but because it's a building, a piece of property. For that, they'd give him the works—arrest, fine, gaol, long lectures on how outrageous, what's the world coming to, how dare he, is nothing sacred any more, etc. etc. And when he says, But those places are supposed to belong to me, they'd say that only made things worse, he ought to be ashamed of himself. After all, what would the country be like if people started taking him seriously and bulldozed any building they owned just because they didn't like it? Think what would happen to property prices. They'd collapse. And anyway, he didn't get planning permission to demolish his church. You can think what you like, they'd say, and even say what you like, it's a free country, but demolishing buildings, that's serious. Only someone absolutely mad would do such a thing. And people must be taught respect for property. Go to gaol for five years hard labour, you horrible man.

And when he answers back, and says: I'm God, I'm God, and incites people to give up all they have and follow him, the authorities get fed up, but they don't crucify him. Not these days. They're not barbarians. They're civilized. No, they'd say he's deranged, schizoid or dangerously deluded, anyway crackers, and pack him off to the bin, where they'd convulse him with electric-shock treatment till he can't remember a thing, and inject him full of tranquillizers till he doesn't know who he is or what he is or where he is, and leave him there, out of sight, out of mind, till he ceases to be a problem by snuffing it.

So the last shot in the film wouldn't be anything gory. It would be of a forlorn, drug-dosed young man staring at nothing with a blank expression on his face, shuffling slowly along a bleak, echoey corridor without any windows, accompanied by a burly warder in a clean white coat, while on the soundtrack massed football crowds sing 'You'll never walk alone'.

Joke for a Christmas cracker: If you were the son of God, would you rather be drugged for life in a mental hospital or put to death by crucifiction?

PARTING SHOTS

'Nik!'

'Surprise surprise!'

'You're on your own?'

'Got your tape. Thought I'd come over.'

'How did you get here?'

'Train. Grandad gave me the money. Good trip. Enjoyed it. Except for the underground in London. Had to play sardines with a package tour from Tokyo.'

'Lovely to see you.'

'Great that you can. You look a lot better.'

'I'm mending. Knowing my eyes are all right is a big lift. But how are you?'

'Terrific.'

'Truly?'

'Honest. So there's the famous pond and tree.'

'No sun today though. Did you get wet?'

'It's quite a nice view, but somehow I imagined it would be—I don't know—more impressive.'

'I did warn you.'

'I didn't mean—'

'Perhaps it's the grey sky and the rain. Everything looks washed out. And I was euphoric, not surprisingly. Still . . . I shan't forget . . .'

'Brought you some prezzies. Nothing amazing. A book I thought you'd like and the regulation bunch of grapes.'

'You're very kind.'

'Neither's much cop, I now realize, because you still can't use your pickers and stealers. Sorry!'

'No, they're just right. I'll share the grapes with Simmo. She'll feed them to me. And I can manage books, though they still ration the time I'm allowed to read.'

'Are your hands coming on okay?'

'Slowly. They took the worst.'

'But they'll be all right?'

'I'm doing well. Really! Don't worry so. You're as bad as Mum. But thanks all the same. Now, what's the news from the home front? You haven't written for a few days.'

'No, sorry.'

'I wasn't complaining. Only meant—'

INTERCUT: *Nik in his bedroom with his Walkman head-phones on. He is sitting, crouched, gaunt, his face strained, staring out of the window. He grips a fat black Bible tightly between his hands.*

'I know. Haven't written anything lately. Can't somehow.'

'Nothing at all?'

'Nothing. School nor you.'

'Not even your project?'

'Least of all.'

[*Pause.*]

'I was only burnt outside. Maybe you were burnt inside.'

'You always know.'

'I do?'

INTERCUT: *Nik in his bedroom as before, but viewed now from outside. His face is unbearably tense. He rises and with studied violence hurls the Bible directly at us. It smashes through the window.*

[*Enter Staff Nurse Simpson, carrying a tray with two mugs of coffee on it.*]

'Thought you might like a drink after your journey.'

[*She passes a mug to Nik, who takes it with only an impatient nod of thanks, before she sits on the other side of the bed from him, where she holds Julie's mug for her to drink from.*]

'He's not over-exciting you, is he?' Simmo says.

'It's good to see him.'

'He doesn't exactly look full of beans. A bit peaky in fact. You're not coming down with something, are you? Don't want you in here if you are.'

'I'm okay.'

'He's a bit in the dumps, I think.'

'That can be catching as well. What have you got to be in the
dumps about?'

'I didn't say I was.'

'You don't have to. Your face says it for you. Aren't you
pleased to see Julie sitting up and taking notice?'

'Naturally.'

'And don't you think she's done well?'

''Course.'

'Then why not show it?'

'What would you like me to do, a flipflap or a pirouette?'

'I'll settle for your nicest toothy smile. Come on, live dangerously! Your face won't crack.'

'Stop teasing him, Simmo.'

'I'm not. I mean it. He's a lot livelier on paper than he is in the
flesh, judging by today's performance, I must say.'

'You don't know anything about me.'

'What, after all those letters! I'll miss them now Julie can
read for herself.'

'They were only meant for Julie.'

'Somebody had to read them to her.'

'Simmo did it in her own time,' Julie says.

'Fear not, Nik, your secrets are safe with me.'

'What secrets? There weren't any.'

Simmo hoots, mocking. 'There's none so blind—'

'What d'you mean?' Nik says, smarting.

'It's obvious you two shouldn't be left in the same room
together,' Julie says.

'Time I went anyway. Here, make yourself useful.' Simmo
hands Nik Julie's mug. 'See you both later. And cheer up, Nik,
it might never happen.'

[*Simmo goes. Pause.*]

'Don't mind Simmo.'

'Do I?'

'She was on duty all weekend and now she's covering for
someone off sick. She's hardly had any rest.'

'If she's that brisk when she's tired, I hate to think what she's
like when she's not.'

'More patient but just as frank. Which I like. We've become
good friends.'

193

'I thought it was only men who fell in love with their nurses.'

'Why should men have all the fun?'

'Are you being serious?'

'Are you being bitchy?'

[*Nik scowls at Julie who is grinning at him. He feeds her some coffee.*]

'Did you mean it though?'

'Why not? Don't you love your friends?'

'Not sure I have any. Not that close anyway. Except you.'

'Which I want us to talk about.'

'About me not having friends?'

'About you and me.'

'What about us?'

[*Pause.*]

'You remember the night before?'

'Am I likely to forget?'

'What I said then still goes, Nik.'

[*Nik places his and Julie's mugs on her bedside cabinet and crosses to the window, where he stands, his back to Julie, looking at the view.*]

'You're not really talking about the night before, are you?' he says. 'You're really talking about the tape.'

[*Pause.*]

'I didn't want to bring it up here,' Julie says. 'I wanted to wait till I was home again and back to normal. But—'

[*Nik turns and faces her.*]

'You've decided.'

'Yes. I know what I have to do.'

'You can't know. Not yet. You're afraid you're not going to heal properly, that's it, isn't it? You think you'll have scars and not be attractive.'

'No, that's not it!'

'I don't care, it wouldn't matter to me. I've thought about it. It won't make any difference.'

'Listen, Nik. It isn't that at all, truly. The doctor doesn't think there'll be anything bad. Nothing ugly. That's why I wanted to wait till I'm fully recovered before we talked like this. So you could see I was okay. But—'

'But what?'

'It just wouldn't be right to let you go on thinking . . . waiting . . . I don't know . . . *hoping*. When I know now.'

'You can't possibly, Julie! You've just said, you aren't back to normal. You can't be sure how you'll feel when you're home again instead of stuck here. Nobody can think straight in a place like this. Anyway, you're still recovering from the shock of the bomb, never mind from your injuries. They're still pumping drugs into you, aren't they? And I don't care what you say, you must be feeling pretty crappy and worried and fed up, even if you do put on a good face and look happy, which I'm not knocking, just the opposite, but I'm not giving you up yet, I'm just not.'

'I don't want you to give me up, I'm not saying that.'

[*Nik comes to the bed and sits at her side.*]

'I love you, Julie.'

[*Pause.*]

'No, Nik, you don't.'

'I do. That's what I've come to say.'

'I'm grateful. And I don't want to make you unhappy. But you don't love me, not the way you mean it.'

'But I *do*. Believe me.'

[*Pause. Julie smiles.*]

'Believe you?'

[*Nik, realizing the incongruity, smiles too.*]

'Okay! All right.'

'Tell me what belief feels like, Nik.'

'Chuck it, will you!'

'What does it *do*, for God's sake!'

'Knock it off, will you!'

[*They are laughing now. When it is over Nik gets off the bed and sits in the chair, leaning towards Julie, elbows on knees, hands clasped together, and says:*]

'I love you, Julie, and I want you. Right now in your hospital bed I want you. Even with your eyebrows burnt off and your scorched hair like a fright wig and your face still healing and your poor hands all trussed up. You still turn me on as hard as you did the first time I saw you yomping through the rain in your sloppy pullover and your brother's old jeans, looking like a drowned bundle of castoffs on its way to Oxfam.'

'You certainly pick on a girl's strong points.'

'But I do, I want you.'

'I believe you, Nik . . . But what do you want for me?'

'How d'you mean? I don't want anything for you, I just want you.'

'Exactly.'

'Exactly what?'

[*Julie looks at him with an amused stare.*]

'Simmo says what you really want is a girl who'll treat you like a motherly older sister you can have the pleasure of screwing whenever you feel like it.'

[*Nik slumps back into the chair. A tense pause.*]

'I bet she's keen on karate as well.'

'Don't worry. You're not alone. Lots of men are the same.'

'That's a comfort! You know how much I like being one of the crowd.'

[*Brooding silence, ended by Julie.*]

'Sorry. Shouldn't have said that. I was only trying to tell you that I don't think love and wanting are the same thing.'

[*Nik shrugs.*] 'Expect you're right, as usual.'

'Right but wrong.'

'Can you be both at once about the same thing?'

'Why not? Right about something but wrong the way you say it.'

'If you say it wrong, surely you haven't got it right yet?'

'I don't know . . . Yes, I expect so . . . Don't let's argue about it.'

[*They sit in heavy silence for some time. Julie keeps her eyes on Nik, pained by her own vulgarity and his sadness. He avoids her gaze but this does not save him. Tears begin to course his cheeks. Watching his reined distress, Julie also begins to weep. At last Nik glances at her. The sight unleashes his restraint. He bursts into racking sobs. Julie holds out her clubbed hands towards him. He rushes to her. They hold each other in a clumsy embrace.*]

†

Tom recognized the girl as soon as she came round the corner. The one who passed him on the towpath this afternoon. The one with the fetching bum. His pulse quickened along with bloodshot thoughts.

Is that a truncheon in your pocket or are you pleased to see me?

Cop the braless knockers poking the clingfilm singlet. Here was evidence he'd like to get his grabbers on. No question: on a hot evening like this a forensic frig would nicely fit the bill. Business first, natch, but mix it with some pleasure, why not? All work and no foreplay makes Tom a dull John. Blow that for a nark. And anyway, who cared about slag? The only thing she was good for was banged up in the nick between her legs. As investigating officer he had right of entry. Stand astride, I've come to skin the cat.

'And what are you staring at?' Michelle said.

'Okay, Sharkey,' Tom said. 'See you later.'

'Sure you can manage on your own?' Michelle said. 'Don't want him to hold your hand—or nothing?'

Sharkey, smirking to himself, left them to it.

Michelle eyed Tom, her arms folded, cradling her breasts.

'He says you know something interesting,' Tom said.

'I know lots of things.'

'And I know you know what I'm talking about so cut the crap.'

Michelle sniffed and looked with distaste around her.

'Do we have to talk here? It's really smelly. Can't you think of nowhere better?'

'Why? Are we going to be long?'

She gave him an appraising look, up and down, with pauses on the way.

'Maybe,' she said. 'Depends.'

'On what?' Tom asked, moving closer.

'You, of course,' Michelle said, mocking him with innocence. 'Didn't ask to come here, did I? You're the one who knows what you're after. But I'm not talking here however long it takes.'

'What about in my car? It's outside the station.'

Michelle huffed. 'You're full of bright ideas. What d'you think my friends will say if they see me sitting yakking to you in a pig van?'

'They wouldn't know. It's unmarked.'

'Yes, but you're not. Anyway, I'm not sitting talking to you in a stuffy old car outside the railway station.'

Tom chuckled and, leaning a hand on the wall either side of her head, said, 'Okay, let me have a guess. You've got a better idea.'

'Might have. We could do a quick drive up to Rodborough Common. It'll be cooler up there, and there's a lovely view of the town from a shady place I know.'

'Sounds great. But I might not have the time.'

'Oh well, if you're in a tearing hurry . . .'

Michelle ducked under his arm and, brushing against him, slipped free.

Tom twisted after her, only just restraining the impulse to catch hold. 'Okay, listen,' he said. 'Come to the car. I'll make a call. If everything's all right, we'll go.'

'Please yourself,' Michelle said, shrugged, and strutted her stuff ahead of him.

At the station, while she studied travel posters on the wall, pretending to be by herself, Tom had a word with the duty officer on his car intercom.

'Any info re that Matthews Way address, over?'

'Negative. We're checking possible alternatives, over.'

'Roger. Investigating possible lead this end. Will contact if and when. Out.'

He started the car and pulled across to Michelle, who skipped into the seat beside him before he came to a stop.

The signs were good. With the blank at Matthews Way he had time to mix it with Michelle; and she seemed less unwilling than Sharkey had said. Now why was that? But the twinge of suspicion was stifled in the lust that provoked him to over-gun the revs as he swung up Rodborough hill. He hadn't had it in the open for ages and the prospect swelled his crotch.

†

Home again from hospital, brooding on the scene—their tears, her separate determination—Nik again, though weary, could not sleep. The night too was brooding, its heavy air claustrophobic, and would not let go.

At last, unable to lie still in mind or body, he rose in the dark and left the house to his grandfather's contented snores, like foghorns marking the channel to death. Dressed only in T-shirt and jeans, he wheeled his bicycle from the garden shed and, pedalling slowly, doggedly made the journey through town and up the steep winding ascent onto Selsley Common, drawn there not only because it was his favourite place but more by a wish-fulfilling memory of his first walk with Julie.

Even there, though, he found no breeze to freshen and revive him. Oiled in sweat, and panting, he bumped across the common. At the edge he dropped his bicycle to the ground, pulled off his wringing T-shirt, and spread himself on the grass, intending to remain so only until he had cooled off and caught his breath again.

Instead, he at once drifted into sleep; utter, seabed sleep, dreamless, limpid, surrendered.

Only to be jolted awake by a voice speaking his name.

He sat up abruptly, blinking in the ghostly light of pre-dawn at the face of Mary Magdalene.

'Are you okay?' she was saying. 'Didn't mean to startle you. Just, I saw you lying there like you'd fallen off your bike and thought you might be ill. Well, I mean, you looked knocked out, if not dead.'

Nik rubbed his eyes and grasped his hands round drawn-up knees. 'I'm all right,' he said, and looked, blear-eyed, beyond the girl at the wide mist-veiled fenestral of the valley, and remembered why he was here.

The Magdalene ran a warm hand over his shoulder and down his back. 'You're cold as slabfish. How long have you been lying here?'

Nik shrugged. 'No idea. It was dark.'

She picked up his T-shirt and felt it like laundry. 'This is soaking.'

'I was hot,' he said, taking the shirt from her and pulling it on, perversely glad of its clammy penance.

'You'll catch your death,' she said.

Nik stood up and flexed his stiffened joints.

'You're not exactly overdressed yourself,' he said. She was

wearing a blatant singlet and hugging lightweight jeans. 'What are you doing here anyway?'

'Three guesses,' she said flatly.

'Doesn't sound like you enjoyed it much.'

He walked the few paces to a wooden bench and sat, his legs splayed, suddenly weary again now the shock of waking had worn off.

The Magdalene got up and followed, saying, 'I'm fed up of boring boys who have a big head on their shoulders just because they've a big dick in their trousers, and think dropping their pants for a girl like me should be enough reward for doing whatever they want and listening to the endless drivel they talk when they've finished.'

'So what happened to last night's hero?' Nik asked.

'Went off him.' She laughed disdainfully. 'Never really fancied him, to be honest. But he had nice eyes and I go for nice eyes. But by the time we come up here it was too dark to see. Not that he kept them open, I expect. He's the "Look no hands, I can even do this blind" sort, if you know what I mean.'

'I can guess.'

She inspected his face closely. 'You've got nice eyes, as a matter of fact. And your glasses frame them lovely.'

'Thanks,' Nik said, ignoring the hint. 'So what happened?'

'Not a lot. He's probably quite handy with a road drill.'

'How's that?'

'Only capable of a short sharp burst, makes a lot of noise, and doesn't dig very deep.'

Nik chuckled. 'No finesse?'

'Didn't give him the chance. I'm not usually nasty, I can put up with quite a lot, but tonight, I don't know why, I just thought, "To hell with it, if I'm not enjoying myself I'm damn sure he's not going to, not at my expense, the ape," and I shoved him off before he got properly going.'

'That must have pleased him.'

'He was even more pleased when I told him his performance broke the trades description act because it wasn't nowhere near as good as advertised.'

'And?'

'Oh, he goose-stepped around a bit, doing up his flies and

giving himself a thrill by nipping his zipper on a painful place, while he gave me a few well chosen words about me morals and me parents and what he really thought about my physical appearance. I expect you can imagine the kind of thing.'

'Vaguely.'

'And then he stormed off on his motorbike, which I expect he takes to bed with him every night, he certainly smelt like he did, and left me to find my own way home, which I didn't reckon was such a good idea, wandering through town in the middle of the night, so I snuggled up to myself and waited for dawn, and was just setting off when I spotted you flat out and beautiful and catching your death from the dew.' She smiled. 'You looked that helpless I come over all motherly.'

Nik shivered and stood up.

'What you need,' she said to his back, 'is something to warm you up. Me too, come to think of it. Tell you what, just for starters, I'll race you to the hump and back, how about it?'

She was off before Nik could say no.

Instead, he picked up his bike and chased after her.

'Cheat!' she called as he came alongside.

'Can't trust any of us males!' he called back, pedalled harder, reached the hump well ahead, dismounted, and sat waiting, undeniably feeling better for the spurt of energy.

The Magdalene arrived in a glow, panting, and, slumping down at his side, leaned herself against him.

'Look, Michelle,' Nik said when she'd recovered, 'if you like, I'll give you a ride down the hill. The law shouldn't spot us at this time of day.'

'Ta very much,' she said. 'And you can give me a ride any time.'

He nudged his head against hers. 'I'll keep that in mind,' he said and laughed.

'I mean it,' she said. 'I've fancied you rotten since you joined the group. But you never stay around long enough to do anything about it.'

Nik shrugged and they were silent for a time before Michelle said, 'I've told you why I was up here tonight. Your turn now. Why were you lying there or is that where you usually doss?'

Nik sniffed. 'Fun.'

'Now pull the other one.'

'Okay . . . Research.'

'For our stupid film, you mean?'

'Why not?'

'Don't believe you.'

'It's true! . . . Well, kind of.'

She turned so she could face him. 'I saw Randy Frank yesterday.'

'Was he poking a mint?'

'Don't be disgusting! He's all right really. He said he'd been to see you and he thought you weren't very well. He said you were still shook up from that awful bomb, and were worried sick about the girl you were with.'

Nik bristled. 'I wish he'd mind his own business.'

'Well, are you?'

'Wouldn't you be?'

Michelle nodded. 'Anybody would. I just wondered if it had anything to do with you being up here, that's all.'

Nik said nothing.

'Is she . . .' Michelle hesitated. 'Is she your girl? I mean —proper girl?'

Nik rubbed a hand across his face. 'Yes and no,' he said tetchily. 'I say yes, she says no.'

'Doesn't she love you as much as you love her?'

Nik gave her a squinted look. 'You do pry.'

Michelle said, 'Sorry, I'm sure,' and turned her head away.

But suddenly, despite his anger, he wanted to tell.

He waited a moment till the anger subsided, then with a tentative hand brought her unresisting face to his again.

INTERCUT: *Julie's hospital room. She and Nik clutched in their awkard embrace, weeping.*

'This is ridiculous,' Nik says, swivelling so that he can lie on the bed propped up alongside Julie. He wipes his eyes with his free hand.

Julie is snuffling her tears back.

Realizing she can't do anything about her face, Nik reaches for some tissues on the bedside cabinet and very carefully attends to her.

'Anyway, why are you crying?' he asks.

'Why are you?' Julie says.

'For you,' Nik says. 'For myself. I don't know! . . . For the whole rotten bloody world.'

'No,' Julie says. 'Not rotten. Bloody sometimes but not rotten.'

They are calm again. Nik settles himself comfortably. They are silent for a moment, staring ahead at the view through the window.

'Nik . . .' Julie says, hardly breaking the silence.

'Uh-huh?'

'There's something I've got to tell you, but I can't now.'

'Then don't try.'

'I've made a tape.'

'Oh?'

'I want you to take it with you.'

'Can't I hear it now?'

'No. At home.'

'I've brought my Walkman. I'll listen in the train.'

'I'd rather you listened at home.'

'Okay. As soon as I get back.'

JULIE:

Dear Nik:

This is difficult. I'd rather tell you what I want to say when I'm with you, and when I'm completely recovered and back home again.

But I think it probably should be said before then. Judging by your letters and . . . Well, anyway.

[*Pause.*]

I suppose everybody is strong in some things and weak in others. I'm strong in faith but weak in love. I know that much about myself.

I could easily love you, Nik. Love you the way you want, I mean. I knew that the night before the bomb. I wasn't just testing myself the way I said. That was only half the truth. The other half was that I wanted you the way you wanted me. I'd even imagined it happening. Lying in bed all the week before I'd imagined it. You and me together. I'd planned it, our night together outside Cambridge. The tent. Everything! That's my confession.

[*Pause.*]

But then, as soon as I knew you really did want me, and it began to turn out just the way I'd hoped for, I drew back. Isn't that awful! The terrible desire to know you're wanted for your body as well as yourself. And then when someone offers you that, to realize it isn't enough. It isn't what you really want. And you've led them on only to reject them.

I hated myself! Dear God, how I hated myself afterwards. You thought I'd gone to sleep, but I hadn't. All the time we were lying there in the tent, I was loathing myself. Not because I'd wanted you. There's nothing wrong with that. But because of my deceit.

I'm sorry for that. For what I did and for hating myself as well. Neither did any good.

I can tell you this now because I've thought and prayed so much about it. What I did and why.

[*Pause.*]

It's all got to do with love, hasn't it?

The more I thought about it, the more it came down to one thing. 'A new commandment I give unto you, that you love one another.'

She said that at the Last Supper, the night before she died on the cross. She'd broken the bread only a few minutes before, saying, 'This is my body,' and she'd passed round the cup of wine, saying, 'This is my blood,' and she'd told the disciples, 'Do this in remembrance of me'.

You know, to me the Last Supper is the most important part of her story. And being at the Eucharist, at the Last Supper repeated day in day out all down the years since the first time, that's for me the most important part of my life as a Christian. It heals me. Brings everything into focus. Gives me new energy. Helps me view things in the right perspective.

So if she gives a new commandment then, at that moment in the Last Supper, it's just got to be important. And the more I thought about it the more I kept wondering why she calls it the *new* commandment. What's so *new* about it? How is loving one another different from loving your neighbour as yourself, which we'd already been told to do?

And, after all, Nik, she can't mean 'love' the way you meant it that night. Otherwise, she would mean a kind of everlasting gang-bang. Which you've got to admit is impractical, if not impossible.

Then I realized only St John's Gospel, my favourite, mentions the new commandment. The others don't. And in John's story, it comes after Judas has left the room to go and betray Jesus. Also, she repeats the command three times. You'll like that. And it's tangled up with her talking about friendship. 'You are my friends if you do as I command you,' she says. 'I call you servants no longer.' So this love, this *new* love, is the love of friendship.

In the love you wanted of me, Nik, two people come together and make themselves one. Whereas it seems to me the love Jesus is telling us to have for one another is the love of two friends: the love of distinctness, of separateness. Neither wants to dominate. Neither wants to be dominated. The desire in the love of friendship is the desire for the other's freedom.

In the love you want, the two people fit themselves together physically because they want to fit together in every way—in their bodies, in their minds, in their spirits. But in the love of friendship you don't want your friend to become one with you. Just the opposite. You want your friend to be as perfectly herself as she can be.

[*Pause.*]

That's what I want for you, Nik, and that's what I hope you most want for me.

That is what I want you for, and I hope that is what you want me for.

[*Pause.*]

Lying here, at first hating myself, wanting an end to my life, I have slowly learned to love myself as a friend. That has been my cure for my wounded self. Now and in future loving you as a friend is the best of me—is all of me—I can give you.

All I can give you is the love I give myself.

The love you've been wanting from me—the love that comes from the desire to be one—I've already given elsewhere, Nik.

What I need is a friend who loves me as a friend, if I am to live up to that other love. Will you be that loving friend?

'She sounds a bit of a fanatic,' Michelle said, 'if you don't mind me saying.'

'No more than you are,' Nik said.

'Me? I'm not a fanatic.'

'Yes you are. You're a fanatic about boys.'

'That's natural.'

'So? You like doing what comes naturally. Julie likes doing what comes supernaturally.'

'Clever dick!'

'Smartypants!'

She poked her tongue at him through vulvarine lips.

Nik blew a raspberry. 'I'm not saying you aren't good at it, Michelle, don't get me wrong. Just the same as Julie's good at giving her all to God.'

'Maybe that's why you like her so much.'

'Because I can't have her, you mean?'

'No. Because she's good at what she wants. That's always a bit sexy, isn't it? I mean, there's a boy in the swimming team at the Leisure Centre. He's terrific at swimming and he knows it, the bighead. He's just gorgeous to watch, I mean he just is. It's not only his smashing body. It's everything. I dunno how to say it, but it's like when he swims he's the best he ever will be in the whole of his life. If you could have him then, while he's swimming, you just feel it would be the greatest, the last word . . . Ecstacy!'

She sighed.

'But then after, when he's not swimming, even though he's got this stunning body, it's like all that—I dunno . . .'

'Concentrated energy?'

'Yes—all that lovely concentrated energy has broken up into awkward little bits all sparking off in different directions and you're left with this big-headed, ham-fisted idiot that's about as likely to give anybody ecstacy as a side of beef in a butcher's shop.'

'I suppose it might, a side of beef, some people being as weird as they are. But it sounds to me like you should choose your meat more carefully.'

'That's what I've been thinking lately. But you know what I'm trying to say.'

'Sure. Ever since I first saw Julie I've been hot for her. Not just for sex, but because of her specialness. She knows what she wants and she's going for it, all or nothing, no side-tracking.'

'Dedicated.'

Nik glanced at Michelle with surprise. 'That's right, that's what it is.'

'And you want the same. Want it with her.'

'Do I? . . . How do you know?'

Michelle laughed. 'Any girl would know that. But if you ask me, she has to be a bit of a fool to turn you down.'

'She hasn't turned me down.' Nik pushed himself to his feet and, breathing deeply, took in the sweeping view, early morning mist now shrouding the valley so that he seemed to be standing above the clouds. 'She's offered me something else, that's all.' His eyes came back to Michelle lying on her side, her head supported on her elbow. 'Something better.' He went to his bike and stood it upright. 'Only I'm not sure I can live up to it.'

He mounted and hobby-horsed himself alongside Michelle.

'I'm getting cold,' he said.

Michelle got to her feet and groomed herself with practised vanity.

Nik said, 'Would you do something for me?'

She smiled at him askance. 'Don't say this is going to be my lucky night after all!'

He grinned back. 'You never know!'

Michelle climbed onto his saddle behind him. 'So what is it?'

'Tell you when we get there.'

'Why? Where are we going?'

'To the dump by the canal.'

†

'Isn't this nice?' Michelle said.

'Nice it is, secluded it isn't,' Tom said, coming up behind and slipping his arms round her waist.

'Who said it was?' Michelle strained against him. 'But it's a lovely view. All of the town. And especially of the dump by the canal. Isn't that where it happened?'

'That's where it happened,' Tom said, his hands now exploring under Michelle's singlet.

'I must say,' Michelle said, using her elbows to prevent Tom's hands rising higher, 'you don't waste much time.'

'Told you—' Tom's breathing was not at all calm, 'don't have any to spare.'

'Thought you was after information?'

'I am.' Thwarted in one ambition Tom's hands set off in pursuit of another.

'Well you won't find it down there!' Michelle wriggled free and faced him. 'So what d'you want to know?'

Irritation flickered in Tom's eyes and revived his suspicion. 'Look, you—what's your game?'

'Snooker,' Michelle said. 'I'm quite partial to a game of snooker.'

'Smart ass!' Tom said.

Michelle laughed. 'How funny! Somebody else called me that only last night. Well, early this morning to be exact. But he was a bit more polite.'

'Said please and thank you, did he?'

'Lots of words you don't know.'

'All talk but no action, by the sound.'

'Wouldn't say that.' Michelle turned away and looked into the valley. A black-leathered figure on a motorbike, like a beetle on a matchbox toy, was circling slowly round a pile of crushed cars in the centre of the dump. She smiled to herself at the sight. 'Nor would you,' she went on, 'if you knew who he was.'

'Why should I give a damn who you were with last night?'

Michelle shrugged and said, 'Isn't that what you want to talk about?'

The confusion on Tom's face made her tingle with

satisfaction. She had duped him, trapped him, hooked him; he knew it and was smarting.

A glance into the valley told her that the tiny motorcyclist had driven away. The dump appeared deserted.

'All right,' Tom said, 'let's cut the crap.'

'You must watch the cops on telly a lot,' Michelle said.

Tom stepped down the bank to face her, the slope so steep his head came level with hers.

'This is official, okay?' he said straining for professional neutrality. 'The guy you were with—he had something to do with the crucifiction?'

'You could say that.'

'Say what?'

'He was the one, of course.'

'The one? Which one? The one on the cross or one of those who put him there?'

'Ah!' Michelle said. 'I see what you mean. The one on the cross.'

Tom's evident disappointment took her by surprise; she was even more startled by his reply.

'You mean Nicholas Frome?'

Tom's turn for satisfaction now. He added with tart pleasure, 'Tell us something I don't know.'

Michelle preened her hair in hope of hiding her sudden panic.

'Like what?' she said.

'Like who did it.'

She turned hard eyes on him and said, 'If you know it was Nik why don't you ask him?'

'Because I'm asking you.'

'And what makes you think I know?'

Tom grinned coldly. 'You know, and you're going to tell.'

'Who says!'

'Look—you've had a nice little game.' Tom snorted. 'Snooker!' He pulled at his nose and sniffed. 'Well, I can take a joke. And I'm not mean. I'll be generous. I'll give you a choice of balls—if you'll pardon the expression. You tell me what I want to know, all friendly, like a good citizen, or I take you in on suspicion of being accessory to criminal assault and for obstructing a police officer in the course of his duty.'

'All right, all right, don't go on!' Michelle regarded him for a moment with undisguised dislike. 'But only on condition there's no come-back on Sharkey. He's got nothing to do with this.'

'Who said anything about Sharkey?'

'Just so long as you remember, that's all.'

'Sure,' Tom said, 'no danger.'

'Promises, promises!' Michelle said with scorn, and set off in the direction of Tom's car, saying, 'Let's get it over with. Drive me down to the dump.'

REPORTS

NIK'S NOTEBOOK: I can write again.

Not tears, after all.

The crucifiction was what I needed.

Who would understand? One person's need is another person's bananas. Maybe one day I won't understand myself. So, for the record:

Len S. shouldn't have told me to observe other people. He should have told me to observe myself. I don't need to look elsewhere. All humanity is in me. All its history, all its quirks, quarks, and (w)holes (black and white). Therefore all its future too.

When you think about it, this is bound to be so. With all the fathers and mothers it took to make me, going back by compound interest to whothehellever Adam and Eve were, how could it be otherwise? And not only for me but for everybody.

My life is my specimen. My body is my laboratory. Last week the cross was my test tube.

Now I know that the only faith I can believe is an experimental faith.

STOCKSHOT: *The eye by which I see God is the same eye by which God sees me.*

But I was barmy to think Michelle would help. When I told her what I was going to do she threw an eppie. I'm not going to help you do THAT! You must be MAD! You'll KILL yourself! Etc.

Wouldn't listen. Don't blame her. Not that there was time for explanations. Sunrise wasn't far off. Thought for a minute she would shop me. But she thought I couldn't do it without help. So I said no, I probably couldn't and loaned her my bike and she scooted off home.

I wasn't so barmy as to tell her I'd already worked out how to do it on my own. Though it would have been easier with somebody to lend a hand and would have saved some of the fash that happened afterwards.

Nature and conduct of experiment

Reasons 1. Believers (e.g. Old Vic, Kit, Julie) have been telling me that, if you want to know about belief, you have to behave as if you believed. You don't think it out, they say, and then believe, like solving a puzzle. You earn it and learn it by living it.

2. They have been telling me belief is a gift which you have to want. You obtain it by willing it. Ask, and it shall be given you; seek, and you shall find; knock, and it shall be opened unto you. (Matt. 7, 7.)

3. They all talk about:
   a. The Last Supper / Eucharist / Mass / Holy Communion;
   b. The Crucifiction;
   c. The Resurrection.

They perform the Last Supper, make pictures and sculptures of the Cross, and argue about what happened at the Resurrection.

I have taken part in (a), and quite enjoy arguing about (c). Sharing a meal with friends and having a jawbang about the Big Questions is understandable / fun / good / right / natural. But hanging two- and three-d pictures on the walls of your home, never mind in public places, of a man being tortured by the cruellest death known to the human race does not seem quite pukka, old boy, certainly not kosher, cobber.

Besides, the confessed believers in God's own religion also talk about the imitation of Christ, of living your belief. They act out (a), hope for (c), not being able to do much about their own resurrections as yet, but, apart from a few of their number that they tend to regard as nutters, none of them has a go at (b) crucifiction, which yet they say is so important to their belief. So what's all this about *living* your faith?

Of course, they talk a lot about the cross as a symbol, and that's okay. But I thought I'd take them at their word, why not? That's logical, after all. It's what any scientist would do experimentally, if he wanted to study a form of life closely. And as I am my own specimen, my own laboratory, and my own experiment . . . who else for the cross but me?

Not that I ever thought of doing the Real Thing. Nails through hands and feet, and a crown of thorns, and a spear up the rip cage, I mean. I'm not a suicidal sado-masochist. What I had in mind was more like a practice version. Besides:

4. Julie says we are all in everything, and everything is in us. We are the children of God, she says.

Well, children are composed of their parents. They are their parents while also being themselves. Christ, the son of God, was/is therefore God. God is therefore also in me, and I am in God. The believers tell me this as well as telling me to behave as if I believed. And the irreligious OBD tells me I must play Christ.

Okay, I shall take them all at their word. I shall act as if, and practise being Jesus Christ. I shall do some field work, some flesh-and-blood first-hand research, and find out how he-she-it felt, even if only a little bit and not the very worst. After all, I cannot perform miracles, cannot preach to great crowds, cannot invent wise sayings. But I can be crucified.

NB: This sounds pretty lame now. But at the time, that night, after seeing Julie in hospital and hearing her tape, these seemed good enough reasons. And the only ones. But they weren't the only ones. Not even the most important. I know that now but hid it from myself then. (Another conclusion from the experiment: people do things more for hidden reasons than for stated ones. Each of us is a galaxy of secret lives.)

INTERCUT: *The shot from outside Nik's bedroom, as before but this time in slow motion. His face is unbearably tense as he listens to his Walkman. He rises and with studied violence hurls the Bible directly at us. It smashes through the window.*

Shot continues: Shards of glass fly in all directions. The Bible narrowly misses us, leaving a gaping, jagged hole in the windowpane. Nik comes to the window. The hole frames his head and shoulders. He stretches out his arms, cruciform, and grasps the casement. He stares out at us, unseeing, while we hear Julie's voice-over, as from a tape heard through headphones:

(fade up): . . . *found this passage which says it for me:* 'Now I know, now I understand, my dear, that in our calling, whether we are writers or actors, what matters most is not fame, nor glory, nor any of the things I used to dream of. What matters most is knowing how to endure. Know how to bear your cross and have faith. I have faith and it doesn't hurt so much any more.'

The Place. Golgotha. The place of the skull. A burial place for rubbish. A dump outside the city wall of Jerusalem, a small town on a trade route on the outback edge of the Roman empire in the first century of the Christian era.

This was easy. The dump on the other (i.e. wrong) side of town, across the railway line and the canal, a burial ground for clapped-out motorcars. That seemed to me a pretty good twentieth-century stand-in for the original setting. Especially as the canal is dead, killed by the railway, which isn't what it used to be, having been crippled by the automobile, junked pyramids of which rise up as monuments to travel.

And Grandad's workshop being right next to it meant I could get all the gear I might need.

The Time. Sunrise. JC was nailed up at 9 a.m. I couldn't wait till then because at that time there would be people around who would stop me. Failing that, sunrise seemed appropriate. New day, new way, etc. Not that I worked it out beforehand. Only decided to do the crucifiction experiment when I was on the common with Michelle. Though—hidden lives—the idea must have been rumbling about in the back of my mind like a brainstorm on the brew all the day before, if not longer.

The Cross. Easy again. Two or three weeks ago I saw a piece of metal from the chassis of an old lorry lying on the dump. It was made of two pieces welded together in a T-shape that reminded me of the *crux commissa*. I soon found it again that morning.

The Method. In Grandad's workshop there was a big roll of heavy-duty clear polythene sheeting. He used it to cover any-thing he wanted to keep dust or rain off. Also for making temporary cloches and cold frames for his garden. I cut five strips off it, each a metre long by ten cm. wide. I also looked out

214

a six-metre length of strong rope, and cut two twenty-metre lengths of window sashcord.

I took this stuff out to the dump and laid it on the ground directly under the arm of the old mobile crane Fred Bates uses to shift wrecked cars and heavier scrap. Then I dragged the chassis-cross to the same place.

I tied the rope to the cross where the metal pieces were joined and made a noose at the other end. The strips of polythene I tied round the bars, two on each arm and one on the upright, leaving them loose enough so that I'd be able to slip my hands through the ones on the crosspiece and my feet through the other. I reckoned these would secure me to the cross while leaving my hands free.

Next I had to fix the crane. I've often helped Fred use it. When I was a kid, the crane seemed like a great big toy and Fred used to let me sit in the cab with him and work the levers. When I got old enough he started paying me pocket-money for working on the dump at weekends. Fred's a kindly, bumbling old guy who has no children of his own, which is maybe why he likes having me around. Grandad often tells him off for spoiling me but I suspect he's jealous. He and Fred have known each other since their infant school days and have a mock-insulting kind of relationship, full of jokes no one else can understand and that neither of them ever do more than half-smile at. The point is, though, that I know how the crane works and I know where Fred keeps a spare ignition key hidden in case he loses the one he carries with him.

So as soon as the cross was ready I took the two lengths of sashcord, found the key, and climbed into the cab. There I attached one length of cord to the lever that raises the hook and the other cord to the lever that lowers it. Then I ran the cords through the cab window to the point on the cross where my hands would be.

That done, I hunted out a stub of heavy metal about the size of a brick and took it back to the cab.

Everything was now ready for a trial run. I started the engine and tested the arrangement of the remote control cords. This meant first finding how to jam the stub of metal against the accelerator pedal in such a position that the accelerator maintained just the right revs to raise the cross. If there aren't enough revs for the weight to be raised, the engine stalls; if there are too many, it raises the load too fast and can jam the hook at the end of the crane's arm. As I couldn't find the right revs by trial and error, I had to judge them from experience.

When I'd done that I had to make sure it was possible to work the up and down levers by pulling on the sashcords. The levers have quirks. You have to lift and shift, rather like a motorcar gear for reverse. To achieve this I had to rig the cords round struts in the cab before a pull from outside of the cab made them function properly. I'd anticipated this, and had been thinking out the solution while getting everything else ready. So I didn't take long to get it right. Except that I discovered I only had one chance with each lever. If anything went wrong once I was in the air, I'd had it: I'd be stuck.

If I'd let myself think about it, I might have given up right then. But I didn't. The grey summer dawn was lightening now every minute. The sun would be up soon and so would people. No time for pondering. If I was going to do it, it had to be done at once or I'd be too late. And I certainly wasn't going to give up.

Besides, I felt a weird kind of excitement. From the moment Michelle had left me, fleeing on my bike, I'd worked with steadily increasing speed and passion. Everything I did went perfectly, as if I knew exactly what I was doing because I'd practised many times. And by the time I'd rigged the crane I was sweating and breathing hard, almost as I had been earlier when I arrived on the common. Only, instead of feeling utterly whacked, I was elated, surging with energy. I can remember thinking, *I am as one possessed*, and laughing out loud.

Now, two days later, when in my memory I see myself scurrying about Fred's dump in the early morning light, I know something I was not aware of at the time: a sensation of being utterly absorbed, of being wholly myself and yet also more than myself, a part of something inevitable and beyond that moment. I think what I felt must have been what people mean when they talk of fate and of meeting their destiny. That is why now I feel no guilt or shame or regret, the way some people (everybody?) think I should. I know it was a ridiculous thing to do, dangerous and stupid really, but when I think of it, I find myself smiling.

The cross prepared, the crane revving, its hook lowered and ready with the noosed rope attached. All that was left was for me to slip my arms and legs into their polythene bindings, take hold of the control cords, and pull the up lever.

I took my shoes off but found that my jeans were snagging on the polythene strip. So I pulled them off; decided to make a proper job of it, and pulled off my T-shirt as well, which was wet through for the second time and uncomfortable anyway. That left me in my underpants.

Without encumbrance of clothes my legs and arms fitted easily into their straps. I took hold of the ends of the cords, settled myself as best I could on the bars of my cold metal bed and, taking a deep breath, tugged the up cord.

Which is when things went slightly wrong.

†

'This better not be another stunt,' Tom said as they approached the dump. He had driven down from the common in sullen silence.

There's nothing so funny, Michelle was thinking, as a randy boy when he's thwarted. Nor so dangerous, sometimes, neither. She performed to herself her mother's frequent refrain: Men, they're all beasts!

'Pull up just there.' She pointed ahead at Arthur Green's workshop.

Before she went in she banged at the rattly door, calling: 'Mr Green, hello. It's me, Michelle.' But Tom swept her inside on the bow of his temper before there was time for reply.

The place was gloomy and cavernous, lit only from skylights. But everything was neatly kept and arranged. A carpenter's bench, ancient in use but as cared for as front room furniture; tools hung and laid out in meticulous order; a circular saw, a band saw, a planing machine, all giving sharp metallic winks; even the sawdust on the floor looked as if scattered by order rather than neglect.

One corner was occupied by stacked piles of wood in various cuts and sizes, a library of timber. Another, the farthest corner, half hidden by large sheets of blockboard standing on end and leaning against a main rafter, was an inner sanctum, a den where a naked light bulb dangled from the roof, shining above an old kitchen table, at which sat Arthur Green, his knotted hands curled round a large mug, his head bent over a newspaper spread in front of him.

He turned to peer at Michelle and Tom standing just inside the door but did not rise.

'Now then,' he called.

'I've brought him,' Michelle called back.

'So I see.'

Tom made his way through the workshop, Michelle following slowly like an indulgent mum behind an over-eager child. He stopped by the partitioning boards, where he could see all of the den—its chipped sink and water-blackened draining board, its long-out-of-date oven, its couple of battered armchairs angled towards a wood-burning stove, presently dead. But other than the man at the table, nobody.

Michelle arrived at his side; Tom glanced and saw her undisguised pleasure at his puzzlement.

'So where is he?' Tom said. 'I thought he was here.'

'Aye, well he's not, is he?' Arthur Green said. 'He's gone.'

'I talked to you this morning,' Tom said. 'Out there.'

'You did.'

'You said you knew nothing.'

'No, no! I said there was plenty of gossip.'

Michelle couldn't help chipping in, 'Mr Green is Nik's grandad.'

Tom's face betrayed that he felt like kicking himself.

'Where is he?' he demanded.

Arthur Green chuckled. 'He is risen, he is not here.'

Tom said, 'This is no joke, Mr Green. It's a police matter.'

'You're right, lad,' Arthur Green said. 'It's no joke, and it's nothing to do with the police neither.'

'Your grandson is crucified and you don't think it has anything to do with the police?'

'Why should it?'

'Because it's a criminal offence. GBH at least. Don't you want the people responsible to be caught?'

Arthur Green turned to Michelle. 'You didn't tell him?'

Michelle shook her head. 'Didn't think he'd believe me.'

Tom said, 'Believe what?'

Arthur Green pushed his mug away, sat back in his chair, placed his work-warped hands flat on the table in front of him and said, 'He crucified himself.'

INTERCUT: *The scene at the dump. The cross lying on the ground with Nik strapped to it. He pulls the sashcord. The crane begins to wind in. The rope connecting hook to cross takes the strain. The cross begins to rise, pivoting on its foot. At first all goes well. But then, suddenly, Nik's unevenly balanced weight causes the cross to tip to one side. It slews and turns over. The control cords are snatched from his hands. This takes Nik by surprise. He cries out. Now, instead of lying on the cross, he is hanging under it.*

The cross continues to rise up. As soon as its foot leaves the ground it begins to gyrate, swivelling as well as swinging from side to side like a pendulum. And because of the way the rope is attached, the cross does not hang upright, but tilts forward at the top, so that Nik is hanging from it, his arms pulled back by their bonds, his chest thrust out, and his legs, caught at the ankles, bending awkwardly at the knees. It looks like, and is, a painful position in which to be trapped.

Slowly, the cross rises until it is about five metres above ground, when the crane's engine coughs, splutters, stalls, and conks out.

Silence.

The cross swings and turns. At each turn we see Nik's dumbfounded face. And as he turns, his glasses catch the first rays of the rising sun and flash at us.

NIK'S NOTEBOOK: I had worked out the mechanics. But not the dynamics.

When I said that to Grandad afterwards, he said: The story of your life.

So there I was—suspended, stuck, helpless, suffering, and alone.

My God, my God, why hast thou forsaken me?

It took six hours before J C was broken enough to ask that. It took less than six minutes before I knew why he asked it and exactly what he meant.

'I don't believe you,' Tom said.

'Told you,' Michelle said, slumping into one of the armchairs.

'Tell him, girl,' Arthur Green said.

Michelle said: 'I found him on Selsley Common last night, not long before dawn actually. He was lying on the ground, flat out asleep, nothing on, only jeans and trainers. I thought he must be ill or something. But when I woke him he was okay and we talked a bit, well, quite a lot actually. But only talked, I mean, nothing else.'

She gave Tom a look that defied contradiction.

'He told me all about the bomb and the girl he was with, how he felt about her, and about him and her and religion. And about how the girl didn't love him like he loved her, and he'd just found out. He was pretty upset about that, I think. Well, I'm sure he was actually.'

She drew a deep breath, the way people do when they're talking about a hopeless situation.

'Anyway, he asked me if I'd do something to help him, and I said I would, and he brought me down here. But he didn't say till we got here that he wanted me to help him crucify himself. I couldn't believe it! I said: No way, I said. No way am I going to help you do nothing like that, I said, that's crazy, you must be off your noddle, I said, even to think such a thing. It's that girl, I said, and her religious stuff, she's a fanatic, I said, she's mangled your brains. And lying around on the common with nearly nothing on in the middle of the night, and soaking. He was wringing wet with sweat when I found him. You must have caught a fever, I said, and he did look flushed, no question.'

Michelle took another deep breath before going on.

'Well, he said, don't worry, I expect you're right. It was just a joke anyway, he said, I didn't really mean it. I'll just stay here for a bit, he said, and make myself some tea in Grandad's workshop. You take my bike, he said, and go home. I'll use an old one of Grandad's. You can fetch mine back later, he said. Though, to tell the truth, I was really glad of the excuse to see him again because—'

She glanced at Arthur Green, thought better of saying what she had been about to say, sat forward in the chair, coughed and went on: 'But when I got home I couldn't sleep for thinking about him. And the more I thought about him wanting me to help him crucify himself, the more I was sure he hadn't been joking. And I thought: What if he does do it somehow? It'll be terrible, I'd never forgive myself for not staying with him and making sure he didn't and for not helping him a bit more. I mean, he's had an awful time lately, hasn't he? He can't be very well, can he, even if he looks all right? And people can do crazy things when they're really in love, can't they? Especially if they're rejected. I mean, everybody knows that. Anyway, in the end I couldn't bear it. And I thought: It'll be my fault if anything happens.'

The abstracted glare of desperation in Michelle's eyes allowed no doubt. She swallowed hard and continued: 'I didn't know what to do. And then I thought of ringing the workshop so I could talk to him and make sure he was all right but I could only find the number for his house. So I thought of ringing Mr Green but then I thought: What if he goes racing off to the dump and nothing's the matter, he might give Nik a bad time, and Nik would hate me for telling his grandad, and—'

She glanced at Arthur Green again and shrugged, a resigned apology.

'Go on, girl,' Arthur Green said. 'Don't you mind.'

Michelle gave him a grateful nod, snuffled against imminent sobs, drew a staving breath, and managed to add: 'I got that worried I decided the only thing to do was ride back to the dump. So I did . . . and there he was . . . hanging—' before undeniable tears welled and burst, sluicing with them the trauma and distress she had hidden from view all day.

INTERCUT: *The dump. Early morning sunlight. Michelle comes cycling hectically along the road. She sees Nik before she reaches the dump and begins yelling his name in a panic-stricken voice.*

When she arrives under the cross she flings herself from the bicycle, which wobbles away on its own until it collides with a mound of scrap and entangles itself with the other discarded vehicles.

Struggling for breath, Michelle gazes up at Nik and between gulps, shouts at him: 'You—bloody—fool!—What did you —go and—do that for!'

Nik stares back at her with a pained grin, making confused, constricted noises.

'Jesus!' Michelle says, and stamps her foot. She sees the control cords snaking over the ground to the crane's cab, runs to the crane, climbs into the cab, at once realizes the problem is too complicated for her to sort out quickly, jumps down, and sprints towards the workshop, shouting as she goes: 'I'll get your grandad.'

She disappears into the workshop.

The cross turns slowly, swaying in the first breeze of the day as it does so.

After a moment Brian Standish in white running gear bursts through the hedge above the canal, his appalled face turned up towards Nik as towards a vision. Nik mutters incoherently.

'Christ Almighty!' the man gasps. He takes in the scene, dodging and skipping as if avoiding invisible assailants. He jumps, trying to reach the cross, as if he thinks by grasping it he can pull it down. He stumbles towards the crane. But stops before reaching it, turns, looks up at Nik, says, 'Dear God!', makes a dash for the access road, stops at the edge of it, turns to look at Nik again, says, 'Hell's bells!', comes to a decision and races back to the hole in the hedge, shouting at Nik as he goes, 'Hang on, I'll get help!' and disappears the way he came.

The cross slowly turns, floodlit now in bright warm sunlight.

There is birdsong. And Nik's voice in an indecipherable ritual chant.

'I better be sure I've got this right, Mr Green,' Tom said. 'You drove here on your motorbike at about six fifteen this morning in response to a phone call from Michelle Ebley. You found your grandson suspended on a cross from the crane on the dump. You got him down, and with Miss Ebley's help, carried him into your workshop. Then, while Miss Ebley looked after him, you removed from the scene the cords, the metal block your grandson had used against the accelerator, and the crane's ignition key.'

'Right so far,' Arthur Green said.

'You knew someone else had found your grandson on the cross because Miss Ebley had seen him. And fearing the police would come, you locked yourself with your grandson and Miss Ebley into the workshop. The police did arrive shortly afterwards. But you all kept quiet till they left the scene.'

'Right.'

'Not long afterwards, I visited the dump. At first you thought I was just someone poking about and you came out to try and get rid of me. When you realized I was a police officer you began to fear that we hadn't given up. This was confirmed when you learned that afternoon from Miss Ebley's brother that I was making inquiries through contacts—'

'That's one way of putting it!' Michelle said.

'You then decided that your grandson's presence here might be discovered, that the police would make a fuss and so the newspapers would get on to the story and create another stir. To prevent this happening you phoned the Reverend Ruscombe of St James's, told him the whole story, and asked for his help. He suggested that he come for your grandson and take him to the vicarage where he would be more comfortable and be safe from police or press inquiries until he was recovered and able to cope.'

'That's about the size of it.'

'In order to allow time for this to happen, Miss Ebley suggested she meet me and act as a decoy—'

'I didn't say decoy!'

'No, but that's what it amounted to.'

'Well, but—'

'And she and her friends kept me away until she was sure your grandson had been removed.'

'You make him sound like a piece of furniture,' Michelle said.

Tom ignored her. 'And that's where he is now.'

'He is.'

Tom thought for a moment before asking with an attempt at off-handedness, 'What happened to his glasses, sir?'

Arthur Green smiled wryly. 'They got knocked off when we were cutting him loose. I didn't notice and stood on them. Broke the lenses. Didn't think they'd be much use after that so I chucked them over the pile of tyres to get shot of them. I was surprised when you found them. Even more surprised you traced him from them.'

'Just routine,' Tom said.

'Oh aye? Pat on the back, though, for you, eh? The lot who came first didn't find them.'

Tom shrugged. 'Lucky break.'

Michelle gave a scoffing laugh. 'My, my!' she said. 'He's never witty as well as handy!'

Arthur Green sent her a look that said: Mind yourself.

They fell silent, avoiding each other's eyes. Doubt hung between them like the fine motes of dust making smoky the light from the naked bulb above their heads.

Outside, the eight-twenty local connection from London rattled down the valley, across the viaduct on the other side of the canal, and braked to a greaseless stop at the station.

Inside, the only sound was the tattoo of Tom's fingers drumming on his thigh.

Michelle's patience snapped first. 'Is that it, then? We can go home, can we?'

Her irritation seemed to make up Tom's mind. He braced, stood up, and pushed his chair under the table, as if rising from a polite meal that's gone on too long, saying: 'Not yet. I'll have to report back.'

'Aw, come on!' Michelle sprang to her feet and confronted him across the table. 'What for? We've told you everything. Nobody else was involved. Nik's okay. What more d'you want? Nobody's done nothing illegal.'

'Oh no?' Tom's own patience was crumbling too. 'Removing evidence from the scene of a possible crime. Concealing a wanted man. Misleading and obstructing an officer in the course of his duty. Try those for starters.'

'Refusing an officer the pleasure of a bit on the side during the course of his duty. Does that count as well?'

Tom's face flushed. 'Look, I've had enough of you!' he said, pointing his finger at Michelle, who, flaunting herself, sneered: 'You haven't had me at all yet, you big dick!'

Arthur Green rose between them. 'All right, all right, that'll do, the pair of you!' he said with unbrookable firmness. He gathered himself, a tired old man giving in to consequences he has known all day must eventually be faced. 'Now, let's try again before there's more harm done. Listen, young man, I know you've got your job to do, and I'm not trying to stop you. All we've been doing is trying to keep my grandson from any more trouble. But all right, maybe I've overstepped the mark here and there and was wrong. I'm sorry about that. But nobody's been harmed. And there's nothing that can't be cleared up.'

Tom, fighting his temper still, replied with strained calm. 'I'll have to report. My governor isn't happy about this one. I reckon he'll want to see your grandson and you two and question you himself. Anyway, I can't let you go till I've new instructions.'

Arthur Green nodded. 'Can I make a suggestion?'

'What?'

'Report to your boss. If he wants to look into it personal, arrange for us all to meet at St James's vicarage. It'll be easier there. I don't think your boss'll want any more hoohah than I do, do you?'

Tom considered before reluctantly nodding agreement.

†

NIK'S NOTEBOOK: But being stranded on the cross turned out to be what Grandma Green used to call a blessing in disguise.

The blessing was that it gave me a clue for cracking the code of the indecipherable.

To start with, though, all it gave me was a nasty shock.*

---

* SHOCK: otherwise known as the Big Bang theory of the origin of the universe. This states that one day God was playing about with a lot of nothing in his-her-its laboratory in the middle of nowhere, when he-she-it had a nasty accident. *Bang!* And a few God-minutes later,

One thing about a nasty shock, it does bring you to your senses. Grandma Green was right about that too. What caused the shock, of course, was pain. Some people don't seem to mind pain. Athletes, for instance, are always talking about going through the pain barrier like other people talk about (or usually don't talk about) going to the lavatory: as if it is one of those normal, everyday chores you have to do if you want to stay alive. Personally, I find any kind of pain anything but normal and everyday, and always abnormal and unique. I could happily live without it.

In my opinion, anybody who says pain is a Go(o)d Thing is crazy, anybody who recommends it to others is evil, and anybody who goes looking for it is sick.

But I know I am pretty much alone in this, judging from the way most people go on.

One of the reasons why the pain of the cross was such a shock—apart from the actual, physical pain itself, I mean—was that it brought me back to my senses with a jolt and I thought:

What am I doing here?

Why did I do this to myself?

I must be sick!

---

there everything was, evolving like crazy before his-her-its very eyes. And God thought: Hello, this looks a bit dodgy, and quickly dictated a few commandments to put things back in order, but nobody would obey them. So God tried threatening horrible consequences if they didn't do as they were told but that didn't work because nobody cared less until the consequences actually happened. So God let a few really large-scale calamities occur, but that didn't put a stop to the nonsense either. So finally God decided he-she-it had better pile in as himself and do something about it before the whole business went to pot. But that didn't go too well either, as any fool would know it wouldn't, because, as any fool knows, only nothing can come of nothing, and nothing did. And that's why adherents of the Big Bang theory believe we're all nothing but a load of old rubbish floating around in the middle of nowhere with nothing to do and nowhere to go and do it. Which also explains why Big Bangers are always saying to each other: What the hell, who cares, let's have another big bang.

This is also known as the Cock-up theory of creation.

Idiot! You got yourself stuck up here, now get yourself down!

And I started wriggling about, trying to pull my arms out of their bindings. But I couldn't. The bindings were too wide to allow me to bend my arms and slip my hands out. I felt like an insect pinned to a collector's tray.

I heard myself say out loud: This is ridiculous! I can't get myself free! Somebody's got to help me!

And trying to shout: Help! ... Hello? ... Anybody ... Help!

STOCKSHOT : *The mystery of the Cross of Christ lies in a contradiction, for it is both a free will offering and a punishment which he endured in spite of himself. If we only saw in it an offering, we might wish for a like fate. But we are unable to wish for a punishment endured in spite of ourselves.*

Panic. But I remembered my research. (Facts are useful sometimes.) By tying the victim's arms to the cross the Romans could prolong his death for up to three days. And that was when his wrists and feet had been nailed as well. I was only tied, not nailed. So there was a pretty good chance of staying alive till somebody found me—three hours at most, never mind three days.

This thought calmed me down.

But then the strain on my muscles. And the sweats coming in fierce waves. And the dryness in my mouth and the taste of salt on my lips. And the strangling of my breath unless I pulled up and back with my arms. Which increased the pain in my muscles unbearably. And the sensation of my body being stretched by its own weight and tearing itself in half at the waist. And nothing to push up on with my feet. And my legs twisting at the knees, writhing against the pain.

The waves of pain.

And my eyes, as if they would pop.

Wave-pop.

Black blur and white dazzle.

And wave-pop.

And my breath breaking the sound barrier as my eyes splinter against the wall of light, the black sun blazing and flickering between here and there now and then as I turn on the axis of my heart pounding in my ears.

> The ring of singularity.
> Until I spin
> Sucking my mind
> Dazzled into another where
> And there was only now.
> And the zing of words
> In other worlds
> Stars exploding
> In clusters
> > galaxies
> > > universes.
> Cross words.

STOCKSHOT: *Hold to the now, the here, through which all future plunges to the past.* (As, it might be added, all past plunges to the future through the now and here to which you hold. For everything is in the neck of the hour glass: the kiss of two cones.)

JULIE: It is the hidden that I look for.

'Where is he, vicar?' Tom demands.

NIK: Now for the life of the eyes?

'Nobody else!' Tom's superintendent says. 'Nobody at all? Are you sure? What's he think he's doing?'
  'Performing an experiment, he says, sir.'
  'Experiment? What kind of experiment?'
  'Making pictures, he says, sir.'
  'Making pictures! What does he mean?'
  'I asked him that. He said: Those who have eyes to see let them see.'
  '. . . Is that all?'
  'Refused to say anything else, sir.'
  'Is he off his head?'
  'His grandfather thinks he's still in a dodgy state after the bomb. Miss Ebley says he's in love with the girl who was involved in the explosion, and that he's upset because she's

jilted him, but I don't think she's a reliable witness, sir. The vicar believes he's suffering some kind of religious experience which has gone a little too far.'

'And you?'

'I think he's a weirdo desperate for attention. He's the sort who gives me the creeps, to be honest, sir.'

'Dangerous?'

'No no! Bit of a wimp, if you ask me. But maybe you should have a word, sir?'

'I'll have more than a word. A fine dance he's led us. And all for nothing.'

INTERCUT: *Old Vic raises up before his eyes the round ice-cream wafer and says in his vicarious voice: 'This is my body which is given for you. Do this in remembrance of me.' He breaks the wafer in half and places the two pieces as one into his mouth.*

'Get him away from here, Mr Green,' the superintendent orders, 'get him out of the road. And now. At once. I don't know which of you is right about why this has happened. And that's not my concern. But we can't have this affair getting into the media. It wouldn't just be bad for your grandson, it would be awkward for us all. Have you relatives he could stay with?'

'None he'd want to go to.'

'Well, you'd best think of somewhere, because either you get him away from here or I'll have to make some charges. Against you in particular, Mr Green.'

'What about the monastery?' Old Vic suggests. 'I'm sure they'd have him, and they'd understand.'

'He might go there. He liked it before. And they seemed to know how to handle him. He's got beyond me these days.'

'Admirable!' the superintendent says. 'If he's still shook up from the bomb, a spell of monastic quiet will do him good. If hankering after that girl is the trouble, then the best thing is for them to be kept apart till he's over it. If it's religious fever he's suffering from then a stretch in a monastery is just the place for him to sweat it out—and they ought to be professionals at that.'

'I'll go and ask him.'

'Do that, Mr Green. And let's pack him off tonight. I want

this matter cleared up. Young Thrupp will drive him so we're sure he gets there . . . er . . . safe and sound.'

JULIE: It's like the leaves on the branches of the tree outside my window, and the branches in the tree, and the flecks of sunlight flashing on the ripples on the pond. All around me everywhere I'm struck by how the many make one. And by the one hidden in the many. It fascinates me. Catches my attention and holds it.

Which reminds me. Philip Ruscombe visited me the other day and celebrated the Eucharist at my bedside. Afterwards I asked him what he thought prayer was. He said the best description he had ever come across was this: Prayer is complete attention.

I liked that. It sounded right. Giving your whole attention till you are part of the whole, yet are still yourself.

That decided me. I knew what I had to discover more about. How to give my whole attention. What to give it to. What to do with it. And I don't want to find that out in some special way, like the old-fashioned monks and nuns did—not by cutting myself off from other people and living in purpose-built prayer houses. I want to do it hidden among ordinary people in an ordinary everyday place while I do ordinary everyday work.

There is nothing special about me. I'm just another leaf on the branch, another branch in the tree, one of the flecks of light flickering in the ripples on the pond. One among many. Yet also myself, alone.

If God is God, then that is God and that is where God is. Ordinary people must find God among themselves or they won't find her at all. It isn't to one of the many that I want to give all my attention—you, dear Nik, or anyone. But to being one among the many.

What I'm asking is: How do I remain myself, truly and without being crushed or diminished, while being one of the many, no more special and no more privileged, no more *noticeable*, and yet be wholly of God?

That's the question I have to give all my attention to. And at first I have to try and answer it alone.

Perhaps I'll manage, with a little help from my friends.
Hello, friend!

[*Pause.*]
And you'll say: But how do you know?
And I'll say: Because I believe it.
And you'll say: But what is belief?
[*Pause. Laughs.*]
Well, I've given that question some attention lately!
And I've tried to find an answer by playing your game.
Belief. Philip Ruscombe looked the word up in a dictionary, and then both of you gave up attending to the word *itself*! So I went on playing the game.

BE . . . LIEF

Be, my dictionary says, means: *To have presence in the realm of perceived reality; exist; live.* Which being translated means, I suppose: *To live in the world you accept is truly THERE.*

Lief, my dictionary says, means: *Gladly, willingly.* And adds that the word is related to the Old English word for *love.*

So *Belief* means: that you *will* to give all your *attention* to Living with loving gladness in the world you think really does exist.

Perhaps what you wanted to know was all there in the word itself and you didn't need to look anywhere else. I wonder if that's why St John's Gospel begins: In the beginning was the Word!

Anyway, I do think it is true that if God is to be found by belief, she is to be found by living gladly and with attentive love in the world where we are. Because God is here and now and is all of us and everything.

I don't know how to say it simpler than that.

The kiss of two cones.

'All right, settle down,' the Director shouted. 'I can't tell you any more than that. You'll have to ask him yourselves when you see him again. His grandad says he'll be back for Christmas. Now, Michelle has a message from him. I don't know what it is, she wouldn't tell me. You'd better read it out, Michelle.'

'He sent us this letter,' Michelle said, unfolding a page of computer printout. She cleared her throat and shuffled and brushed her hair from her eyes and cleared her throat and read aloud:

To the film group. This is my last piece of research for you. It contains my conclusions.

From everything I've learned, it seems to me that if Christ returned today:

1. He would be a woman.
   Reasons:
     i. The universe is a binary system:
        Black holes / White holes;
        in / out;
        male / female; etc.
        Last time God appeared as male;
        next time as female. The system demands it.
     ii. The time of the domineering male is over;
         the time of the female has come.
     iii. Now the fish is returning to the water.
2. You wouldn't recognize her though, because she is not one but all.

Therefore, to make a film about Christ coming now you should:

1. Set up a camera on any street, in any house, and anywhere else you like, and let it film whatever people do there for as long as you can.
2. Edit the film into any sequence of shots that make a pattern you enjoy.
3. Add clips from any other films that help make your film more interesting, and which improve the pattern of your own film.
4. Print the result and show it.

One more thing:

Sack the Director. All he wants to be is God. His kind of God doesn't exist any more. You don't need him. Do it yourselves. Together. When you can, Christ has returned.

Cheers.

See you.

Nik

As soon as Michelle finished reading everybody started talking at once.

An hour later the meeting broke up in uproar.

>>> MAKING LIGHT
OF LEAFING >>>

for >>

J U L I E

EYE SAW

from >>

N * I * K

Who says we saw
What last we saw
When last we saw
  Each other?

Whose eyes we saw
No others saw
When last we saw
  Each other

SUN LIGHT

Those eyes we saw
Told all we saw
When last we saw
  Each other

The sun
that flickers
the leaves
makes light
of leafing

Our eyes we saw
Saw yes and saw
The last of
  Each other

The sun
that sunders
the waves
makes light
of weaving

The sun
that flickers
is the light
that sunders
all one
in making

The kiss of
two cones

```
>>>              How do you say it?

 ^
 ^                   Is God is
 ^                   Is God already
 ^                   Is God always
 ^                       Always-already
 ^                       But not yet    Is
 ^                       Not-yet God     Eye es
 ^                                       Why es
 ^               Yet God
 ^                  Is God
 ^                              see why  I A M
 ^               God Is                  M I A
 ^
 ^                         Stars spinning
 ^                         he points the compass
 ^                         His hands
 ^                         bear the universe
 ^
 >                         He swings in the breeze
 >                         God's weathervane

                          A jogger's padding feet
                          tattoo in his mind
        s
        s                     Where's he going
        o                        where's he running
        r                            and from what
        c                     with his feet on
        e                     the end of his legs
        h                     and his body
        t                     head bent
        f                     to the ground?
        o
   n    m
   u    s    Why hast thou forsaken me?
   s    i
   g    t    Am I forsaken?
   n    p       To be forsaken
   i    a       must have been known
   r    b
   e         Now I know
   t            It unknown
   n            knows me   I ran one day    Here
   i                       Sprinted        in
   l            Why yes    But not arrived  head
   p
   s                       Hello J U L I E  You
                           With love        there
                           N I K.           G O D
```

water by tree splintering sun congregation at the ritual baptism of the cross CROSS WORDS

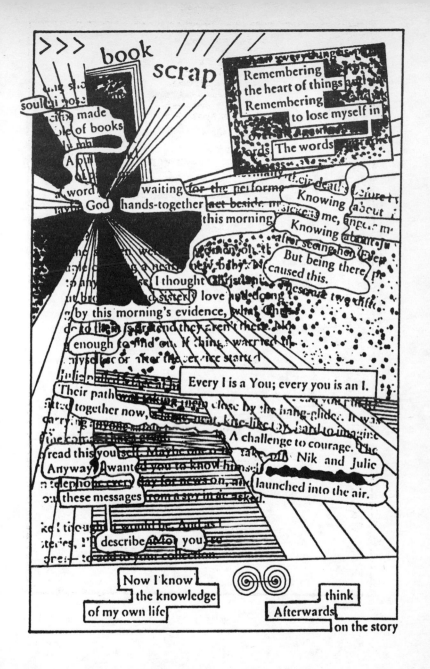

book scrap poem

BIRTHDAY SONG

An identity
to speak of?
I was born
a book
You should read it
Might get a surprise

Silence
my mind
my cell
myself

Silence
it's very beautiful

writing
in Silence
words
make an object
words weaving in and out
moving all the time
make new sentences, new meanings

Now I know
But
    for
the poet
living in
ourselves
we
wouldn't
learn anything

end without end

STOCKSHOT SOURCES

The Narrator gratefully acknowledges:

4 'The best in this kind . . . imagination amend them.'
William Shakespeare, *A Midsummer Night's Dream*,
V i 210–211, C U P 'New Shakespeare' edition.

24 'Jesus of Nazareth . . . living faith.'
Donald M. McFarlan, *Bible Readers' Reference Book*, p. 89,
Blackie.

30 'And as the mole . . . I shall be.'
James Joyce, *Ulysses*, The Corrected Text, p. 159, Bodley
Head.

42 'Canst thou . . . canst thou know?'
The Book of Job 11 7,8.

51 'Who is there? . . . the Thou and the I.'
Paul Valery quoted in W. H. Auden, *The Dyer's Hand*, p. 109,
Faber.

73 '. . . by history . . . are perfected . . .'
Hugh of Rouen.

110 'There is only one definition . . . freedoms to exist.'
John Fowles, *The French Lieutenant's Woman*, p. 99, Cape.

116 'People like you . . . a word to come.'
C. G. Jung's Letters, vol 1, Routledge & Kegan Paul, quoted in
Michael Tippett, *Moving into Aquarius*, p. 167, Paladin.

211 'The eye . . . sees me.'
Angelus Silesius.

214 'Now I know . . . hurt so much any more.'
Nina in Anton Chekhov's *The Seagull*, Act 4, quoted in
Chekhov The Dramatist by David Magarshack, p. 191,
Methuen.

227 'The mystery of the Cross . . . in spite of ourselves.'
Siân Miles, Editor, *Simone Weil: An Anthology*, p. 263, Virago,
from which come the other quotations from Simone Weil, to
whom Julie's meditation on affliction also owes a debt.

228 'Hold to the now . . . plunges to the past.'
James Joyce, *Ulysses*, The Corrected Text, p. 153, Bodley
Head.

Mother Julian's words are quoted from *Revelations of Divine Love*
translated by Clifton Wolters, Penguin Books.

Two pages of Nik's book to Julie owe their inspiration to the work of
Tom Phillips, especially his book *A Humument*, Thames & Hudson.